A CAGE OF ICE

DUNCAN KYLE was born in Bradford, Yorkshire, a few hundred yards from the house where J. B. Priestley grew up.

He started his career as a junior reporter on the *Bradford Telegraph and Argus*, later going on to the *Leicester Mercury* and the *Yorkshire Post*. In the mid-fifties he joined *John Bull* magazine – which later became *Today* – in London and from there he went on to become editorial director at Odhams where he wrote his first novel, *A Cage of Ice*.

It was the success of this book which persuaded him to become a full-time writer and to fulfil his long-held ambition to live deep in the country. He now lives in Suffolk with his wife and three children.

He has written six novels, each more successful than the last: *Black Camelot* (published by Collins in 1978) is the latest.

DUNCAN KYLE

A Cage of Ice

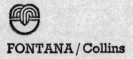

FONTANA / Collins

First published in 1970 by William Collins Sons & Co Ltd
First issued in Fontana Books 1972
Ninth Impression January 1979

Made and printed in Great Britain by
William Collins Sons & Co Ltd, Glasgow

PROLOGUE

It is night on the icecap. The Arctic wind scours up flakes from the vast, smooth whiteness and carries them within itself, screaming. Nothing else moves in the endless snow-scape, for at this place, six thousand feet high, even animals equipped for survival are deprived of the one outside element necessary to life. There is no food, so there is nothing but the wind and the snow, the cold and the dark.

And man.

Beneath the snow, a movement, a lifting. A small mound swells and breaks and through it ploughs a dark rectangular shape, pushing the snow arrogantly aside. It turns, roaring, and disappears into its lair. Now at the mouth of its tunnel there is light. The tunnel is long and straight. Its floor is crystalline like sand and along its walls run the arteries upon which man's life depends. They carry power, without which man will die; and heat, without which he cannot live; they carry man's capacity to talk to other men, to melt the water, warm the food and chill the drinks.

This is Camp Hundred.

Four years ago, in the brief summer, Luke Chance came here in a giant tractor which drew behind it, like a goods train, wagons called wanagans mounted on ski runners. One carried a Peters snowplough of the kind used in Switzerland to clear the Alpine roads. When Chance had picked the site, the snowplough cut trenches in the icecap, flinging the loosened snow out through its chimney into a raised strip along the edge. When the plough was fifteen feet down, curved corrugated iron sections bridged the trench, and the loose snow was piled on top. Now there was shelter in which construction work could begin. Chance controlled, planned, organized in a desperate race to finish Camp Hundred before winter, and when winter came he had won. He had been here ever since, professing to detest it, yet going away for rare leaves with obvious reluctance. The standard tour of duty was six months, and men left with sighs of relief.

Chance was in the bar now, diluting eight-year-old bourbon with two-thousand-year-old water from the deep well, the day's work behind him and an evening of bridge pleasurably in prospect.

'Signal for the Colonel, sir.'

Chance turned, hand out. He placed the glass on the bar as he read the message through twice. It said:

COMMANDER HUNDRED UNIDENTIFIED AIRCRAFT APPROACHING HUNDRED FROM DIRECTION POLAR SEA—FAILS REPLY TO SIGNALS—FIGHTER INSPECTION SUGGESTS RUSSIAN RECONNAISSANCE PLANE OF BEAR TYPE—CRIPPLED AND LOSING HEIGHT—RADAR TRACKING—STAND BY

MICHAELSON USAB THULE.

'How's the radio, Corporal?' Chance asked.

'It's OK, sir.'

'See if you can raise General Michaelson. I'll come through in a moment.'

'Yes, sir.'

Chance looked at the identification tape sewn above the corporal's left breast pocket. 'Hainey.'

'Sir?'

'That looks like the start of a lousy beard.' He grinned.

Corporal Hainey grinned back. 'I'm working on it, sir.'

'OK.' Chance picked up the glass, drank without hurry, giving Hainey time, walked out of the Officers' Club, across the main tunnel and into the radio room.

Hainey looked up. 'They're getting him, sir.' He listened and then. 'Here you are, sir. Headphones or speaker?'

'Speaker.' Chance waited, then a voice said:

'Colonel Chance, General Michaelson.'

'I'd rather talk than teleprint, sir,' Chance said. 'Anything new on the aircraft?'

'No question it's coming your way. Down to eight thousand feet now, range forty miles. Losing height all the time. Maybe twenty miles east of you.'

'Is it Russian, sir?'

'Reckon so. If it comes down—'

'You want us to see what we can find?'

'Yes. Sorry, Chance. It could be important.'

Chance said, 'The Corps of Engineers is always happy to help out the Air Force, sir.'

'Seven thousand, same course. Good of you, I must say. The Air Force appreciates it.'

'The Air Force doesn't have to do it.'

6

Michaelson chuckled briefly. 'Maybe that's why . . . Still coming down. Doesn't look as though they've been doing anything at all except head for land. Stand by.'

Chance lit a cigarette thoughtfully. The weather on top was murderous: high winds, blowing snow and not much moon. It would be a nasty trip, complicated by the fact that there wasn't a trail anywhere east by north. 'Come on, Tovarich,' he muttered. 'Get her nose up and fly home.'

'Not much more than six thousand eight,' Michaelson said. There was a long pause. 'She's off the screen, Chance. I'm afraid . . .'

'I understand, General. We'll need a hell of an accurate fix, though.'

'We're getting it. BMEWS is on it. Stand by.'

Two minutes later the fix was through. Chance checked the co-ordinates on the big map in the radio room, then reached for the Tannoy switch.

'Chance speaking. There's an aircraft down twenty-two miles east-north-east of here. May be Russian. We're going out there. I want one big tractor and a sleeping wanagan, two 'dozers and two—' he stopped, wondering how many crew the Bear might carry—'no, three Polecats. Crews to tractor tunnel now. And I'd be obliged if the doctor will switch off his hi-fi and join us. That's all.'

He walked quickly to his quarters and put on his Long Johns, Grenfell cloth trousers, jacket, fur hat and parka and the big white felt boots, then hurried to the tractor shed. The extractor fan in the roof was whirling, forcing the diesel smoke out into the night. He watched the sleeping wanagan being dragged across and coupled to the massive ice-orange tractor, glanced round at the little, fast-throbbing Polecats, then climbed into the cab of the bulldozer nearest the doors.

'Open up,' he shouted. 'Wagons ho!'

His voice was lost in the din of engines, but the waved arm had meant advance since the days of the cavalry. In all the vehicles hands enclosed in double mittens worked the track levers. The convoy began to roll through big doors that led into the end of Main Street and to the base of the ramp, where the bulldozer lowered its blade to push the snow aside, an operation known at Camp Hundred as 'sweeping the doorstep'. The heater was blasting warm air into the cab as they came out on to the surface.

Chance wondered how long the journey would take, and what sort of condition the aircraft's crew was in. Even if they had survived the crash, men not equipped for the Arctic would not last more than minutes, without shelter of some kind. He thought what it must be like out there, shuddered, and deliberately switched his mind to the problem of getting there. Twenty miles didn't sound far and in any normal terms it wasn't. Damn it, some men could run it in around two hours. But these were far from normal conditions and he had known times when a twenty-mile journey might take a week, if there were crevasses in the path and a white-out reduced visibility not to yards, not to feet, not to inches, but to zero. He wished he could simply send the Polecats' rapid, tracked personnel carriers blinding off there. They might make it in less than an hour. But they might not; might instead vanish down one of the deep crevasses that the constant plastic flow of the icecap opened and closed and the wind covered treacherously with thin bridges of snow. You were in them before you knew they were there, which was why the two bulldozers and the tractor were cabled together; at least, if the leading vehicle plunged, the other two could take the strain and, even if they couldn't haul it out, could hold it until the crew climbed clear.

The train of vehicles edged forward, drivers peering hard through their windscreens at the shapes of the vehicles in front. Between moons in the five-month night, there was very little to see except the lashing snow patterns in the headlights.

After five miles. Chance switched on the radio. 'Chance to Hundred. Chance to Hundred. Over.'

'Hundred to Colonel Chance. Signal good, sir. Our directional fix has you two degrees too far south.'

'Two degrees?'

'That's right, sir.'

He lowered the microphone and bawled at the driver, 'Steer left, Jablonsky, we're too far south.' He glanced at the compass, wishing it were more reliable. In these latitudes, proximity to the magnetic North Pole produced unpredictable deviations. After a few minutes he hand-signalled an order to straighten and spoke again into the mike. 'OK, Hundred?'

'OK, sir.'

'Keep watching, Hainey. I'll transmit every minute.'

'Roger, sir.'

For seven miles they kept on line, Chance making his

sixty-second calls and waiting for the direction-finder's verdict. They were doing well: twelve miles in not much more than an hour . . .

Suddenly the tractor jerked, hurling him forward against the screen. The thickness of the fur hat and parka hood took some of the force from the impact, but it was painful all the same. He dragged himself back into his seat, holding himself there against the force of gravity. Jablonsky, strapped in, had reacted quickly, disengaging the engine from the tracks, but the 'dozer was now canted over at a forty-degree angle.

Chance waited, praying that nothing was wrong with the cable, which must now be stretched taut. He looked out of the side window at the unbroken snow, then out of the windscreen at the headlights glinting on the white wall of the crevasse. It was impossible, yet, to know its depth, but the angle of the lights illuminated the wall for a good twenty feet. A little jerk came, followed by another, and the headlight beams tilted up a fraction. There was nothing to be done except wait, and hope that the drivers of the tractor and the other 'dozer didn't let any cables slacken. Working together and with a slow, straight pull it should not be too difficult, but that kind of manoeuvring, easy to specify, was difficult to carry out.

'Reverse the tracks, sir?' Jablonsky yelled.

'Next time you feel the pull. And slowly, Jablonsky. For God's sake don't crumble the edge.' The big white felt boots were clumsy and sensitive control was needed if the fifty-four-inch tracks were not to chew away the compacted snow on which the bulldozer rested. Enough power to lift, too little to scrape, that was the requirement. He felt a slight change in the level of the cabin and watched the driver's hands and feet working the levers and pedals. His eyes switched to the wall of the crevasse as the line of the lights climbed slowly, picking up the precipitation layers that marked the years. They were moving back.

'Keep it like that, Jablonsky!' The tracks were not slipping and inch by inch they edged backwards. He waited, sweating. It wouldn't take much: the weight of the tractor was immense and the snow beneath it still comparatively soft. If the shoulder cracked off, and slid into the crevasse, the tractor might go with it, and with the kind of jerk that could snap a cable. But it was all right this time. A moment later Chance was flung backward against the back rest of his seat as the tractor slammed level and Jablonsky raced the

9

engine grinding the tracks into the snow surface, moving it clear.

'OK. Halt.' Chance opened the door and, as the massive track stopped turning, stepped on to it, jumped down and stood deliberately in the glare of the lights, waving the other machines forward, then halting them in a line a few yards short of the crevasse. He opened the tool compartment in his own tractor and took out a handlamp with a length of cable attached, plugged it into the socket, tied a lifeline round his shoulders, and walked slowly forward to the edge. Everything depended now on how deep it was. Crevasses could be anything from a few feet to many fathoms in depth; a few yards or many miles long. A long, deep crevasse was a hell of a hazard. The only way to pass it was to go round, and there was danger every minute as you tried to track its course, thrusting a rod into the snow, knowing that you might be standing on a snow bridge and any second you might vanish. He stamped his feet hard as he approached the edge. An overhang now was unlikely; the lip had, after all, borne the weight of the tractor. All the same, it paid to be careful. Feeling the lifeline slacken, he jerked it hard as a reminder to the men to keep it taut, then shone the beam into the crevasse.

Thirty, maybe thirty-five feet deep, and the walls narrowing to meet at the bottom; well, it was worse than he'd hoped, but not as bad as it might have been. Width, maybe fifteen feet.

Chance went back and gave instructions to Jablonsky and to Martin, who drove the other bulldozer, then went and sat in the heated cabin of the tractor watching them work. The fifteen-foot blades of the bulldozers could handle eight or nine cubic yards of snow at a time and they began to scrape it forward to the edge of the crevasse, tipping it over the edge, maybe a ton at a time, gradually filling it. He glanced at his watch. Already twenty minutes had been lost, and filling and packing the crevasse could take at least an hour. He didn't give a plugged nickel now for the chances of any men stranded out there.

After a while he got out again and walked to the edge. The two bulldozers were working well and the snow was piling up but it was the narrow base of the crevasse they were filling; as the level got higher, progress would slow. He turned, incautiously, as the roar of engines behind him heralded Jablonsky's approach, and felt the blast of the wind on his face. Hastily he turned his back to it and pulled at the drawstring of his parka hood, tightening it until it formed a two-inch ring forward of his face. His breath would warm the air space and his face was safe now from windchill.

The big diesel engines roared in the night as the 'dozers manoeuvred back and forth, each pass of the big blades piling more snow into the abyss. Chance had been through this before, so many times. Impatience got nobody anywhere. The drivers were working desperately hard, but it was like filling a bucket with a teaspoon. The best thing was simply to let it happen, not to look too often; a watched crevasse was never filled. If you succeeded in thinking about something else for a while, then went back, there was pleasure and reassurance in seeing how much had been done.

He radioed Camp Hundred. 'Ask Thule if there's any kind of signal at all from the wreck,' he told Hainey. 'Tell them to listen out on all distress frequencies.'

'Roger, sir.'

He waited and a few minutes later Hainey was back. 'They've had the intercept station covering it, sir, ever since the radar track disappeared. No signal at all.'

'Thanks, Hainey. Out.'

He lit a cigarette, waiting, wanting to go outside and look, forcing himself to sit tight until the butt was an inch long. There was no profit in hurry: another crevasse exactly like this one, or bigger, might be waiting a hundred yards beyond, and the same process would have to begin all over again. Finally he climbed out of the cab, tightened the parka hood again, and went forward. The snow was now near the top, a few more minutes should see it level, and he stood watching as the level climbed, feeling the cold beginning to get to him and stamping his feet and swinging his arms to stimulate circulation. The drivers needed no instructions on procedure; both had done this many times before, and even when the snow came level with the lips of the crevasse, they would go on piling it higher to allow for compression when the vehicles began to move forward. As the piled snow came higher, Chance kept a careful check on his own body, moving his fingers inside his gloves, his toes inside his boots, contorting the muscles of his face. Frostbite sneaked up on you; that was why it was so dangerous. The first numbness on eyebrows, nose, cheekbones or chin was too faint even to feel.

Now the piled snow stood clear of the edge and he waited until it piled five feet high, then waved one of the Polecats forward. It came quickly, then halted at the edge of the crevasse. Chance walked over to it and opened the door.

'Gently, a foot at a time. It's going to be compressed under you and you may tilt forward. If you do, stop and wait to be pulled clear.'

'Yes, sir.'

The Polecat waited until its cable had been connected to the tractor, then edged on to the piled snow. Its nose lifted as the tracks forced it forward and upward, then began to lower gently as its weight compressed the snow; lifted again on the next crawl forward, then lowered. It reached the other side quite quickly, but the Polecat was light, not much more than two tons; the 'dozers and the tractor were nearer twenty. Chance waved the Polecat back on a line parallel to its first crossing, then waved the bulldozers forward to pile in more snow. He repeated the operation five times before he dared risk moving the bigger vehicles forward, but at last he went back to Jablonsky's cab.

'Let's give it a whirl, Jablonsky,' he said.

The sweating driver moved the levers and the 'dozer inched forward. As it came to the edge, then rolled on to the piled snow there was a moment's pause, then its nose tilted down a fraction. Jablonsky looked at him. 'One more foot,' he said. The nose tilted more. They were at an angle of maybe ten degrees. 'A couple more passes with more snow,' Chance said, and Jablonsky reversed the tracks and backed out.

A few minutes later they were crossing and the bridge was marked with fifteen-foot-long flagsticks rammed deep into the snow.

When they were all across, Chance waved them on. A look at his watch told him that more than two hours had elapsed since they had left Camp Hundred. There was not the remotest chance that anyone could have survived two hours in these conditions, but he had orders to reach the wreck, and the convoy was capable of doing it.

They rolled forward steadily, Camp Hundred's direction-finder keeping them on course. One more crevasse held them up but it was no more than a dozen feet deep and the bulldozers filled it in a few minutes.

Forty minutes later, Chance looked at the mileage meter: they must now be getting close and Hainey reported they were dead on course. He switched on the big light mounted on the roof of the cab and began to swing it in a low, searching arc. Visibility was not much more than two hundred yards on either side and Heaven alone knew how far the crashed aircraft had slid on landing. He ordered Jablonsky to stop, got out, and drew all the vehicles up in line abreast. It was a risky procedure, opening up all the vehicles to hazard, but if they were going to find the plane it was the only way.

The six vehicles, a hundred yards apart, began to edge slowly forward. Chance looked at the blowing snow that made racing patterns in the beams of light and wondered how long it would take to obliterate all trace of the crashed aircraft. If the fuselage had really been flattened and the tailplane smashed, it could conceivably have vanished already, but usually, when an aircraft crashed, something was left: a wing, a tail, pointing skywards.

A few minutes later he saw the lights of a Polecat flash on the right wing of the line and turned towards it, then saw before he reached it a deep trough already half-filled by the blowing snow that could only have been caused by a large object gouging its way powerfully across the icecap. The question was, which way? But it was easier to go ahead than turn, so he followed the track away to the right. As it happened, he was right. After two hundred yards the lights picked up a melancholy finger pointing into the night sky, and they raced forward.

The big jet was in several pieces. God alone knew how much scattered wreckage was already hidden under the snow, but the long fuselage, its back broken and bent, lay like a massive lump of dark pipe.

There could now, Chance thought, be little danger of fire; either it had burned already, or it would not burn at all. Jablonsky took the bulldozer close to the port side of the aircraft's body and Chance jumped out, carrying a handlamp.

He climbed into the broken fuselage carefully, easing past the jagged, ripped plates, and shone his lamp along it. Nothing here, except a tumbled pile of drums that might have held oil. He moved cautiously forward towards the cockpit, pulled the broken door away and stepped through.

There were five of them, sitting strapped in their seats, bodies bent grotesquely. Pilot and co-pilot had been thrown forward, jack-knifing in their harnesses; the radio operator lay against his set; the navigator was almost on the cabin floor, his charts blowing sharply in the wind that sliced in through the smashed windscreen, and another man, sitting behind the pilot, had smashed his head against the back of the seat in front.

Not one, obviously, had survived the impact, and in that they had, Chance thought, been lucky. Offered the choice, he would himself have chosen to die quickly in the crash rather than freeze to death waiting, hoping for help and knowing that, if it came at all in this God-forsaken place, it could not come in time.

He turned and walked back along the fuselage. They would collect the bodies and take them back to Camp Hundred; from there they would be flown down to Thule and back, presumably, to Russia . . .

The tractor dragged its wanagan alongside and halted, and in a few minutes the bodies had been cut clear and carried out of the wreck. Chance went back inside once more. He had never before been inside a Russian aircraft and poked around interestedly, but there was nothing unusual. As far as he could see, it was simply a military aircraft, remarkable only for its nationality.

Finally he left. Already the wings, torn off and lying yards away, were almost covered. He walked over to one of them. It was strange to think that these dead, cold things had carried five men high through the Polar night, great jets whining to meet their death here. He strolled on, seeing the humps of the engines, now partially snow-covered, soon to be gone for ever in the Greenland icecap.

Then he tripped and almost fell. He bent and examined the thing he had stumbled over: a long, flared pipe with a fish-tail end. With his felt boot he kicked the snow clear. Anything could be anything in modern machinery, but this reminded him of crop-dusting equipment he had seen on a farm in Kansas. Chance grinned. Whatever else they might have been doing, they hadn't been dusting any crops!

Two hours later they were back at Camp Hundred, the tractors silent in their shed, the bodies lying in a storage tunnel, and Chance was back in Main Street, heading for the Officers' Club. He walked in, ordered Old Grandad and drank. Then he glanced down. The white felt of his snow boots was black with oil. No, it wasn't oil. He brushed at it with his hand and now the hand was black, too. He wondered momentarily what it was and then knew. It was simple carbon. There must, after all, have been a fire. Perhaps in one engine.

He'd finish his drink before writing the report . . .

CHAPTER ONE

It wasn't a nice night. All day the sleet had been alternating with cold driving rain and finally they'd agreed to fall together. I'd spent twenty increasingly damp and miserable minutes trying to pick up a cab but all the empty ones had gone wherever cabs go when the weather's foul, leaving only the others with their single passengers smug in the back. You can spend hours like that: stepping hopefully into the street every time a yellow car approaches, then leaping backward as soon as you can see it's taken and before the tyres make the rain water into a curtain and try to drape it over you.

So I cut my losses and walked, with my heavy overcoat putting on weight and my lightweight trousers dripping into my shoes. There was a time when people dressed for the seasons but machinery and marketing boys, particularly the marketing boys, decided that proposition needed confusing.

So now in summer air conditioning blasts icy air at you anywhere indoors, and in winter the heating bakes you. Maybe it keeps lightweight suits selling in the winter time and tweeds in June; it certainly doesn't make for comfort.

It's a long way from Grand Central up to East 75th but after a while you get so wet and cold and damned determined, that Masoch might find you interesting. I like that 75th St apartment, but I'd been wishing it was at 46th. So when I got there all I wanted was a drink and a hot bath in short order, before I plunged out again, this time equipped to drench a few sodden pedestrians myself.

I went in through the swing doors shaking myself like a wet retriever and headed for the elevator.

Bob's voice said, 'Oh, Professor Edwards.'

I stopped and turned. He was coming out of his sentry-box grinning at me.

'Doctor Edwards will do.'

'It says Professor here.' He was prodding a letter with a spatulate forefinger. 'Congratulations. Couldn't have happened to a nicer bloke.'

'Yes,' I said. 'Thanks.'

Bob and I were the only two Englishmen in the place and he was given to holding my elbow and reminding me of it.

I took the little stack of letters from him and almost ran into the elevator. Water dripped off me on to the carpet, but at least there was a nice downdraught of warm air. I took my hat off and basked for the one point four seconds it took to reach my floor. With the prospect of a hot bath in front of me I drew my door key like Bat Masterton, went in at a gallop and turned on the water.

I slung the letters on my desk, hung my overcoat in the heated cupboard and prescribed myself a fine mixture of two parts J and B to a half part of water, swallowed half of it, and began to take my clothes off. If there's a greater pleasure in this life than lying in a hot bath sipping good scotch, I wish somebody'd tell me about it. One day I'm going to do a little monograph on the delights of the bath and I shall point out that neither asses' milk nor all the perfumes of Arabia compare with the simple, Sybaritic wonder of warmth within and warmth without.

It took maybe ten minutes to get the chill out, but I gave it half an hour, just to be sure, topping up the tub from time to time with an educated foot that had turned taps ever since it had learned to walk. I got out, wrapped myself in a towelling robe, wiped the steam off my watch-glass and realized time was sliding. I wasn't exactly late but a certain crispness of action would be in order. I headed for my bedroom where all those nice dry socks and clean shirts were waiting, then remembered the letters, wondering idly who'd promoted me Professor.

The top one was from the *Reader's Digest* offering me a lifetime of untold pleasure if I'd buy a pile of records of unforgettable concert favourites; there was an unmistakable request for dollars from the electricity people, two insurance circulars, and a stack of muli-coloured literature from assorted drug corporations who didn't beg but demanded a few minutes of my precious time, promising it was necessary to the continued good health of my patients. And profitable. They didn't say to whom. In any case, they were on a bum steer. I didn't have any patients. Some computer somewhere had sniffed out the magic 'Dr' and passed it on to all the other computers and I was back under the paper shower. The hell with it. I'd look later.

I went through and assumed a nice sober suiting to re-assure all the medical academics that I was neither irresponsible nor chasing their wives, put on a trench coat, and prepared to leave. It's impossible to wear a belted trench coat and a hat without looking like a bad imitation of the late and much-missed Bogey, and I caught a glimpse of myself in the mirror. I clenched my fist and stuck my forefinger forward and my thumb up. 'Reach,' I said. 'Perfessor,' I said. I still don't know what picture the line came from, but he'd said it sometime. Naturally it struck a chord and I went back to the desk and found the letter. It was addressed, sure enough, to PROFESSOR EDWARD, FAGS. That was three mistakes in three words: one, I was entitled only to doctor; two, my name was, and is, Edwards with an 's'; three, I was a surgeon, not a geographer. It bore all the hallmarks of a hungover typist at the keyboard terminal and I'd have thrown it away if I hadn't noticed the postmark. *Mockba* it said. It was dated two weeks previously. Late or not, I challenge anyone to walk away from a postmark like that.

I slid my thumb under the flap, tore it open, and pulled out a small booklet. I crunched the envelope into the waste basket and looked at the paper in my hand. It was printed and in Russian and I wondered what it was and who had sent it. Flicking through it told me nothing; there was no letter enclosed, no compliments slip. I slipped it into my pocket as a conversation maker for the evening.

I took the elevator down to the basement garage and found the MG sitting looking skinny as ever One of these fine days a big Lincoln wouldn't even notice me as it sucked me in through its air intake, but until then I was one of the sporting nuts who liked to shift the gears myself and have a rev counter to advise me on the proper moment. I was glad, all the same, that I'd retained some sanity and bought a hardtop. The MG gave a delighted snarl as I started up; it growled between the other cars and up the ramp to the street. I turned through the system and headed crosstown towards the park.

The partnership between sleet and rain had broken up. The sleet had obviously been making overtures to a blizzard and been taken on as a junior partner. Big fat soggy snowflakes were hitting the windscreen stickily and clinging until the wiper blades pushed them away and piled them up round the pillars, but they didn't have the strength to do anything to the road, which was merely wet, shiny and treacherous. All the same, they didn't help visibility and I slowed to thirty miles an hour. It's a loathsome speed in a little car with a manual gear box because you never know whether you should be in third or top and you fidget between them like an old cat confronted by two firesides. In top you wait guiltily for the beginnings of judder and in third you keep asking yourself why the hell you're using all this extra fuel. As far as I'm concerned it's the only argument for automatic shifting, and I suppose it's the reason why big city people either have automatics or give up driving altogether. But I wasn't a big city man; I was country bred and I learned to motor on roads where suspension and handling and steering mattered, and I hoped one day to be back among them instead of heading through these Manhattan defiles towards a square park where the muggers and rapists and junkies roamed and the skyscrapers on the East side reminded you all the time that these trees and this grass were invaders among the steel and glass and masonry.

I never drove into the park, particularly in the dark, without breathing a little prayer that no moisture was dripping on to the distributor head, and that no speck of dirt was working its way up through the fuel system to clog the carburettors. Stop in Central Park at night and you're in trouble: the collection of civilization's by-products lurking in there will steal everything you have and then stomp you for fun. I wondered sometimes whether the muggers themselves were ever nervous about going in there. If nobody else turned up, did they mug one another?

I turned in there, thinking about the evening in front of me. There's a starchy formality about dinners in New York that you don't get anywhere else I'd been. Maybe New England is even stiffer, but I don't know New England, or want to, and I like my meals to be cheerful. The gentlemen who liked to think of themselves as the leaders of medicine in New York always reminded me of the bottles they brought up from their cellars for these occasions: cobwebbed, crusty and full of years. Their encrusted wives were still inclined to call you Young Man and generally to speak as though every word had an initial capital. Many of them had clawed their way upward and clawing had become a habit; you'd go a long way to find a bitchier crew, male or female, than the medical establishment. It was mildly astonishing that I wasn't wearing a tuxedo, or rather it wasn't because I didn't have one. If tuxedos had been specified they'd have had to get along without me.

Traffic was pretty light. I suppose everybody had got

home and decided to stay there among the Martinis and the heaters, turning the dial to escape the commercials. It's a better game than watching the programmes, and I'd once managed to go twenty-three minutes without encountering one product or sponsor. Anyway, I was gliding easily through the park, listening to the newscast and hoping that something stronger than sherry would be available, when a car came howling up behind me with its headlights full on. The light burned blindingly back at me from the rear view mirror. I flung up a hand to mask it, but it was too late: I was badly dazzled. I decelerated and braked instinctively, not wanting to hit a tree head-on even at thirty, and sensed that the headlights were swinging out to my left. I remember thinking that if he broke the ordinance about overtaking in the park, at least he wouldn't hit me as I slowed.

But he did. As he came alongside, the big sedan swung across the road, hitting the side of the MG hard and noisily with its rear wing. The world seemed to swing and I was totally disorientated. Badly dazzled, I wrenched the steering-wheel round desperately to what I hoped was straight, and trod on the brakes. Those ten-inch servo-discs, bless them, bit hard and even, stopping me fast and in a dead straight line.

That was when the windscreen shattered. One second it was there, as clean and clear as the snow and the wipers would allow; the next it had crazed to opacity. I punched it hard, forcing the chips of safety glass out on to the bonnet, and through the hole and my own partial blindness saw the rear lights of the sedan vanishing down the road. I punched again at the glass, knocking a hole eighteen inches wide in the screen, and looked around. The MG was clear of the carriageway and on the grass, but at least it was still on all four wheels and the motor was running. I clipped it into reverse and moved back on to the carriageway, then went through the gears, whipping the agile little car forward in the hope of catching the guy who'd hit me.

I needn't have bothered. Aside from the fact that there's more than one exit from the park, he'd had a flying start and must have gunned his four litres away as soon as he knew he'd hit me. I wasn't even sure what I was looking for, not even sure his car would be much marked, and in any case, it's difficult to see the right rear wing of a car driving in front of you. I came out of the park with a cold face, cold hands, a lapful of damp snow that had blown unhindered through the shattered screen, and a filthy temper. I thought it was some hit-and-run citizen who'd skidded and then made a fast getaway before problems arose with New York's Finest and the insurance companies.

I didn't know. But that's what I thought.

CHAPTER TWO

It was sherry all right. Very dry. I remember a phrase my Scottish grandmother used to use about that kind of thing: she said it pulled your puddocks together. One sip and you walked around hollow-cheeked for a few minutes while all your saliva hurried back where it came from and your taste buds cringed before lapsing into total if temporary paralysis. The sherry came from Spain and they must have felt guilty about it because the rest of the evening's liquor was all native. There was an Alles Amerikanischer Hock from California that was probably bottled by the German-American Bund to demonstrate the advantages Hitler had, and a high density liquid from upstate New York that Nelson Eddy must have been thinking about when he sang 'To Hell with Burgundy' with such high enthusiasm.

The conversation was nearly as unlikely. I'm not one of those doctors who believe a few years in medical school confers eternal infallibility, but getting a degree does require an occasional impulse to flicker faintly across the brain tissue. Post-graduate work actually demands sluggish stirrings of the mind. And here were all these pillars of the AMA, some of them with strings of qualifications so long you had to turn the page of the directory, focusing their attention on Johnny Carson. True, the prices of Xerox Corporation and Col. Sanders common stock did crop up over the ignorant Ohio cheese, but only because they'd slipped half a cent that day and the world was coming to an end. Once somebody asked why I was in the States, but her attention was elsewhere by the time I replied.

It was an evening not just devoid of reward, but of stupefying tedium. I'm well aware of and even approve the convention that duodenums should not be taken to the dinner-table and lumbar fluid kept out of cut glass, but I had retained a dim hope that music or medicare, even the ethical questions raised by transplants, might edge in, somewhere upstage left. I spent hours saying yes, apparently thoughtfully, to the blue-crested eagle on my left and mm-m-m equally pensively to the brightly-coloured parakeet on my right. There was no danger of saying the wrong thing; neither of them expected either debate or disagreement. And it left me free to wonder how deep the snow had drifted in the MG. I'd tucked a newspaper over the windscreen, and it was held in place by the wipers, but New York being New York, some friendly passer-by would have had the presence of mind to remove it.

At about midnight, when they'd got around to what Johnny had said to Candice Bergen and how neatly she'd blocked that brilliant gambit, I thought my face needed a change before it set permanently in the expression of polite interest it had been wearing with increasing discomfort.

'So soon?' my hostess asked. Her voice was going through an exercise that had become a reflex, but her eyes were disinterested. My host, a geriatrics king who was beginning to need his own attentions, murmured something about '. . . again, My Boy'. The door opened and I was free, free, free, I tell you. It must have felt like that when you left San Quentin.

The snow had stopped. Maybe the boredom was universal. I let air flow into my lungs a few times, tied the belt of my Bogey-coat, and set off to count the wheels of the MG. This time they were all there. The newspaper had gone, of course, but it must have lasted almost until the snow stopped falling because I didn't have to take a shovel inside with me. All the same it didn't take the water long to get through both mac and pants. I drove home hoping I never became enuretic. When I drove down the ramp into the garage, fortune gave me two great big glittering smiles. Not only was the parking space beside the elevator free, but the elevator itself was there, doors open. I was out of the car and into the elevator in one easy, serpentine wriggle and punched the button. Somebody else wasn't so lucky. I heard a hand bang the outer door as it closed, but one of the advantages of automatic elevators is that they relieve you of any genuflections in the direction of manners.

The elevator doors opened and I crossed the hall, key ready, and went in to my apartment, feeling the usual warm pride of ownership. Well, not ownership exactly, leasemanship or something like that. Here I was, John Edwards from

Kendal, Westmorland, with an apartment in the East Seventies and mine, all mine, as long as I could pay the rent.

The warm feeling disappeared and suddenly all the rest of me was as cold and clammy as the seat of my pants. I didn't go in any further. Instead I closed the door and pressed the call-bell beside the elevator. Somebody had been in there while I was out; maybe someone was still in there; and if they were, the armaments could be anything from knives and zip guns all the way up to howitzers. I'm not especially nervous, but at times like that it helps to have a friend's support.

I contributed to Bob's support and now it was his turn to reciprocate. When the elevator door opened he came out on the double, though I wasn't sure for a moment whether it was Bob or not because the top half of his head and one eye were hidden by bandages. The other eye glittered angrily. Bob Roberts was a London bobby who'd retired and come to the States to be near his daughter. He didn't fluster.

'What the hell—?'

'Somebody hit me,' he said. 'Took me keys. I didn't know which apartment—apartments p'raps. Was it yours, Professor?'

I wasn't going to correct him again. At least, not then. 'Yes,' I said. 'Are you OK?'

'Just a bang on the head, sir. I'm all right. Is anything missing?'

'I don't know. I opened the door and closed it quickly.'

Bob smiled, put his hand to his hip and pulled out a miniature version of a New York cop's night stick. 'Truncheon,' he said. 'Just in case.'

I'd hate to face an armed man with it, but he obviously didn't mind. I opened the door and we went in together, clipping the lights on.

All I'd seen earlier had been a couple of cushions on the floor, but I expected chaos and I was wrong. The apartment had been gone over and it was clear it had been gone over thoroughly, but there was no destruction. We went into every room and opened all the closet doors, but whoever had done it had gone.

'Anything missing?' Bob asked.

I looked around. It didn't look like it. I have a silver cigarette box that belonged to my father and it was still there, open, on top of my desk. I checked the gold cufflinks in my bedroom and they were still there too. I don't have any Rembrandts.

'Nothing I can see.'

'Drugs, sir,' Bob said. 'Do you keep any on the premises?'
I shook my head.

He shrugged. This must have been about the millionth
break-in in Bob's life and the first fine excitement had long
gone. 'P'raps they thought you were someone else. Came in
here by mistake, like.'

'P'raps,' I said. 'Thanks, Bob.'

He said, 'You'd better let the police know, sir. Even if
there's nothing missing. They know about me already,' and
he touched the bandage with a certain pride. 'Once a copper
always a copper.'

'Yes, I'll do that. Thanks, Bob.'

'I don't suppose they'll come tonight. Not if there's nothing
missing.'

'No.'

'But they'll be round in the morning, I expect.'

'Yes.' I was suddenly tired. 'Thanks, Bob.'

'That's all right, sir.' He didn't want to go and I saw
which way that eye was looking. He had a point.

'Drink?'

Innocent surprise and pleasure. The thought had never
crossed his mind. 'Well now, that's very nice of you, sir.'

I poured two cruiserweight whiskies. 'Water?'

He sniffed it approvingly. 'No thanks. It always seems a
shame somehow. Good health, sir.'

From the way the scotch disappeared I judged he'd been
watching Westerns. He put the glass on the table. 'Good
night, sir.'

'Night, Bob, and thanks again.'

'Thank *you*, sir.'

He went out and I watched him go, admiring his nerve.
In all senses of the word.

I added water. I always do, just to cut the edge. I don't
like that feeling that you're swallowing a garden rake. That
whisky went down quickly, at least by my own standards,
and I poured another. The feeling you get when someone's
broken into your home is a strange one, prickly and animal.
Nests, lairs and homes of all kind are sacred. When you
find someone's been in uninvited this crawling feeling comes
slimily out of the subconscious and all sorts of things happen.
Spines tingle, flesh creeps, hair stands on end, just as everybody always says they do.

This cosy little nest in the East Seventies that was slowly

beggaring me suddenly didn't seem quite so snug any more, in that strange way familiar things change somehow when you look at them from a new point of view. All this furniture that was only part of living, just background, had suddenly acquired the sharp, clean outlines of unaccustomed objects, turned maybe not cold, not hostile, but somehow watchful.

I peeled off the sober, soaking suiting and thought a shower might help, but it didn't. I stood there, under the hot water, looking at the curtain and thinking of a movie called *Psycho* which contained an imaginative shot of blood mixing with water and swirling out of a bathtub. Hitchcock. He'd be sleeping soundly somewhere having given the heeby-jeebies to half the population of the civilized world. If he was, he didn't deserve it.

I gave myself a sadistic rub-down with the hardest towel I could find, put on pyjamas, slippers and dressing-gown and crept round the apartment closing stable doors. There were two big bolts and a chain on the front door and I fastened them all. It's a pity you can only barricade yourself in and have to leave a place in a condition of maximum insecurity to go out. Somebody ought to work on it: Ingersoll, Yale and Towne, somebody like that. It's a whole new marketing concept, worth a fortune. For somebody.

I didn't sleep. I tried hard, but your body knows when you're trying and refuses to co-operate, even when you pretend you're not trying. There's no deceiving that mental monitor. He knows what you really want so he gives you something else; if you really want to read a book, he clangs your eyelids down like steel shutters; if you really want to sleep late, he'll have you clear-eyed at cockcrow.

Let me sleep, damn you, I told him. The hell with you, he said. Look, I said, feeling the sheet wrinkling like a rubbing board beneath me, I'm going to sleep. No you aren't, he said. How can you when your arm's all scrunched up like that? So I straightened my arm and took it out from under the pillow. See, he said, the pillow's too low. I didn't want to think, but he made me, tangling the bedclothes around till I felt like a trussed turkey. So finally I gave up and lay on my back staring at the ceiling with my mind clear and clean and ready to go, the way it always ought to be and never is in examination rooms.

It had been quite a night. Airline pilots say flying jets consists of long hours of boredom punctuated by moments of sheer terror, and that's how it had been. I looked round my bedroom and after a while there was just enough light to let me see shapes and outlines. It was very still, yet not long ago somebody had been prowling round, opening drawers and cupboards, stealthing across the carpet.

But who? And why?

That part of the East side is like Fort Knox. Maybe they don't push the stuff round on trolleys but it's all discreetly guarded. There are lots of ladies who like to believe diamonds were taken out of the ground to be worn, not shoved straight back under the care of Chase Manhattan or First National. Those few blocks to the south of my apartment probably house as many good paintings as the Prado, more jewels than the Tower of London, and enough small but valuable antiques to keep Parke-Bernet auctioning till Gabriel blows. Just living there makes a man into a target.

But my apartment wasn't in one of the plushier blocks and from the little I know of crooks they don't much like wasting their time. If it was a thief, then he'd gone away unrewarded and hadn't minded much; he hadn't even kicked over the odd chair in irritation. Which was surprising when I thought about it. I'd heard so many times about burglars who showed their disapproval by smashing the place up. Hopheads and the like were, by all accounts, much worse; they did nasty things on the carpet and wrote on the walls if you were out, and worked you over comprehensively if they happened to catch you in.

So who?

It hadn't been my night, that was for sure. A lunatic driver in the park, and a burglar sapping Bob to get the keys to my apartment—

I sat up very straight. They couldn't, they surely couldn't, be connected? Then for no good reason I thought of somebody trying and failing to catch my elevator up from the garage, and of my shattered windscreen. My scalp crawled.

I switched on the light, mostly for reassurance, and tried to piece together these little incidents which had crowded suddenly into my gentle life. I'd walked home in the rain, bathed, had a drink. Maybe it was the Cutty Sark people who didn't like my drinking J & B? I'd got into the car and driven properly and responsibly in to the park, where a big car, going fast with his headlights full on, had smacked the MG in the side. Then the windscreen. I had assumed it was just a flying pebble that crazed the glass. I continued to think of what had happened, as exactly as I could. And the answer was nothing. Nothing else at all until I brought the MG back in to that parking space by the elevator, then slid inside quickly. And someone had wanted to join me. Then this . . .

But no! It wasn't in that sequence at all. Whoever had been in this apartment had been here *before* I brought the car back.

I tried to think what they could have been after, always supposing anybody was after anything and all this wasn't just my imagination over-reacting to a long evening during which it hadn't been required. Bob had talked about drugs and I certainly knew plenty of cases where doctors' homes had been broken into by junkies looking for stationery or prescription forms. But this was an apartment, not a doctor's office, even though the board in the lobby did say *Dr J. Edwards.*

If we looked at the black side, and I was doing just that, the run-in with the sedan and the shattered windscreen had happened *before* Bob was knocked unconscious. Then the break-in. Then the elevator. What could be deduced from that? That having failed to fill me in in the park, they had rushed back, broken into my apartment, found nothing here, and then waited for me in the garage, but because I'd been so quick, they'd missed me?

It was crazy. I'd been seeing too many movies: the roads were full of lousy drivers, and made of loose chippings, for God's sake. And everybody was burgled once in a lifetime. It was just my turn, that's all.

I was sleepy now, but I checked the bolts and bars again all the same, before I climbed back into bed. This time the monitor opened his black door and let me through.

It wasn't for long. At six o'clock my eyes opened very wide indeed and I made the transition from sleep to total wakefulness faster than a big Univac could add two and two. My mind must have been doing some arithmetic of its own, and it had made four. I slid out of bed feeling exposed and vulnerable and went over to where my suit was hanging. The paper was still there, still in Russian, still incomprehensible. Could it be coincidence that this had arrived the same day the other things happened? It could, of course, but . . .

I began to turn the pages, looking for a message of some kind; a marginal note, maybe; anything that might indicate why it had been sent to me. There was nothing. I took it to my desk and went through it again.

I didn't know anybody in Russia, why should I? I hadn't reached the level where the Academy of Sciences extended invitations to me to demonstrate my surgical skill in Moscow. I hadn't even reached the stage where I was invited to meet visiting firemen from Puerto Rico, let alone Russia. And most of my friends were happy enough where they were, except maybe one or two in Vietnam, and hadn't got to the point of hiding from the taxman behind the Iron Curtain.

So who could have sent it? I turned to the waste basket and searched among the drug circulars for the envelope. I went into the kitchen and checked there. I hadn't been into the kitchen last night, I was sure of that, but I checked all the same. Then I checked the bedroom and all my pockets and went through the waste basket again, and the drawers of my desk.

The envelope had vanished.

CHAPTER THREE

It was not a pleasant feeling, and I sat there feeling it for some time. However you boiled it up, took it down, looked at it or tried not to, somebody had broken into my apartment to get that envelope. To get it, they had been prepared to injure Bob. If you took the other events into account, they'd been prepared to do a whole lot more, but I was sticking to certainties and being very sober about it. It wasn't difficult. I looked down at the paper. If they were ready to commit armed robbery for the envelope, what would they do to get their hands on this? Wishing that I understood what was in it, I turned the pages again, holding each one up to the light in case there was something I hadn't noticed before. There was. One page was missing; had been torn out quite jaggedly and close to the spine.

I felt a momentary panic, imagining somebody must have entered the apartment while I was asleep; but I had already checked the door and windows and they hadn't been interfered with. Furthermore, the paper had been with me ever since Bob had given me the post when I came in last night. I had only left it on my desk while I bathed and dressed. But the envelope had still been sealed then, so if anybody had sneaked in to snatch it under cover of the clouds of steam, they'd have been able to take both paper and envelope, and would presumably have done to. That meant effectively that it hadn't left my possession since I'd got it. So what about the torn page? Any other time I'd have assumed it was a momentary aberration of the printing press, and maybe it was, but it didn't seem safe to assume it.

So what about the page, and what about the envelope? And why me? I got out the list of tenants provided 'for my social pleasure' by the public relations counsellor of the property corporation which owned the building, to see whether there was another Edwards under this roof. I already knew there wasn't and the list confirmed it. An even bigger list of names, thoughtfully provided with the telephone, lay on my desk. I picked it up and turned to Edwards. There were pages and pages of them scattered all over New York and I was tempted by an engaging thought of the first Edwards, who begat Edwards, who begat Edwards and so on, until now there were Edwardses busily begetting all over the five boroughs and everywhere else doubtless, throughout the civilized world. I caught myself being amused and stopped thinking about Edwards who procreated and started looking for Edwards who professed. There was only one and he was listed as ventriloquist with an address in the Bronx. At seven-thirty I telephoned, but he'd been dead eight months and the people who lived there now were called O'Hara and sounded like it. I worked my way through those lists again until my vision was dancing, but there wasn't another Professor Edwards. What else had it said on that envelope? Some letters after his name, but what were they? It was a G for a C or some such literal. I remembered: FAGS. He would be a professor, it was fair to assume, of Geography.

It made sense that the letter had been intended for somebody else; certainly it made no sense at all that I had received it. Maybe it should have gone to 75 East 60th Street or something; it hadn't been a particularly accurate piece of typing, and those numbers could confuse anybody. A further thought struck me: perhaps the good professor had an unlisted number. I dialled Information. They wouldn't give me the number if it was unlisted, but they might confirm the existence of a Professor Edwards.

Those girls are pretty good: polite, brisk, efficient, and they usually come up with the goods. But then they are not usually asked what I was asking.

'May I help you?'

It sounded stupid as I said it, but that didn't stop me. 'I want to know if there's a Professor Edwards in the New York telephone area.'

'Yes, sir. What's his first name or initial?'

'I'm afraid I don't know.'

'Do you have his address?'

'I'm sorry.'

There was a little hiss on the line. It might have been static but I doubted it. 'Edwards?' she said, hoping she'd misheard.

'Professor Edwards.'

'I'll call you back on it, sir.'

'Maybe New York state, or New Jersey.'

I gave her my number and hung up, suddenly feeling an urgent need for coffee. I went and made some, swallowed one scalding mouthful, then took it back to my desk. The phone was off its hook before the first ring was completed.

She said, 'You don't know anything else about him, sir? Where he's a professor. Something like that?'

'He's an FAGS.'

'What's that?' she asked quickly. She must have thought I was a hoaxer or worse.

'Letters after his name.'

'After? Not initials?'

'Sorry.'

'Well, sir, I'm afraid there only seems to be one Professor Edwards listed in New York, and he's in the Bronx.'

'I know,' I said. 'He's dead. The O'Haras live there now.'

She was hanging on to her patience with laudable determination, and I sympathized.

I said, 'I wonder . . .'

'Yes, sir?' but guardedly.

This time she did sigh, but it was only a momentary lapse. 'It's very difficult without an initial or even a district, sir.'

'I know, I'm sorry.'

'I'll call you,' she said.

I returned to my coffee and my thoughts, then turned on the set to get the news and weather. There had been two murders in New York City last night, which was about par for the course. There had also been a revolution in one of the Arab countries and a tanker had broken in half in the Gulf of Mexico. I realized suddenly how small-time my troubles were, but they didn't feel that way. They still felt like big troubles.

I remembered that in spite of Bob Roberts's urgings I still hadn't told the police about the break-in, so I called the Precinct.

'Address?'

I told him.

'Any valuables missing?'

I hesitated. That envelope was obviously valuable to somebody, but I doubted if he'd see it.

'As far as I can see, all that's missing is an envelope.'

'Anything in it?'

'No. It was in the waste basket.'

'And that's all?'

How could I tell him any of the rest? If I'd mentioned the car he'd probably have tried to book me for dangerous driving or failing to report a collision, and he'd be able to quote statistics on the incidence of shattered windscreens.

'The doorman got mugged.'

'Oh yeah, I heard. I wouldn't worry. Happens all the time.'

'Not to me.'

'To everybody,' he said, firmly. 'I'll report it. Call us if anything else happens.'

I was beginning to feel a mite helpless. The Information girl would obviously be some time, so I showered and shaved and dressed. Wondering. And waiting.

She called back in half an hour. 'I've found a Professor Edwards, sir.' There was triumph in her voice.

'Great!' I said. 'Where?'

'Rochester, New York, sir. Professor Francis Xavier Edwards, DD St Saviour's Seminary.'

My heart sank. 'He's the only one?'

'In New York or New Jersey, sir. Will you make a note of the number?'

I couldn't say no. I made the note, thanked her, and dumped the note only after I rang off.

I paced up and down for a while pretending I was thinking, but what I was really doing was delaying walking out of that door. I didn't feel particularly safe where I was, but I felt a hell of a lot safer than I would anywhere else. I avoided it for a long time, while I ate some cornflakes I didn't want, and wondered what to do next. But finally I had to go.

I looked round the place for something to give me a little reassurance, but it's remarkable how little there is in a modern apartment. People in difficult situations in the movies always have something: farmers lift shotguns down from the wall, garage men pick up large spanners, fathers of families swing baseball bats. I had nothing. I remembered that line in *The Prisoner of Zenda* where Rupert of Hentzau tells Rassendyll, 'I can't get used to fighting with furniture,' and wished I could take a big couch with me, or an icebox; anything big to hide behind.

But there was nothing. Plenty of ties, table napkins, wooden spoons and table lamps, nothing else. So I left with only a raincoat and a little cushion to put on the driving seat because it was likely still to be wet.

I slid back the bolts and chains on the door, feeling both nervous and stupid, then turned the latch and opened the door a crack, half expecting it to be smashed back at me. It wasn't though, and I stepped cautiously into the hallway which was deserted except for Martha, the cleaner, polishing the floor blocks at the other end. Closing the door behind me, I crossed to the elevator and pressed the button. The doors closed and down it went, quickly and silently. The elevator stopped two floors down for a couple to get in, then went on to the ground level, where they got out, chatting cheerfully, leaving me wishing I could have asked them to ride on down with me. I put my finger on the button marked 'Garage'.

A little jerk and the doors were opening again. I looked out at the cars, then stepped forward looking to right and left quickly in case anybody was flattened against the outside wall, out of sight. The MG wasn't five yards away and there seemed to be nobody in sight. Taking a deep breath, I skipped across to it, slung in the cushion and climbed in. Behind me the elevator doors closed with a soft whirr. I felt very alone.

I looked through the hole in the windscreen. Nothing moved. A quick glance through the side windows showed nothing either and I looked up to check the rear view mirror and met my own eyes. Getting in and out of an MG is something of an art, but I had mastered it long ago; one thing I never did was to knock the mirror out of line. So who had? I put a hand to adjust it and that was when I saw, reflected in it, the hole in the roof lining.

It wasn't a big gash: maybe four or five inches long, though I didn't turn round to measure it, and there wasn't much doubt, at least in my mind, what had caused it. I stared at it for a moment, certain now that it wasn't a pebble that had crazed the screen, but a bullet. It must have hit the screen, passed through, and lodged in the roof lining. Maybe it had even passed through the metal.

I banged out the screen to improve forward vision. As I did so, the wing mirror came into view, and in it I could see something. Twenty, maybe thirty yards away, on the other side of the garage, a man was sitting in a Buick. It was impossible to tell if the motor was running, but there was no doubt what he was doing: he was looking my way. I continued to bang out the glass chips, keeping an eye on him. He didn't move.

I adjusted the rear view mirror again, so that I could see him more clearly. He may have been blinking, but otherwise he was motionless, just sitting there, thirty yards away, staring at the MG. And somebody had been in the MG during the night!

My keys were in my left hand and I looked at them and then at the ignition switch. Man gets into car, switches on —pouf! I'd read enough newspaper stories about Mafia methods to be familiar enough with the method, though even now it still seemed crazy that somebody had me in mind as the victim. Maybe it wasn't rigged as a bomb, but I wasn't going to find out.

The elevator doors were firmly closed and the sign showed it was on the sixth floor. If it would only come down, I might make a dash for it, but it wouldn't come down if nobody pressed the button, and there was nobody to press it but me. I got out of the car and started going through my pockets as though I had lost something, hoping it looked convincing. Finally I slapped my side as if in irritation, walked over to the elevator, pressed the button and stood waiting. Out of the corner of my eye I saw the door of the Buick open, and he began to get out, moving slowly. He hadn't made a sound. A look at the indicator showed the elevator was descending, and I pushed the button again to make sure the automatics didn't change their electronic mind and programme it back upstairs again. The guy from the Buick was moving towards me. If I'd been Spencer Tracy, I might have convinced him I'd forgotten my keys, but I must have hammed it up a bit too much. The elevator was at the ground floor now, and there it stopped. The man wasn't more than ten yards away and standing close to one of the concrete pillars. I had about as much chance of getting in without him as a California husband of bucking alimony, but it was coming down now, and the G for garage was illuminated on the indicator. I pulled my keys from my raincoat pocket, tossed them in the air and caught them, trying to act as though I'd just found them. I turned away and took two slow casual steps towards the MG, listening to the sound of the doors opening. They stayed like that while I took a couple more steps, then I heard the sound that says they're about to close.

I turned and raced towards them, and as I moved, so did he. There was no question of concealment now: he was trying to head me off, and he had a knife in his hand. The doors were closing, and there were two things I had to do. The first was to get in and punch the button; the second was to make sure he didn't get anything into the anti-trap mechanism on the door's leading edges. I swung my heavy Bogeymac like a flail into his face, heard him grunt, hurled myself in, got my finger on the ground floor button and pushed.

The raincoat delayed him just a second or two, and with the gap no more than a inch wide he threw himself forward. He missed by a whisker, and as I watched those leading edges kiss I could have kissed them myself.

Then the doors were opening again. I tore out into the ground floor lobby, knowing I had very little time; that Mr Buick would be racing for the fire escape or the service stairs. Somehow or other I had to get out.

Bob Roberts wasn't there and the lobby was deserted. I sprinted for the side corridor at the end of which was the janitor's storeroom. I knew that door was never locked and there was a window leading out of the back of the building, but I didn't know whether it was possible to lock the door from the inside.

It wasn't. There was a lock but no key. I closed the door quietly and moved to the window. It didn't look promising. It was an old, metal-framed affair that probably hadn't been opened in a decade, and was divided into small panes of wire-reinforced glass. Grabbing the handle, I tried to lever it down, but it didn't give a millimetre. Tugging and wrenching at it didn't help either. I looked desperately round the little storeroom; any second now that door might open and a man with a knife come through. I was lucky: this wasn't like the apartment upstairs; it was a working area. A bag of tools lay on an old chair and I grabbed a hammer from it and picked up a mop in my left hand. That made things a bit more even. If he did come in through the door, I could stab the mop at him and let him have it with the hammer. Meanwhile the hammer had another purpose. Striking that window handle with it would be noisy, and if Buick were standing out in the hall it would bring him at a gallop, but it had to be done. One hard blow didn't move it. I swung again and saw paint flake where the window joined the frame. Two more blows moved it. I levered the handle down and tried to open the window, but the paint seemed to hold it firmly. With the hammer I started raining blows on the frame, and finally it gave an inch, then creaked open on un-oiled hinges. The noise had been gigantic and I wasn't a bit surprised when the door flew open and Buick hurtled in. I shoved the mop at him clumsily with my left hand, but he brushed it aside. He was looking at me greedily, lips parted and narrowed, the steel in his right hand shining. His heel caught the door and slammed it.

I pushed the mop at him again, but he simply brushed it to one side, and inched forward. The knife was held the professional way, pointing upward, blade up, and his thumb lay on top to steady it. This guy knew what he was doing; he'd be able to carve a sirloin while I was trying to swing the hammer. I lunged forward again with the mop, aiming for his face, and as he moved his head aside I threw the hammer as hard as I could at his chest. I didn't see it strike him, because by that time I was jumping for the window, but I heard a thud and a grunt.

The sill was high, maybe four feet off the ground and I reached for the top of the window, then swung my buttocks up on to the ledge. By that time he'd recovered and was coming for me again. I drew my legs up to my chest and kicked out horizontally with both of them, aiming for his face. I got him too, but it was mutual. He staggered back but I felt the knife slice along the outside of my calf.

There was no time to stop and examine it; I wriggled backwards till I could get both feet on the sill, glanced down and jumped. It was only five feet, but I landed with a hell of a jolt that brought me to my knees. I could feel blood running warmly down my calf and, hoping it was only a surface wound, I turned and sprinted along the alley to the street and just kept on running. Pedestrians turned and stared at me as I ran, and some who were coming towards me did the same; there was no time to go round, so I put my shoulder down and went through like a football player making for the line. By this time, my leg was aching and throbbing and I suspected that all Buick would have to do was to follow a trail of blood. Then I saw it and urged myself forward: a Yellow cab had just put a fare down and was about to move away. I opened the door and fell in. 'Anywhere,' I gasped, 'just drive.'

He just sat looking at me. Then he said, 'You in a hurry, bud?'

I glanced at the identity card by the glove compartment. 'Five bucks a mile, Mr Kronsky,' I said. 'But move.'

'Yessir.' He moved. The cab pulled away from the sidewalk and out into the traffic, and I swung round and stared out of the rear window. A block back I thought I saw somebody running.

'Come on, come on!'

He swung out into Park Avenue, headed south, and I sighed with relief and sank back into the seat, but a twinge from my leg brought me upright again. The trouser leg was already stained with blood and I raised it carefully. Underneath a four inch cut was bleeding steadily. The blood was welling, not pumping, but there was quite enough of it and it needed staunching and stitching. I told Kronsky to make for the Grand Central drugstore in 42nd Street, went in, bought a dressing, some tape, a surgical needle and some sterilized thread, then went back to the cab.

'Drive slowly, Kronsky,' I said. 'Granny's doing some embroidery.'

He turned in his seat and looked at me. 'Jesus!'

'It's my problem,' I said. 'Just drive.'

He was instantly suspicious. 'Just what's going on here, bud?'

I took out my wallet and dropped it on the seat beside him. 'My name's John Edwards. I'm a doctor. I've had a little accident.'

'Yeah?' He didn't believe me.

'Look at the wallet, Kronsky.'

I didn't watch him doing it; I was too busy threading the needle, but at intervals of wincing as I shoved the point through my own skin, I could hear him shuffling the papers and letting the foldaway credit card holder flap open. If that didn't convince him, nothing would.

'Okay, bud. Here y'are.' The wallet arrived back on my own seat with a thud. 'How in hell'd you get that?'

'It was for talking too much,' I said savagely.

He shrugged. 'OK. Where d'you wanna go?'

Where *did* I want to go? Not back to my apartment, that was for sure. I thought of the paper in my pocket. The best thing would be to try to find out something about it. Maybe I could get some clue what all this was about, but five bucks a mile now seemed a high price.

'Take me to a Hertz station,' I said. 'Now shut up. This is delicate work.'

He shut up and drove.

I'd done neater stitching. This job looked like a four-year-old's first try at a sampler, but it had closed the wound. I put the dressing over it, taped it in place and pulled the trouser cuff down to my ankle. There's this much to be said for dark, sober suits : they disguise bloodstains pretty well.

By the time we arrived at the Hertz place I'd calmed down a bit. Kronsky turned and said pleasantly, 'That'll be twenty-five.' It left me desperately short of ready cash, but there are times when it's nice to have credit cards. This was one of them. Ten minutes later I was taking the Chevrolet out into the street. Compared with the MG it rolled with all the precision of a hog in a swamp, but it was about a thousand times less conspicuous and had plenty of power to go with the bubbled floor rubber and the bent ashtray. I watched the rear mirror carefully, wondering if somehow I'd been followed. I didn't see how I could have been, but this whole business was so damned unlikely I wasn't prepared to doubt their capacities.

CHAPTER FOUR

I drove to Columbia University, parked the Chev and made my way to the library. I stood in the doorway looking around, glancing over my shoulder from time to time at the main entrance to see who followed me in. I kept it up for a few minutes, but they were all obvious students; you could tell by the hair. I've never seen so much hair. Both sexes wore it long and you could tell the men from the girls by their beards. They were all right when they were up and walking, but the kids sitting working in the library must have felt as though they were looking at their books through screens. Most of them lifted a hand every few seconds to brush some strands away, then retired again into the undergrowth.

But I wasn't here either as coiffeur or trichologist. I walked across to the counter and a girl came forward, a library girl, big black glasses and hair done up in a bun. Cary Grant always takes off their glasses and tells them to let their hair down, and when they do, they turn out to be Sophia Loren. I'd tried it once, long, long ago, and the girl had looked even more like a long-nosed anteater afterwards than she had before. So I wasn't tempted.

I took the paper out of my pocket. 'I'd like to identify this paper,' I said.

She looked at it, then at me. 'It's Russian.'

I nodded. 'You can tell that by the Cyrillic characters,' I said. 'But I want to identify it.'

'Who are you?'

'John Edwards. *Doctor* John Edwards.'

She smiled. 'I'll do what I can, Doctor Edwards.'

I waited. I waited for quite a while, then she came back bringing with her a tall, thin, stern young man whose beard was nearing his navel. He looked as though he wanted to be a patriarch and was only waiting for it to turn grey.

'Do you know what it is?' I asked.

'Yes. Institute of Engineering. It's attached to Leningrad University. The title is "Outline of the problems of hydro-electric power supply to the Aktyubinsk region of Kazakh-stan." It's quite old. Nineteen sixty-four.'

'Sixty-four?' I repeated in surprise.

He pointed. 'It says so here.'

I opened the paper. 'Unfortunately there's a page missing. I'd hoped to get it translated, but—'

He interrupted me. 'I wouldn't be too surprised if we have a copy. We do exchange a certain amount of material with Leningrad. Non-strategic. You know.'

'I'd be glad if you'd check.'

'All right.' He left me there and went away, into some distant recess, but this time I hadn't long to wait.

He stalked back and said, 'It's in the catalogue, but I'm afraid it must be in use. Somebody signed it out.'

I said, 'Is it signed out often?'

'I shouldn't think so.' He reached for a book and flicked the pages. 'It was taken out last night. Five-forty p.m. to be exact.'

'By whom?'

He frowned at me, but my expression must have told him

it mattered. He looked at the book again. 'Somebody called John Smith.'

'At five-forty last night?'

'Yes.'

'Any way of knowing when it was last out?'

'Does it matter?'

'It might,' I said. 'It might matter a lot.'

He checked for me, and said eventually, 'I don't think it's been out at all. It doesn't even seem to have been translated. At least, there's no record.'

'Thanks,' I said. I turned away, and as I did so something caught my eye, something that hadn't been there before. A few faces had been turned my way, looking at me idly, and they hadn't looked away as I turned. But one had, and in that sea of luxuriant young hair, a bald spot shone out like a fried egg in a blueberry pie. The face was kept well down as I went by and I looked at him out of the corner of my eye; whatever the book was, he wasn't reading a word.

I walked slowly out of the library, into the lobby, then broke into a run, down the steps three at a time, racing for the car park. I started the Chev as though this were Le Mans and gunned it away. I couldn't really believe they'd got on to me, or imagine how they'd done it, but there was no doubt that I was big in their book. Three men were running towards another car. A Buick.

All the way down to midtown, I tried to keep my eyes on the road and out of the mirror. Once I was there, I reasoned, I might lose them by a bit of judicious filtering in the traffic, but this part of the city wasn't really familiar territory. I couldn't help looking, though, and most of the time I could see him easily, either one or two cars behind. Somehow I had to shake him and it was difficult to see how I'd do it if he kept as close as that. What I needed was traffic that wheeled and whirled and went in all directions. I glanced at the fuel dial. One good thing about rented cars, and there aren't many, is that they fill the tank before you take it out. I turned and headed for Kennedy Airport.

They trailed me all the way out through Queens, and I kept wondering whether they might not come alongside and use a gun, but they didn't; they just sat there, comfortably behind me, for the whole half hour. I did a couple of swift laps round the approach roads, but that didn't shake them either, so I headed straight for the TWA building, stopped the car in the middle of the road, left it with the engine running and fled inside, up the escalator and along the mezzanine. Though I didn't turn to look, they couldn't have been far behind. Still I reckoned I now had a chance if a bit of luck came my way and my leg held out. It throbbed pretty nastily and I was pretty sure one twinge represented a torn stitch, but I plunged on. I rounded a corner and found my luck: a recess with seats in it, and on one of them some visiting Texan had left a checked lumber coat and a big hat. Snatching them up as I passed, I raced into the lobby and out by the entrance signposted Taxis. If they hadn't seen me grab the coat, and I didn't think they had, I might be all right.

I put on the hat and shrugged myself rapidly into the coat then walked slowly away letting my hips roll and hoping I looked more like a cowboy than a Greenwich Village fairy. Not far away there was a line of offices bearing the names of various overseas airlines, and I headed towards them, looking out at the aircraft in the parking area and trying to match the offices with the planes. There was a high Boeing tailplane labelled Varig, so I went into the Brazilian Airlines' office. Quite a lot of other people were there too, which meant a flight had either just come in or was just leaving, so I moseyed in among them and stood quietly, getting my bearings.

A girl said, 'Taxis are available, and there is a bus system which runs from the airport here to the depot. You can also fly direct from the airport by helicopter to the top of the Pan American building in midtown Manhattan.' That was for me. I eased my way through the crowd and told the girl I wanted the helicopter flight. She was charming and efficient, and a few minutes later I was on it, looking uneasily at the other passengers and wondering whether any of them had knives or guns concealed about their persons.

By the time the Manhattan pincushion showed up below, I had worked out my next move. It ought to have occurred to me before, and probably would have done if I had not been quite so shaken up by the way things were building. The elevator at the Pan Am building is the kind that takes your feet to the ground and leaves your guts way back up in the sky, but it couldn't be too fast for me. I hurried out of the building and round to the Commodore Hotel where I'd stayed when I came first to this great throbbing metropolis. There's an onward transportation office tucked nicely away in a corner there, and I wanted to stay nicely tucked away. I also wanted the address of the American Geographical Society and I got it.

The question was how to get up to 156th Street, and how to get my hands on some dough. But the Commodore, may its frontage never grow less, cashed a cheque for me without directly inferring that I was Al Capone reincarnated, and arranged for an Avis car to come around. They'd wanted to call Hertz but I told them I was on the side of the little guy. I lurked in the back of the lobby restaurant drinking coffee and watching the doors till the bell captain signalled that the car was there, then out I went. I could imagine Hertz's computer calling up its pal at Avis and issuing warnings, but I'd sort out the disintegration of my reputation later. I headed uptown.

The American Geographical Society dwelt in one of those hushed, old-fashioned buildings only Academe can manage to have these days. It smelled of furniture polish and you could almost hear the years of grave discussion still vibrating. I told the inquiry window what I wanted and was shown in to see a middle-aged lady called Phelps.

She said, 'I'm not sure if I can help, Doctor Edwards. What is it you want?'

'I'm looking for Professor Edwards. He's an FAGS so—'

'It's safe to assume he's a geographer.' She smiled. 'I can't think of a Professor Edwards, but I'll look.'

She went away into another office and came back carrying a book. 'This lists the holders of chairs in geography in all United States universities,' she said.

I opened it and almost groaned aloud. The universities were listed alphabetically, but not the professors; I'd have to go through the whole thing entry by entry. 'You don't have a card index file of members and Fellows?'

'Oh yes, I've looked. He's not listed. Of course, it could be an error—' her tone said it couldn't, not in a million years it couldn't; errors didn't happen here and they knew all their Fellows like they knew the longitude of Greenwich, but a look at her face told me she thought she was humouring a nut.

It was a hopeless search from the start, but it was the only thing I had apart from the paper, and I was determined to look.

'Sit down if you like,' she said. 'Over there.'

I followed her gesture. Over there was an arm-chair under

the window; it was low and nobody would be able to climb out of it fast and unexpectedly. It was also a safe distance from her desk.

Almost an hour later, I was reading the entries for Washington, West Virginia, Wyoming . . . getting rapidly more dispirited. I'd no idea there were this many universities in the United States, and since there were, how come there were so many dimheads about? There turned out not to be a University of Zen. I'd got to the end and there wasn't an Edwards anywhere, which was surprising in itself, if only statistically. I closed the cover with a soft thump and Miss Phelps looked up. 'No luck?'

'No,' I said. 'No luck.'

'I'm sorry. I don't see what else we can do.'

'No.' I hauled myself out of the depths of the chair, walked back towards her and put the book down on her desk. 'You've been very kind. Thank you.'

I stood there, indecisively. It was a big room and books lined the walls, thousands of them, reaching back into time. Some of them looked as though they might be a couple of hundred years old, and the bindings had faded in that strange way bindings have, so that they all looked roughly the same colour whether they were blue, green or red.

I didn't want to leave. Somewhere in this building there had to be some clue to the things that were happening to me. Miss Phelps was looking at me expectantly, and what she was expecting was that I'd go. Quickly. There didn't seem to be anything else to do, but as I turned for the door something caught my eye. I supposed it was because my mind had been focused on the name for so long that I saw it and it registered. It was a new red binding with the titling in gold:

COLLECTED
PAPERS
PRESENTED
TO AMERICAN
GEOGRAPHICAL
ASSOCIATION
CONFERENCE
1966
ED:
WARD.

'Who's Ward?' I almost shouted it and Miss Phelps jumped. I pulled the book off the shelf and thrust the spine under her nose. 'Ward. Who is he?'

'Oh, that's Professor Ward. At Princeton. He's edited several collections of papers . . .'

I reached for the list again, turned up Princeton and found him. 'Edwin Ashley Ward, MA (Princeton); PhD (Cantab, Eng.); FAGS.'

'Do you know him?'

'Oh, yes, I—' she looked at me. 'Yes, he's very distinguished, you know. A member of the council. Our council.'

I said, 'Edwin Ward. What do they call him?'

'Call him? Why, Professor Ward, of course.'

'His friends,' I said savagely. 'What do *they* call him? Do they call him Ed?'

'Well, I suppose they do sometimes.'

'You've heard them?'

'Yes.'

I patted her hand, but only once because she pulled it away sharply the moment my intention became apparent.

'Thank you, Miss Phelps.'

She was still saying 'Not at all,' in a genteel reflex as I went out of the door.

Princeton. Distinguished. He was bound to be. Professors of Geography at Princeton were much more likely to be sent learned papers from the Soviet Union than young and obscure surgeons. I found the car and headed downtown. It occurred to me suddenly that I'd missed today's lecture and that they'd be surprised, but it wasn't the end of the world and I was damned if I'd stop to phone.

I drove down as far as 43rd Street and turned west to the Lincoln Tunnel, through it, then south to the New Jersey turnpike. It was nice to be moving fast; to be going somewhere I might find some answers. I left the turnpike at Exit 9, crossed the Lawrence river, then took the US No. 1 highway south. In not much more than an hour and a half I'd reached Princeton.

It's a great place. There's enough accumulated authority there to hold back the rolling tide of the Disfigure America army. When Princeton was founded a fine situation was chosen and it's a fine situation to this day. The Garden State always seems to me to be principally engaged in growing scrap metal and power lines rather than tomatoes, but Princeton still hasn't even a factory in it. When you see a place like that, Ivy League stops being a term of abuse.

I headed for the campus and asked a strolling young gentleman where the Geography Department might be. He heard me first time: his hair wasn't screening his ears and he looked the sort of kid who'd have washed them, maybe even that morning. It made a change. He told me politely.

I suppose I hadn't been taking much notice of the time, or I'd have realized that academic effort would have ceased in order to give the alimentary tract its chance. The sound of champing jaws wasn't exactly audible, but it was implicit in the stillness. Ever-optimistic I went into the building, looking for Professor Ward's office, found it and knocked. There was no reply. There wouldn't be. The next door was marked *Private* and was locked too, and when I knocked on it there was that curious hollow sound that unfailingly tells you when a room's really empty.

There was nothing for it but to wait. At two-thirty a girl came along the corridor, fishing in her handbag for her keys, found them and opened the door of Ward's office.

I said, 'Is Professor Ward about?'

She turned, startled. She had an intelligent face: blue-eyed, clear-browed and framed in shiny fair hair that got its nightly hundred brush-strokes. One day I'd get myself an assistant this pretty.

'Your name, please.' Her voice was low and cool and she gave a nice impression of competence.

'Edwards. Doctor Edwards.'

She walked over to her desk and picked up what was obviously an appointments book. 'Do you have an appointment, Doctor Edwards?'

I said, 'No, but I'd like to have a talk with him. It's rather important.'

She closed the book. 'I'm sorry. Professor Ward only sees visitors by appointment. He has a very busy schedule. I'm sure you'll understand.' She softened it with a smile, but she meant it.

'Then I'll make an appointment. How about two-thirty?'

She frowned. 'He's lecturing this afternoon, again. He was—' She stopped.

'He was what?'

'It doesn't matter.'

'Like hell it doesn't matter. What?'

'Nothing, Doctor Edwards. He was due to lecture this morning, too.'

'And?'

'He didn't.' She was trying to hide it, but she was worried. My intensity had communicated itself, twanged some chord of concern in her mind. 'He, er . . . He hasn't been here at all today.'

CHAPTER FIVE

Something very heavy bounced inside my stomach, and I looked at her, watching that clear brow cloud over.

I said, 'He missed a lecture this morning?'

She nodded.

'Does he do that often?'

'No.'

'Never?'

She shook her head. 'I can't remember his doing it before. Professor Ward—' Her voice died away.

'Is what?' I demanded.

She said, 'He's . . . sort of precise. Doesn't believe in being late or anything.' She was giving me a picture of a pedant and she corrected it hurriedly, chin up. 'Professor Ward is an extremely courteous man.'

'Could he have been called away? University business of some kind?'

'He'd have let me know. Doctor Edwards, perhaps you'd tell me what all this is about.'

'Has he a family?'

'He's a bachelor. Please, Doctor Edwards.'

'I'm sorry. Barging in like this.' I didn't want to tell her, get her involved. 'It's just that I want to see him. I've driven out from New York, from the AGA,' I lied. I suppose it was only a white lie.

'The AGA? Nothing's usually that urgent.'

'Did you call his home?'

She nodded. 'There was no reply.'

'When was that?'

'I called several times.'

I thought for a moment. 'Miss—?'

'Macdonald, Jane Macdonald.'

'Miss Macdonald, if he'd been delayed or anything, he'd call you?'

44

'Yes.'

'And if he were intending to lecture this afternoon, what time would he be there?'

She looked at her watch. 'Now.'

I said, 'Will you make two calls? Find out if he's turned up, and find out if he's had lunch on the campus.'

I waited, listening and watching her, admiring her neatness and efficiency and several other things. She didn't take long, then she hung up and turned to face me. 'He didn't eat here and he's not turned up for his lecture.'

'Where does he live?'

'I'm not sure if I should . . .'

'Then give me the phone book.'

She relented and gave me the address and directions how to get there.

As I left, she said, 'You'll call me if there's anything?'

Her directions were clear enough but it took me a while to find it all the same. It was in one of those districts where the street signs are discreet to the point of anonymity and the names of the houses don't appear on the gates. I'd driven past the street twice before I realized this was it. I turned into the street and drove slowly along, looking for the Japanese cherry she'd told me about. We must both have forgotten that Japanese cherries aren't evergreens. Furthermore, arboriculture isn't my territory. Ahead of me a car pulled away from the kerb and drove away sedately. It was a sedate street.

But finally I saw it and turned into the driveway, stopped the car and got out. The gravel crunched under my feet as I walked towards the four steps that led up to the front porch. It was one of those big, old, white-painted, wooden houses with louvred shutters on the windows and plenty of both space and charm. Businessmen's homes are painted oftener, but I'd settle for one like this. The bell was set in the door pillar and I pressed it. Hearing no ring, I pressed again, wondering whether the bell was simply quiet or whether it didn't function any more.

I waited. There was no answer, so I rang again, and this time I did hear it ringing gently somewhere in the depths of the house. Still there was no movement, no sound anywhere. It was like the room at the university; you can tell, somehow, when a house is empty.

There was a big bay window to my right and I tried to see into the house, but all I could see was a piece of furniture against one wall. I went back to the gravel and stood on tiptoe, but the wall beneath the window was too high and I couldn't see a thing. Turning, I crunched round to the side of the house and worked my way towards the rear. There was a big, pleasant garden, bare now in the winter time, but screened by tall old trees that would make it secluded and peaceful and still in the summer, and there were woods stretching away beyond the end of the garden.

A couple of steps led on to a wide terrace, crazy-paved and with ornamental shrubs let into gaps in the stone. French windows led on to it. I went up and put my face against the glass, and looked in at a sitting-room of some kind, with two big old couches, chintz-covered and comfortable, and several large, deep chairs. It was empty. I put my hand on the door lever, tried it experimentally, and was surprised when it moved and the french window swung open towards me. The air inside was warm from the heating; lived-in air with a slightly musty warmth that testified to huge numbers of books in the house. It also meant the heating hadn't been turned off. I went cautiously inside and across to the door, remembering Jane Macdonald's description of him and hoping Ward wasn't one of those people who went round the house before he went out, locking doors and fastening windows because that was what the insurance companies recommended. The fact that the french window had been open suggested he wasn't, but I was relieved all the same when it opened easily: I moved out into the hall, which was deserted, and stood still, listening. All houses make noises, of course, and this one was not an exception, but the only sounds I heard were normal ones: the soft whirring somewhere of a heater pump, the tick of a big grandfather clock by the door. Otherwise it was very still.

'Professor Ward.' I didn't call loudly first time. The old boy might be there and perhaps sick, and a strange voice bellowing in the house would be a nasty shock. There was no answer, though, and I called again, more loudly. Still silence.

I was facing the front door. Behind me a flight of handsome, white painted stairs curved upwards. To my left were two doors. The first led into the kitchen and I went in on tiptoe. It was clean as an oyster shell: all the surfaces unencumbered; no dirty cups or plates, and drying towels draped in the warm above the stove. I touched the stove cautiously, but it was quite cold. Leaving the kitchen I went in to the next room, the one I'd tried to see into from the steps outside, and found myself looking at a handsome oval table with a dozen striped Regency chairs around it. The heating was on in there, too, and I was glad I didn't pay the gas bills. But the heat was all there was.

I tiptoed up the stairs, rather badly, and they creaked a bit, but there was no other sound and nobody came out and then I was on a wide, white landing, graceful and light. There were several doors and I started at the right, going into and out of several bedrooms that revealed nothing except that none of the beds had been slept in. There was a big, warm closet stocked with sheets, towels and blankets, and a bathroom with a kind of opulent antiquity: huge bath with a dolphin spout for the water and a tiled floor with cork mats all over it. It made me think of Abraham Lincoln. The smallest room was likewise, tall and fluted and anatomically not too good; I'd hate to live in that house if I had constipation.

When I came out, that looked like the lot, but then I saw there was another door. I'd missed it because it was papered to match the walls into which it was set. I opened it and stepped inside.

He was sitting in a chair, head tilted to the right, a newspaper open on his knee.

'Professor Ward,' I said softly.

He didn't answer, didn't move.

I said it again more loudly. Still there was no response. I moved forward into the room and touched his shoulder, and as I did so his arm moved, but not much. You don't spend the years I've spent learning your way around the human body without knowing how it should feel. There should be some give in the flesh. There wasn't. And if he'd been asleep, that arm would have fallen more limply. I put my hand on his forehead, and my fingers touched cold skin and hardening flesh.

He was very dead.

I know, as well as the next man and better than most, what you're supposed to do when you find a corpse, especially if you have some reason to suspect that it became a corpse by other than natural means: you're supposed to touch nothing, not even the carpet if you can help it, withdraw to the nearest telephone, and let the police know about it. I didn't. I wanted to know whether the Grim Reaper had told Ward it was time or had been given some assistance. Given a laboratory and some help from a pathologist I might have found out, but I couldn't find a thing. Ward's face didn't look exactly happy; he hadn't died wearing a beatific smile, but it wasn't the sort of face that wore them anyway. In death he looked as he might have looked in life: grave, distinguished, with a slightly weary air and brows that had been constructed for authoritative eyes to glower beneath. Rigor mortis had set his hands and they were gripping the newspaper tightly, but they weren't clutching it desperately; he had been holding it fairly naturally when he died. I opened his jacket and looked at the material of his shirt, looking, maybe, for bullet holes or knife wounds. Blood, anyway. But there was nothing so dramatic, and when I tilted his body forward there was no hole or cut in the smooth material of his coat. It was beginning to look like natural causes.

I turned to the door, intending to behave like a good citizen and call the police, but two things got in the way. The first was his desk, a big, handsome mahogany affair with a tooled leather top in red. Papers were scattered all over it. I do mean scattered, and Professor Ward didn't strike me as the type to work with papers all over the place, some right way up and some not. I moved across to the desk, and saw two drawers lying open and paper scattered all over the floor. As I looked, one sheet slid from the desk top, with a soft rustle, to the floor.

I knew then that however the old man had died, Nature had had no part in it. This place had been searched, just as my own apartment had been searched the night before. I was standing there, looking at the mess, when the second thing happened.

A little crunching noise.

I froze for a moment, listening hard, but the sound was not repeated. I dropped to my knees and crawled across to the window, moved the edge of the curtain aside and looked out cautiously. Two men were standing by the gate as though on guard. Both wore hats and dark bulky overcoats and I suspected their bulk hid more than adipose tissue. Two other men were walking slowly and carefully on the grass beside the drive, heading for the door. Parked at the gate I could see a car and I remembered the car that had drawn away as I arrived.

I didn't stop to think, or argue; I got out of that room and down the stairs. Fast. And went back down the hall and into the sitting-room as quickly and as quietly as I could. The french window was still open. I went across to it and looked out, carefully. They hadn't reached the back garden yet. I eased myself out, jumped down the two steps and raced across the lawn into a clump of rhododendrons twenty yards down the garden. Still nobody appeared. I began to edge along through the bushes, the heavy earth sticking to my shoes, but not daring to stop and scrape it off. Then one of the men appeared round the side of the house. He was carrying a gun.

I kept going, trying to put my feet down carefully, trying not to knock the branches, making ground but making it slowly. And watching him as best I could. He stopped and looked at the open french window, then went in purposefully, gun at the ready. As soon as he was gone I did what he must have been expecting me to do: I made a bolt for the other end of the garden.

He must have been waiting, just inside the french window, to see what happened. As I streaked along the grass I heard him shout, and then there was a sharp crack and another thud. I don't recommend patients to do much running on a leg with a four inch gash in it and mine had taken a pounding already that day; it had also stiffened a bit since I'd stitched and dressed it in the taxi by Grand Central. But this was no time to think about the healing process; the healing of that cut was days into the future and my problem was to avoid another and fatal wound in the next few minutes.

A hedge of beeches had been planted years ago at the end of the lawn, and there was a gap in it through which a path went. I raced through and found myself in a big rose garden with rustic arches and poles. I went along it like a greyhound. There was a wall at the other end and the woods lay beyond it. I had an idea that if I could get into those woods I might manage to escape. As I ran I was looking at that wall. It seemed to be getting higher the nearer I got; in fact it turned out to be about six feet, and I was looking for something to springboard me up. The rose bushes ran right to the wall for most of its length, but there was a big compost heap in one corner and what looked like a pile of bricks beside it. I veered towards them, risking a glance over my shoulder.

A man stood framed in the opening in the beech hedge, aiming his pistol at me and I zig-zagged as much as the rose bushes would allow. The heavy earth dragged my legs back and I seemed to be running through glue, but gradually the wall came nearer and I saw that the pile of bricks was a couple of feet high. It looked rickety though and might very easily collapse as I stepped on to it, especially with the great clods of earth making my feet clumsy. I heard the shot, but felt nothing and assumed he'd missed; I'd read once that ten yards is about the limit for accurate shooting with a pistol and hoped it was true. I raced for the pile of bricks, jumped on to them with one foot and hurled myself at the top of the wall. A scraping, falling noise beneath me told me the pile had collapsed, but my weight had not been on them long enough to bring me down with them.

A quick heave and a twist and I was sitting astride the wall, glancing back again. Two of them were hurrying after me, but they still had forty yards to go to the wall and if you have to run, heavy overcoats aren't the best things to run in. I slid down the other side of the wall and raced for the trees.

My leg was aching badly now and all I could think of was getting far enough into those trees to be able to stop and give it a minute's peace. If it had been summer I'd have thought about climbing up into the branches, but all the leaves were under my feet now in a damp, slippery yellow carpet, and the branches were bare. If I'd climbed I'd have been knocked down like a sitting quail. There was no way of knowing how far the woods extended, but I hoped it was all the way to Ohio and that somewhere in among the trees I'd be able to stop and try to breathe.

I stumbled and cursed and then fell against a tree as the pain stabbed my calf. Behind me there was a shout and a quick look back told me one of them was over the wall and the other was on top. I plunged on, working my way round to the right, hoping that the thick carpet of leaves hadn't decayed enough to make my track easy to follow.

Another quarter mile brought me to a narrow track, just wide enough for one vehicle. Why it ran through the woods I couldn't imagine, but obviously it must lead somewhere. The surface was made of concrete, so I supposed there must be something at both ends. But which way to go? I had been going right, so on an impulse I went left for about a hundred yards, then ran off it again into the woods on the other side. When I was well clear of the road, I stopped and waited. By now I could scarcely breathe, my leg was throbbing wildly. And I was lost.

CHAPTER SIX

I stood there, screened from the road by the trunk of a big oak, sure that the noise of my gasps would carry clear back to them and that the hammering of my heart would knock the tree down. Those two sounds certainly drowned any others for a minute or so, but then I began to get my breath back and my heartbeat slowed to around one-fifty. I stood feeling my limbs trembling involuntarily from the effort, and listening. Among all the other sounds of the woods, it was difficult to be sure what was what, but then I heard a voice. It was fairly faint, but from the tone I judged he wasn't speaking softly and must therefore be at least a reasonable distance away. Another voice answered, briefly and sharply, probably telling the first speaker to shut up. I thought they were probably at the road, wondering which way I could have gone and hoped they were stupid enough both to go the same way. Or maybe, I thought suddenly with a sharp taste like a copper penny rising suddenly in my mouth, they were waiting for the other two to join them before fanning out into the woods.

Stealthily I began to move, still working round to the left, but going deeper into the wood all the time. Every few yards I stopped and listened, and once or twice I thought I heard a twig crack, or a footstep rustle in the leaves, but I kept going.

It was a nightmare. My legs were aching dully in every muscle and my chest felt as though it was containing a megaton burst all by itself. I was drenched in sweat and beginning to feel weak. And those few cornflakes I'd eaten —was it only this morning?—it seemed years before—had had to support the outpouring of a hell of a lot of energy which, if our Quaker friends will forgive me, they don't provide for ever. I dragged myself along, and after a while I realized the woods were thinning. Approaching the less dense area at the edge of the wood, I saw a long field, stretching maybe half a mile ahead of me, and groaned: a long open space was precisely what I didn't want. Out in the open the odds against me would multiply faster than rabbits. The view to the left and right was hardly reassuring either;

similar pastures flanked the one in front of me.

But I had to get out of the woods, somehow. Behind me, though I couldn't hear them, they must still be looking for me, and if I went blundering back I might run straight into one or both of them.

I was looking round, undecided, when I saw a small dot moving along the horizon ahead of me at a regular speed. Then another. In this day and age that can only mean there's a road, and a road was what I needed. I breathed deeply a few times, pumping oxygen into my lungs, then climbed the fence and began to run through the wet grass towards it, praying that I could hold out and wouldn't collapse before I got there. I was beginning to feel like those long-distance runners you see weaving from side to side at the end of a race.

I was perhaps half-way there, and daring to hope I was no longer being followed, when there was a shout, faint behind me. I turned as I ran and saw two figures clambering over the fence. They were still overcoated and I wondered how the hell they were still on their feet. Perhaps they'd had eggs for breakfast. I grinned weakly and staggered on.

How I made it to the road, I'll never know. There was a fence at the end of the pasture and I fell off, once, before I managed to get over, but I climbed painfully up the small embankment to the edge of the road, hoping a car would come soon, and that it would stop.

The first one didn't. The driver took one look at me and trod on the gas. I didn't blame him; I doubted whether, in similar circumstances, I'd have stopped myself for some dishevelled-looking, dirty hobo at the roadside. But a look back at the field told me my pursuers hadn't much more than a couple of hundred yards to go.

I looked desperately both ways along the road. A truck was coming, still some distance away, and I lumbered towards it, waving my arms, then pulling out my wallet to show I had one. As he came near, I saw him pull out to avoid me, and rushed into his path. If I had to die, I'd rather it was under his wheels than the other way. His brakes squealed and I shouted 'Doctor, Doctor,' as loudly as I could.

The driver slid the window back. 'I'm—a—doctor,' I panted at him. 'Urgent. Very urgent.'

'Hop in, bud,' he said, leaning across to open the door for me. As I climbed in to the cab, I looked back along the road and saw the two men had got to the fence.

'Thanks,' I gasped, falling into the seat.

'You look all in, Doc,' he said sympathetically. 'What's nappened?'

I said, 'I was chased. By a bull.'

'Go on!'

'Where are you going?'

'Philly. Where d'you wanna go, Doc?'

'Princeton.'

He looked at me and grinned. 'They won't let you on the campus.'

I looked at him. It had given me an idea. He was wearing a brown coverall and one of those flat caps that Englishmen, golfers and truck drivers wear. 'Will you sell me the coverall?'

He turned and stared at me hard. 'You said you were a doctor,' he said accusingly, and his foot went to the brake.

I pulled out my wallet and showed him.

'Then why?'

I couldn't think of a reason. Cupidity was the best answer. 'How much are they worth?'

'Five, maybe.'

'I'll give you twenty.' Then I grinned. 'With the cap.'

'OK.' His foot went to the brake again, but I said we'd make the change when we found a garage and I could either get a cab or hire a car.

I drove back along the road in the hire car. It was a Chevy this time and I reckoned by the time Hertz and Avis were through with me I'd spend the rest of my life in Sing-Sing. I was spreading their cars over the countryside like a man sowing corn and it's not the kind of treatment they appreciate.

The cap was pulled well down over my face and the coverall, brown with Phoenix Laundry stencilled back and front, ought to prove an effective enough disguise, but today had been enough to make me doubt my own name, and I was keeping my eyes wide open along the road. I identified the field easily enough; I'll never forget that field to the day I die, but there didn't seem to be anybody in it or near it.

I headed back towards Princeton, then remembered Jane Macdonald. I'd promised to call her. I found a gas station, pulled in and went to the phone.

'It's John Edwards. Bad news.'

'Go on.' Her voice was very quiet.

'I'm afraid he's dead. The house has been broken into and he's dead.'

There was a silence, then she said, 'Oh God.'

'I'm sorry,' I said. 'There was nothing I could do. He was dead when I got there. Had been for several hours, maybe since last night.'

'Who . . . how?'

'I don't know. Look, has anybody called asking for him? Anybody you don't know?'

She said, 'You.' I could hear the accusation in her voice.

'I didn't do it,' I said. 'He was dead hours ago. I told you. Look—who called?'

'It was just a few minutes ago.' Her mind was getting its grip back. 'A man telephoned and said he'd sent something to Professor Ward by mistake. A paper . . .'

'And?'

'He wanted to know if he could come round and get it.'

'His name?'

'Robert Smith.'

'Yeah,' I said, 'I'll bet it is. Now listen. Tell the police the Professor's dead. Tell them you've been threatened and that you think somebody's going to break into his office. Tell them anything that will get them to the office. Then come and meet me.'

'No.' I didn't blame her.

I said desperately, 'I'll meet you wherever you say, just so long as there are people about. I don't want to harm you. I just want to find out why he's been killed, and why somebody's trying to kill me too.'

She gasped. 'You?'

'Last night. This morning twice. And just now. But I think I've shaken them.'

She promised to meet me at a drugstore and rang off. I was there in five minutes, wolfing a sandwich and a cup of coffee, in a seat where the racks of paperbacks kept me partly hidden.

She came in a few minutes later, pale and anxious and pretty scared. I emphasize the word pretty, though, and I admired her nerve, but she was looking at me with very doubtful eyes, which had wept a little, quite recently.

I ordered coffee for her, but she didn't wait for it to arrive.

'Just who are you, Doctor Edwards?'

I said, 'I'm just that. I'm a doctor.' The wallet got flashed again.

'Then what on earth—? He's dead? Really?'

'I saw him. At his house. Sitting in a chair.'

'How did he die, Doctor?'

I said, 'I don't know. There weren't any signs of violence.'

Tears were glistening in her eyes. 'He was quite old. Sixty-seven. And his heart . . .' Her voice tailed off and I looked away while she got control again. Then she said, 'Couldn't you tell how he died?'

I shook my head. 'Not without—' I let it hang there and changed the subject. Nobody likes the idea of autopsies. 'His study had been searched. Somebody was looking for something.'

'Searched?' The idea clearly surprised her.

I nodded.

'But for what, Doctor Edwards? What were they looking for?'

We'd go into that later, if at all. First there were answers she might have to questions I wanted to ask. I said, 'He was important?'

'Yes. One of the top men in his field.' She was still thinking of other things, though, and went on, 'How do I know you had nothing to do with this?'

'You don't. Except that we both seem to be mixed up in the same thing. I don't know what it is.'

She was looking at me doubtfully, even suspiciously. I said, 'Somebody tried to run me off the road last night, then shot at me. I was attacked by a man with a knife this morning, then chased all over New York by a bunch of characters who were quite determined to kill me. When I got to Professor Ward's house and found him, they came after me with guns. I got away through the woods.' I pulled up the cuff of my trouser and showed her the dressing on my leg. It didn't look any too good. 'That's the nearest they got.'

I pulled the paper out of my pocket and handed it to her. 'Does this mean anything to you?'

She shook her head. 'It's Russian, isn't it?'

'That much I know. What was Ward's connection with Russia?'

Her eyes widened. 'Why, none!'

'Sure?'

'Quite sure. You can't think he was—'

'Was what?'

'Well . . . working for them.'

'I don't know what I think. This thing came to me by post yesterday, and that's when it all began.'

'It's an academic paper, I think,' she said. 'He got them from all over the world.'

'From Russia?'

She nodded. 'Sometimes.'

'Who from? And why?'

'Just an exchange of information. You know?'

'Who sent them to him? From behind the Iron Curtain, I mean?'

'Geography departments and institutes. That kind of thing.'

I said, 'This one's an engineering paper, hydro-electric schemes. Mean anything?'

She shook her head. 'No. Not engineering. He's—' she corrected herself—'he *was* a geographer. Just that. Though it's a wide-ranging discipline.'

'Friends?' I said urgently. 'Had he friends in Russia. Anyone in particular?'

'Not friends. He knew a few people, I think. He'd been to Russia a few times. Conferences. That sort of thing. But he did exchange papers sometimes with one man. A Professor Komarov in Leningrad.'

The envelope had been postmarked Moscow; I remembered that. 'Who's Komarov?'

She said, 'His name's Frol Komarov. Very important, I think. A member of the Academy of Sciences.'

'How well did Ward know him?'

'Well, they met when Professor Ward went there. And I believe Komarov came here once, but that was before my time. Sometimes I used to send things to him and sometimes he'd send things to Professor Ward.'

'Would Professor Ward be interested in hydro-electric schemes in Kazakhstan?'

'Is that what the paper's about?'

'Yes.'

'I don't think so. He was interested in most things of course, but . . .'

'It's dated 1964.'

'She frowned. 'Then I don't see . . .'

I was saying, 'Neither do I,' when a voice said: 'Are you Doctor Edwards?'

CHAPTER SEVEN

I turned, startled, and found myself staring into the barrel of a gun. The guy behind it was about nine feet tall and eight feet wide, and he had his twin brother with him. They were wearing the same police uniform.

'I asked you a question. Are you Doctor John Edwards?'
'Yes.'
He turned to her. 'Are you Jane Macdonald?'
She nodded.
'OK. Outside.'
I said, 'You don't have to bother with those things.'
'No?' He gestured with the gun. 'Outside.'

I took Jane's arm as we went. There was a big prowl car at the kerb, with almost as many lights as Times Square. We climbed into the back and the car moved off. The giant twins didn't talk at all on the way to the station, but even the way they sat was threatening. We were hustled out of the car and into the station, through one big room and into another, which was smaller, and contained neither windows nor reassurance. One cop went out and the other stood by the door.

A moment later it opened again and another man came in, in plain clothes and a hat. He stood for a moment, watching us.

'Why'd you kill him?'
'Kill him?' I repeated, mechanically. 'I didn't kill him.'
'No? But *you* made a call.' He was talking to Jane. 'Half an hour ago.'
'Yes, I did.'
'You told us Professor Ward was dead and somebody was threatening to break into your department.'
She said, 'That's right. I—'
He interrupted her, 'How did you know he was dead?'
She glanced at me. 'Doctor Edwards said so.'
'And he'd know,' the detective said slowly. 'He sure would know.'
'I found him,' I said. 'I went to his house—'
'Yeah. We were told. Last night. In the early hours. In a blue MG.' He told me the licence number. 'Then again this

afternoon, in a Chevy.'

I felt suddenly cold, and looked up at him. 'It's not true. I—'

'Do you own the MG?' he said. Jane was staring at me, too. She was deeply suspicious now. But there was no way of denying it; they'd have checked the number.

'Yes. It's mine.'

'Like I said, why did you kill him?'

Clammy sweat prickled in my hair. I said, 'The MG's in New York. It never left New York.'

'Sure,' he said. 'That's why it was seen here. Around three o'clock. But we'll play it your way. Where were you at three o'clock this morning?'

'I was—' I hesitated. I had been in my apartment, staring at the ceiling and wondering, but there wasn't a way in the world of proving it. 'I was at home,' I said lamely.

He just stood there, looking at me, while eternity dragged by. Then he said, 'I talked to New York. To the Precinct office. They're still checking, but it figures. Why'd you kill him?'

'I didn't,' I said desperately, 'I was in New York last night. I went out to dinner. When I came back my apartment had been broken into. You can check with Bob Roberts, the porter at the apartment building.'

'Don't worry, bud. We're checking. Meanwhile we're holding you. Suspicion of murder.'

Why didn't I tell him? Because the story wouldn't hold water; because the sequence of events, terrifying though they had been to me, wasn't solid enough to take the weight of a pin. If I pulled out the paper and explained, he'd simply think I was being tricky and obstructive. Mysterious attacks on me for no reason. An old academic paper. They wouldn't mean a thing, unless I could demonstrate some connection, something firm.

'OK,' I said. 'But did you put a guard on the professor's office?'

'Yeah.' He turned to Jane. 'Was it true? Was somebody threatening to bust in?'

'No,' she said. 'That was his idea. All that happened was that somebody called and said something had been sent to Professor Ward by mistake, and they'd like to call round and collect it.'

I said as urgently as I could, 'Put a guard on that office. For God's sake. Somebody will try to get in there!'

He ignored me. 'And what did you say, miss?'
'I said I'd help him in the morning if I could.'

The cell door clanged behind me, and I lay there, tense and miserable, staring at the ceiling. There seemed no way of beating them, whoever they were; however I looked at the things that had happened, they weren't what you might call credible. At seven a tray of food came and I picked at it, but the coffee was good. An hour later they took me out of the cell, back to the small dark room. The chair was very hard.

'Your profession?'

'I'm a doctor.'

'Yeah. Tell me, Doctor, is it easy to do an intravenous injection?'

I wondered why he was asking. 'Not easy.'

'No,' I said. 'But you have to find the vein.'

'You need specialized skill?'

Something in his face told me the news was lousy.

'We just had the first autopsy report on Professor Ward. Guess how he died.'

I waited.

'A massive dose of long-acting insulin. Injected intravenously.'

I shivered, suddenly.

'So here's how we see it,' he said. 'You wanna kill the guy.'

'Why?' I said.

'Who knows why. You just wanna kill him. We'll find out why, later. So you report your apartment's broken into. That establishes you're in New York after midnight. Then you drive down here, give him the injection, and drive back. Today you come here again, pretending you don't know Ward, go to his house, find his body, then you tell Miss Macdonald somebody's tried to kill you. Only trouble is, someone phoned us around four to say that a car had been prowling round, suspiciously. MG. Yours. This ain't New York, Doctor. At that time in the morning folks wonder where people are going.'

I stared at him. It was all sealed up nice and tight, and the people who were after me certainly had all the angles covered. That phone call at four in the morning, after they'd killed Ward, had been a brilliant idea. If they'd managed to kill me this morning in New York, Ward's death would still have been pinned on me. Since they hadn't, the police would do their job for them.

There wasn't much point in telling him the story; he wouldn't believe a word. And he didn't. I went over it in detail, start to finish, and not one flicker of childish wonder crossed his face. Even when I showed him the paper. I went back to the cell and it looked as though I'd be there until the first hearing of the case. Maybe a good lawyer, with the slash in the MG's roof lining to help him and a hell of a lot of ingenuity and expertise, might convince a jury not that I wasn't guilty, but that there wasn't enough evidence to convict . . .

But somebody, somewhere, was awake. I was hauled out of the cell around ten and taken back to that room. I was pretty miserable, and that chair was even harder and my leg was sore. I'd managed to persuade them to let me dress the cut, but they hadn't believed how I came by it.

The detective came in, only this time he had another guy with him, and he didn't like the other guy; I could see that in his face.

'Edwards, this is Henry Mason. He wants to talk to you.'

Mason said, 'Alone.' He said it easily, clearly and very authoritatively.

The detective tried to argue. 'He's our prisoner. Nobody except his lawyer talks to him.'

'So waste time. Call Washington. Call the Governor. Just don't blame me when your job disappears.'

I looked at Mason carefully; nearly as carefully as he was looking at me. His authority was obviously big, but he wasn't: a little grey guy, grey suit, grey tie, grey hair; his skin had one of those pale expensive tans and his nose looked educated.

He waited till the door closed, then sat on the edge of the table. 'They tell me you killed Professor Ward.'

'Who are you?'

'Government.' It could have meant anything from District of Columbia ratcatcher to Bureau of Inland Revenue. 'Why'd you do it?'

I said, 'I didn't.'

'How much do you know about Ward?'

'Probably less than you.'

'We know when a sparrow falls. Tell me what happened.'

I told him. There wasn't much to tell, but he didn't miss a word, a nuance, an inflection. Then he wanted to know why I'd been looking for Ward, and I told him that, too. His beady grey eyes never left my face. I also told him what had happened since I'd got to the police station.

Then he spoke. 'Where's the paper?'

'Out there somewhere. The police have it.'

'Come on.' He swung himself down from the table, walked to the door and tapped on it softly. There was no pause before it swung open. I followed him to the detective office. 'Doctor Edwards is coming with me.'

'But we're holding him on suspicion of murder . . .' the detective protested. There didn't seem to be too much hope in the way he said it.

Mason said, 'If your suspicion crystallizes, you can have him back.' He paused, timing it as Jack Benny would have timed it. 'It won't.' He also demanded the paper and the assistance of three cops.

We drove straight to the University, the Coke-ad cop car leading the way with its siren going and lights flashing all over the place. When we got there, Mason got out of the car, and waved me forward. 'Lead.'

I led, up the stairs and along the corridor to the office. I stopped outside the door of Jane Macdonald's office, but Mason didn't. She looked up, startled and nervous when she saw me, then reassured by the sight of the cops.

Mason said, 'Doctor Edwards didn't kill Professor Ward, but somebody did. This guy who's supposed to be here today, has he turned up?'

She shook her head.

'Where did Professor Ward keep his correspondence?'

She pointed to a row of filing cabinets. 'There.'

Mason didn't even look. 'You opened and filed all his letters?'

'Except the ones marked personal.'

'Many of those?'

'No.'

He snapped his fingers. 'Keys please.'

She was too well-trained for that. So far Mason's impetus and authority had carried him along. Jane Macdonald just sat tight. 'By what authority?'

'Government.'

'Who are you?'

He pulled out a small leather wallet and pushed it under her nose. 'If you want further identification call this number in Washington.'

She opened her bag and out came the keys.

'Call it anyway,' Mason said. 'Ask for Mr Dawson. These fit the desk?'

'No. He always carried his desk keys himself.'

Mason turned to one of the cops. 'I want those keys. Call the morgue. Get them out here.'

As the cop hurried out the Washington call came through. Mason took the phone from the girl. 'I've got a Russian academic paper here. Institute of Engineering in Leningrad. Page nine is missing. Title : Outline of the Problems of Hydro-electric Power Supply to the Aktyubinsk region of Kazakhstan. Date 1964. See if there's another copy anywhere. Anywhere. If there is I want a photostat.'

I said, 'How's your Chinese?' My sense of humour had rusted a bit in the last twenty-four hours and I like to keep it active, but Mason didn't smile; he didn't even pause. He selected the right key from the bunch apparently without looking, and had it in the communicating door to Professor Ward's office.

The office was big and crammed with bookshelves, map racks, storage cabinets. There was a large and very beautiful globe any museum would have lusted after. The office did not look as though it had been disturbed.

I said, 'What about the guy who's coming to collect?'

Mason looked at me as though I were an idiot. 'He won't.' He began to go over the office, but his heart didn't seem to be in it. The desk was what he wanted.

Soon, the howl of a siren outside announced the Cavalry was here, and a minute later the keys were delivered. Mason unlocked all the drawers, took them out and put them on the carpet. He started going through the first one, and I stood watching. He looked up at me. 'Help me, please, Doctor.'

'What are we looking for?'

'Anything.'

There was everything from samples of rock to a bottle of magnesia, and papers, papers, papers. There were mapping pens, coloured pencils, drawing instruments, magnets. There was even an old envelope with a dozen letters in it, signed with the name Geraldine, that testified to another and more romantic Ward before he got the chair and hit the big time. I passed them to Mason, but he recognized their age instantly and put them aside.

We did find a few letters, but they were from friends and relatives and concerned with how James was getting on at school and whether Ed would come to dinner on the 25th.

We found nothing else. Mason took a pencil torch from his pocket and examined the carcass of the desk thoroughly, so thoroughly he almost climbed inside. Then he straightened. 'So we search the books and the cabinets. Miss Macdonald!' She came in quickly, and was told what to do.

While she searched the map racks and the cabinets, Mason and I went through the books systematically, starting with the top shelf and working our way down. There were thousands of them and it was a long, dirty, dusty job. When Jane Macdonald had finished with the cabinets, she came and helped. Two hours later I was beginning to feel depressed, but Mason was carrying on, as alert and intense as when he'd started, flipping the pages slowly, systematically, fingering the bindings carefully. If there was anything there, he'd find it.

It was one-thirty when Jane said, 'Mr Mason.' I turned, and she was holding three sheets of writing paper. Mason didn't exactly snatch them from her, but they went from her hands to his pretty fast. His eyes flicked over them.

'My car,' he said, 'is outside.'

Two hours later, Mason and I were in Washington. He hadn't spoken more than six words all the way. He'd simply put the letters in his pocket along with the paper, and switched his mind from S for search to D for drive. The big Oldsmobile slid easily along the highway in a kind of whooshing silence that was sufficient in itself. Maybe there was some fiendish gadget making soothing sounds below the threshold of conscious hearing; maybe I was just tired. Mason, anyway, was the kind of driver who doesn't frighten his passengers, even when he's breaking the speed limits. Time and distance telescoped and suddenly we could see the Capitol looking like a picture postcard against the pale, cold sky.

One astonishing thing about the United States, at least to people like me who get our knowledge of these things from television and novels, is that you don't have to knock nine times on the door of the barber's shop, pause, whistle a snatch of 'Marching Through Georgia', then give a password. If you want the Central Intelligence Agency, there it is in Washington, a big building wearing a label. I believe the number's even in the phone book. John Doe can call them up.

But if John Doe wants to go in, the checks are thorough and careful. Mason stopped three times at various points in the building to show his card and sign me through the checkpoints, and I turned and faced this way and that way, as instructed, while my face was recorded for posterity.

Finally we went into a conference room. It contained a big table with a dozen chairs round it, and the paraphernalia for overhead projection and all the other display methods that keep IBM and 3M shares among the blue chips.

Another man was there already. He was grey, too, only tall and grey where Mason was short and grey. Looking at the pair of them, it was clear that the word intelligence applied to the men as well as to the work.

Mason introduced us. The tall guy's name was Lawrence Dawson and he looked like one of those men who guide the destiny of the world and wear Rolex watches. Mason said, 'Any luck on that page, Lawrence?' Lawrence, not Larry.

Dawson said no, but there was a call out for it. 'If there's one anywhere, we'll get it. Pity they beat us to the copy at Columbia. Still, if it was at Columbia, someone else should have it.'

I said, 'Who's *they*?'

Mason glanced at Dawson, servant asking master. Master didn't so much nod as lower his eyelids.

Mason said, 'KGB. Committee for State Security.' He didn't need to tell me. I'd heard of the KGB.

I felt that copper penny taste in my mouth again. I'd been scared enough, worried enough, not knowing who was on my tail. If I'd known . . .

'Why?' I asked.

Dawson looked at me, radiating calm. 'Who knows? Apparently something to do with that paper. It seems they didn't want us to have it. Or you.' He smiled. 'You'd like some food, Doctor Edwards?'

'Thanks,' I said.

'Steak?' And when I managed to force the word yes through the sudden flood of saliva in my mouth, he picked up a phone and ordered. 'You can tell us everything while we eat.'

It was a good steak, and a bottle of wine went with it; burgundy whose appellation was Contrôlée and whose body was full. I ate until mine was, and they let me tell the story my own way, listening and not interrupting until I had finished. Then they both went after me like Marshall Hall.

I replied as best I could, but there were a lot of questions I couldn't answer. I asked if I could read the letters.

Mason said 'No,' but Dawson said 'Surely,' and Mason handed them across. There were two letters, not three, but

one of them had two sheets. They were both hand-written.
The first read:

Moscow,
May 13th, 1965.

Comrade Professor,
I am writing to tell you how much I enjoyed our meeting.
I found our conversation stimulating and instructive and
it demonstrated again that minds can meet across ideological
frontiers.
You will be aware that I have been invited to present a
paper on our work in the Caspian Sea to the American
Geographical Society—indeed I imagine that you may have
been responsible for the invitation. I hope therefore to see
you next month when I come to New York, and to resume
our discussions.

Fraternally,
Frol Komarov.

'Good English,' I said.
Dawson said, 'He spent three years at Oxford and two at
Harvard in the 'thirties.'
I turned to the second letter:

Moscow
March, 14th 1969.

Dear Ward,
Thank you for your good wishes. My condition has now
been stabilized and provided I adhere to my diet and have
periodic checks, I should be able to go on working for many
years.
Over-eating is like over-work; one must be careful and
know the consequences of indulgence. It is necessary sometimes to resist the pressures, and stand back and think before
one becomes too carried away.
I still think with pleasure of the conversation we had in
your home near Princeton. If we could work together more
closely than the world now allows, I am sure the result would
be for everyone's good.
I hope that it will be possible for us to meet again one
day, though I am afraid that in my present physical situation
travel is difficult for me.
Please give my regards to the American Geographical Associ-

ation, and know that I remember you with affection.

Sincerely,
Frol Komarov.

I handed them back to Mason. 'Very buddy-buddy,' I said.

Dawson said quietly, 'I'd like to know what the hell they were talking about.'

The phone rang and Mason answered, listened, and put it down. 'They've found a copy at Imperial College, London. It's on the wire now.'

'Good,' Dawson said.

There was nothing to do but wait, but it didn't take long. In a few minutes a fair crew-cut young man who was all bones and brains came in, and handed Dawson a piece of photographic paper. Dawson passed it to Mason. 'It's in Russian.'

Mason took it and began to read. After a moment Dawson said, 'Well?'

'Like the rest of it, so far,' Mason said, 'megawatts and motive power, intensely technical. No, hang on!'

'What is it, Henry?' Dawson asked quietly.

Mason read on silently for a moment, then looked up. 'There's a reference to temperature variation techniques, prognosticated by Academician F. Komarov.' He read on to the end. 'That's all.'

'It figures, then,' Dawson said. 'All straight lines to Komarov. What do we know about him?'

'I'll get it,' Mason said. He walked across the room to a keyboard terminal, switched on and began to type. When he finished there was a soft whirring sound followed by a noise like a handful of tin tacks dropping all at once on to a board, then a length of paper appeared in the print-out terminal. Mason detached it with a practised little tug and walked back towards us. The paper, a bit longer and wider than foolscap, was covered in printing, and the whole procedure had taken less than a minute. He handed it to Dawson, who glanced at it quickly, then slid it on to the 3M overhead projector and switched on. The type appeared on a screen on the other side of the room. That way we could all read it simultaneously.

KOMAROV, FROL ILYICH B 1907 MOSCOW MEMBER SOVIET ACADEMY SCIENCES 1948 TRAINED IN GEOGRAPHY, UNIVERSITY OF MOSCOW 1926-1931, DOCTORATE 1933; READ BIOLOGY OXFORD

UNIVERSITY G.B. 1933-6, GEOLOGY HARVARD U.S.A. 1936-38. QUALIFICATIONS BIOLOGY, GEOLOGY, ENGINEERING. FOUNDED OCEANOGRAPHIC INSTITUTE, KAMCHATKA PENIN. 1945. MEMBER COMMUNIST PARTY SINCE 1925. REPUTED JOINED VOROSHILOV'S INFANT RED ARMY AGED TWELVE 1919, DECORATED BRAVERY. WAR SERVICE OBSCURE BUT REPUTED FULL CAPTAIN SOVIET NAVY. LENIN PRIZE GEOGRAPHIC STUDIES 1945, STALIN PRIZE 1949 NO CITATION. OCEANOGRAPHIC THEORIST, ADVOCATE SEA POWER. DURING ASCENDANCY RED AIR FORCE 1950-55 REPORTED OUT OF FAVOUR WORKING ARCTIC INST. CENTRE NOVOSIBIRSK. BELIEVED RESPONSIBLE DEVELOPMENT MINERAL FIELDS VORKUTA REGION SOVIET ARCTIC : GOLD, DIAMONDS, NICKEL, URANIUM, COAL. SAID PUBLICLY LABOUR REQUIRED SHOULD BE RECRUITED NOT COERCED, INCURRING DISPLEASURE KHRUSCHEV, REGARDED RESPONSIBLE NONETHELESS SWITCH SLAVE TO VOLUNTEER LABOUR SOVIET ARCTIC.

There followed a list of papers he had published on a variety of topics, then the print-out went on:

KOMAROV MADE ONE VISIT UNITED STATES POST WAR, LECTURE AMERICAN GEOGRAPHICAL SOCIETY NEED DEVELOPMENT SOUND COMMUNICATION CHANNELS SEA WATER. STAYED PRINCETON THREE DAYS, GUEST PROF. EDWIN WARD, VISITED BRITAIN ON RETURN JOURNEY MOSCOW, STAYED OXFORD WITH DR JAMES CATTO, ORIEL COLLEGE, ONLY KNOWN WESTERN FRIEND FROM STUDENT DAYS. ...INFORMATION KGB DEFECTOR VLADIMIR IVANOV, BERLIN MAY 1969, KOMAROV DISAPPEARED UNDER ARREST. OFFICIAL SOVIET ANNOUNCEMENT KOMAROV DEAD, APRIL 1969. STATE FUNERAL, POSTHUMOUS AWARD HERO SOVIET UNION.

I said, 'Christ!'
    Dawson was cooler. 'Where does all that get us?'
    'I don't like the smell of the whole damn deal,' Mason said. 'Something's going on. That's for sure.'
    'Conference,' Dawson said. 'Everybody in on this one.'

The room filled rapidly and I watched, fascinated, as the intelligence élite came into the room. *The Spy Who Came In From The Cold* was described as the most realistic of all spy novels: a tale of a seedy and cynical agent, broke, down on his luck, and working in a world whose cynicism was a thousand times greater than his own. This looked like father's night at the Parent-Teachers' Association, or a gathering of sales managers. These guys went home nights and tinkered with cars or hand-drills, grew roses, held week-end cook-outs in the garden barbecue pit. I doubted if there was a gun in the room and that's more than you can say about your friendly neighbourhood PTA in some towns I can think of.

'OK, gentlemen,' Dawson said. 'We've got a picture of something but we don't know what it is. It needs evaluation. It may need action. Mason.'

Mason didn't get up. 'Russia,' he said. 'A document came into the possession of Doctor John Edwards, who's sitting over there.' They all switched their eyes to me and then away again. I didn't have time to bow. 'A sequence of attacks then took place upon the person of Doctor Edwards. He was very lucky to escape with his life. His apartment was broken into, and all that was taken was the envelope in which the document arrived. It is apparent that the letter went to Doctor Edwards in error and should have been sent to Professor Edwin Ward at Princeton University. Professor Ward has been murdered.'

There wasn't even a murmur. Those guys were absorbing information, not reacting to it.

Mason went on. 'We have so far uncovered three documents. The first is the one sent to Doctor Edwards and is a Soviet academic paper dated 1964 on hydro-electric development in Kazakhstan. It appears at this time to have no relevance in itself to the need for intelligence or security activity. However, a page was missing from the paper. Another copy of this paper existed at Columbia University, New York, but it has been removed. The removal of this paper, and an ingenious attempt to place the responsibility for the murder of Professor Ward upon Doctor Edwards, plus the attempts upon Doctor Edwards's life, point to well-organized operators, and the source of the paper points to the Soviet Union. That means the KGB.

'The two other documents are letters written by Academician Frol Ilyich Komarov to Professor Ward. Ward was a geographer, important, distinguished, known internationally. Geography was Komarov's basic discipline also, but he developed toward geology, engineering and oceanography. It appears from the letters that Ward and Komarov had had a dialogue of some kind and had formed some kind of personal relationship based on respect for one another's work and some degree of personal sympathy. Copies of all these documents are now being made and will be available in a few minutes.

'Ward, however, is dead. We know that. We know also that Academician Komarov's death was announced in Moscow in April of this year and that he was accorded a state funeral and the posthumous title Hero of the Soviet Union.

'I believe you will all remember that the KGB Colonel Vladimir Ivanov defected to the West in May of this year. Much of the information he was able to provide under debriefing procedures has yet to be evaluated, but such authentication as we have been able so far to achieve has suggested a high degree of accuracy. Ivanov made reference, albeit a passing one, to Komarov. He said he had heard that Academician Komarov had disappeared and was under restraint working outside the Moscow region. Since the reports of (a) his death and (b) his disappearance were almost simultaneous, it is possible that some confusion exists. It is also possible that there is no confusion.'

Mason didn't round it off, or speculate. He just stopped talking. The folders of copies arrived and were handed round.

'Action, gentlemen?' Dawson said softly.

Suggestions came clickety-click and in order as Dawson switched his eyes to the man on his left, then the man next to him and so on round the table.

'Further interrogation of Ivanov may validate or clarify the question of disappearance versus death.'

'Right,' Mason said.

'Immediate collection and evaluation of all Komarov's available papers.'

Dawson said, 'There's a list in the computer. It may not be complete. Inform all offices of the urgency of the matter.'

'Doctor Catto from Oriel College, Oxford. We should get him over here.'

'Right.'

'Full scale search of Professor Ward's home and office. Interrogation of his friends and colleagues. He may have talked to somebody.'

'OK.' Mason smiled. It was the first time I had seen him smile. It was oddly attractive. 'That may take a little time,' he said. 'Professor Ward had a lot of papers.'

'His house groans with books, too,' I said.

Mason's smile vanished. He didn't want me in this discussion; he didn't actually tell me to shut up, but his eyes delivered the message. While I was still wondering whether to be hurt or angry, somebody else was talking:

'Preliminary evaluation of all intelligence information, especially unexplained occurrences, that might be related in any way to Komarov's work.'

'Right.'

'Action within the Soviet Union to clarify information about Komarov's activities.'

I saw Dawson look up. 'Not yet,' he said quietly. 'We don't know whether it's worth that risk.'

There was silence. Mason and Dawson looked round the table, but no further observations came.

Mason said, 'OK, do it.'

'Nine o'clock tomorrow,' Dawson added.

CHAPTER EIGHT

After you come out of medical school, you do a kind of tour of the joint, learning what ticks and where. As a houseman you're kept busy, and tired. You get to value sleep, and learn to glide smoothly into it when the chance offers. I was a kind of connoisseur of the quiet zizz, the forty minute nap; I knew all the secluded corners. One was in the maternity wing: a side ward with a couple of beds that weren't much in use and were very tempting. I was only tempted once and I lay there for an hour listening to the assorted caterwaulings of about forty lusty infants before I hauled my weary bones upright and took myself off. The expression sleeping like a babe has always since appeared to me to be one of the English language's worse similes. In Washington I slept like a log, a hibernated hedgehog, Rip van Winkle. They gave me this room in the CIA building with a TV set, a bath and, after a little insistence, a bottle of scotch. I pursued my favourite relaxation for an hour and three glasses, happily aware that there was nowhere on earth safer than the place I was in. It soothed me to think of all those checkpoints and security men, the passwords and the picture-taking, the whole huge CIA apparatus standing guard while I lay there with only my mouth above water watching the steam condensing on the tiles. Occasionally I put my glass to my lips and swallowed Uncle Sam's scotch with that little extra pleasure any good taxpayer would feel. I thought, too, of the KGB gnashing its collective teeth somewhere outside, and hoped the penalty for failure was the salt mines. I was very relaxed, very cheerful, almost smug. When I went to bed, finally, between those nice crisp sheets I slept happily for thirteen hours.

If I'd known, I doubt if I'd have slept at all . . .

They woke me next morning with a fat breakfast, crisp napery and the *Washington Post*. There wasn't a word in it about Professor Ward and I wondered what kind of high-powered pressure had kept the Fourth Estate quiet.

When I'd showered and dressed in the nice new underwear and the snowy new shirt some minion had miraculously procured, I went to the hospital and had the dressing on my leg fixed again, looking with proper professional pride at the row of stitches I'd put in: considering the circumstances of the sewing, they weren't half bad. I felt slightly miffed when they were removed and reinserted. Still, the wound was beginning to knit efficiently.

Just before ten, two large men arrived to take me to the conference room. They didn't exactly march me there, but one went in front and one behind and I didn't care to think what might happen if my steps deviated to right or left.

Dawson was waiting. 'Sleep well, Doctor Edwards?'

I nodded cheerfully. 'Like a log.'

Mason said, 'You deserved it.'

I hadn't noticed him; his natural camouflage had hidden him among the grey steel cabinets and it was only movement that gave him away.

The rest of them came in a minute later, fresh-faced and alert, all ready to get to work on the new swimming pool if the head teacher approved.

'OK,' Dawson said. 'What have we got?'

'Station Y had three hours with Ivanov last night, going over it. Drugs, hypnosis, the whole shebang. He's pretty positive about the disappearance. Thinks the phrase he heard was "work under restraint".'

'Right,' Mason said. 'What about Catto?'

'Flying in. No trouble. We asked him to come and he said delighted. Doesn't know why yet. He should be here soon.'

'I'll tell him,' Dawson said. 'What else?'

'Certain of Komarov's papers have been obtained, but only the ones that are on free international circulation. They're scattered round the world a bit, but copies are being transmitted where facilities exist and the papers themselves are being flown in.'

'None in yet?' It was Mason.

'No.'

'Right. The searches.'

'Both Ward's home and office have been taken apart. Nothing additional at all. None of his colleagues we've so far talked to remembers anything strange. One of them did meet Komarov, but all they talked about was Picasso. He remembers it clearly.'

Dawson said, 'What's the all-sources picture?'

'Nothing too clear. Signals intelligence monitors report a few increases in traffic and a few decreases. Nothing critical, nothing big enough to demand immediate report. Increases and decreases all fall within the statistically normal limits. Many of them represent shipping movements. However, a list of all increases has been prepared.'

Copies were passed round the table, but not to me. The PTA read, absorbed, then put the paper with the others in their files.

The same man went on, 'Satellite monitoring shows the usual activity all over the country. New things happening from the Arctic to Tashkent and the Ukraine to Vladivostock. All new rocket silos are, of course, on automatic red flash priority report, as are major radar installations. Shipbuilding activity in East Germany and Poland still increasing, but hulls under construction do not suggest progress beyond the A class hunter-killer nuclear submarines or the Arktika class icebreaker. There is some extension of the Cosmodrome at Baikonur, but this has been previously reported. Much of Northern Russia has, of course, been in conditions of maximum night for several weeks now, and though infra-red satellite photography is improving, it is still open to substantial problems of interpretation. Unexplained dark patches that could be lack of reflection, faults in transmission. Anything.'

Dawson said mildly, 'We don't seem to be getting very far, do we. So let's match the dark patches with the increased traffic and see what emerges.'

A big map was pulled down from a rack of rollers on the ceiling, and several of them went to work on it. Half an hour went by and we all watched the markings accumulate. It had all been very tidy, but now papers and photographs began to accumulate on the floor, on surfaces, in corners.

Jackets came off and discussion became, as they say, general.

Then Brains-and-Bones came in. With him was a little guy, thick-lipped. His skin was coarse and pitted with the remains of severe adolescent acne, his forehead a network of deep, curving wrinkles. He wore big, black glasses.

'Doctor James Catto,' Brains-and-Bones said.

Dawson got up quickly and went over to him, hand out. 'Thank you for coming so quickly, Doctor Catto.'

'Not at all, my pleasure.' The voice was startling; I was expecting a bullfrog croak and hearing instead a clipped, clear enunciation that Noël Coward wouldn't have been ashamed of.

'Let me take your coat and briefcase,' Dawson said smoothly, leading Catto away towards an office in the corner.

'You're very kind,' Catto murmured.

They were in there about two minutes, then out they came again. Dawson must have been telling Catto about Professor Ward's death. It was impossible to tell from Catto's face whether he was affected.

Mason gave Catto a condensed version of what had happened and the information available. He compressed more facts into every sentence than *Time* magazine.

Then Dawson took over. 'Doctor Catto, in the CIA we find it valuable to concentrate several minds upon a problem. Call it brainstorming if you like, but we prefer to think of it as exposing a question to a variety of disciplines and therefore to approaches from several directions at once. What I'd like to do is to ask you some questions while all these people listen. Then let them follow up. That OK?'

Catto's thick lips moved into a smile. 'My lectures frequently appear to be conducted in that way. Please do anything you wish.'

Mason said, 'You know Komarov.'

'Knew,' Catto corrected. 'I'm sorry to say he died early this year.'

'We have reason to believe it's open to doubt, Doctor,' Mason said.

'Really?' He didn't seem particularly surprised. 'I shall be glad if reports of his death have been exaggerated.'

'Do you know what he was working on?'

Catto said, 'Komarov's mind is a remarkable one. He is, or was—I hope it's *is*—a theoretician constructing patterns, rather than a researcher into one deep area. Anything affecting the geography of the Soviet Union or the oceans and seas around it, or the minerals in it, might be dovetailed into some concept of his. He has, for example, been responsible to a large degree for much of the mineralogical development of Northern Euro-Asia. He was also deeply involved in oceanographic studies of many kinds.' Catto smiled again. 'I'm sorry if all this is not very helpful. If you asked me what Professor Dorothy Hodgkin did, I could describe, within my own limitations, the lines her research takes. The same is true of Oppenheimer, for example. Try to imagine that, sixty years ago, you had asked an ordinary mathematician what Einstein was doing. In his own field, or fields, Komarov projects concepts.'

Mason said dryly, 'Such as?' but he was grinning.

Catto laughed delightedly, the big mouth widening. 'I really am willing to be pinned down. This isn't evasion. But you'll have to supply me with specific areas for amplification. He's thought a lot and carried out many experiments, for example, in submarine sound transmission. Then there's the interplay of ocean currents, and interpretation of satellite photograph in the discovery of mineral deposits.' He paused. 'Komarov ranges, rather.'

'Let's try not to range, Doctor Catto,' Dawson said. 'Tell us about Komarov as a man.'

'As a man? Well, now . . . I've known him for almost thirty-five years. He studied at Oxford, you know. You *do* know?'

'We know,' Mason said.

'I thought you might. Well, when he first came over he was a very dedicated man. Brilliant. Quite brilliant. But with Marxism always there, if you see what I mean. One got the impression that he didn't much like people. Loneliness, I've always thought. He's not chatty, doesn't like idle conversation. Either he's involved acutely in something that interests him, or he goes away and reads a book. A dreamer, too, I suppose. Knew Jules Verne and H. G. Wells almost by heart. Always been the same. I send him Arthur C. Clarke's books.'

'You're familiar with his way of writing letters?' Dawson asked. 'You corresponded.'

Catto said, 'Off and on, always. They seem to have let my letters in and his out, even in the worst days of Stalin. Yes, I know his style.'

Mason passed him the two letters. Catto read them carefully, twice, eyes staring behind the glasses, then he looked up. 'Second one's a bit odd. It's not like him to go on about illness. When he told me he was a diabetic, he did it in one sentence, then moved on. And overwork isn't a word in his vocabulary. He's never stopped working. What's more, he adores travel. Definitely odd.'

'You like him?' Dawson asked.

'Oh, very much. Awfully nice man. Completely dedicated Marxist, of course, but a humanist, too. He used to quote that line of Shaw's about hating the poor and wanting to abolish them.'

'Principle?' Dawson said.

The thick lips moved into a reminiscent smile. 'Reeks of it. I can't imagine how he survived the Stalin period. Refuses absolutely to have anything to do with exploitation. You know what he did at Vorkuta?'

Dawson said, 'A little.'

'Insisted on volunteer labour, not people from the punishment camps. The thing is, it worked. No sabotage and considerable enthusiasm. I sometimes wonder if that wasn't at the back of Khruschev's virgin lands policy. Am I rambling, or being helpful? It's so difficult to know.'

I found myself grinning, like everybody else in the room. It was impossible not to like Catto, not to be charmed by that beautifully-modulated voice.

'It's helpful, Doctor Catto,' Mason said. 'I'm not sure yet just how, but it's helpful. Keep going.'

'Keep going? Well, I'll try. Let's see . . . well, he believed passionately in justice, you know. Surprising in a way. Demands absolute academic freedom, but then we all try for that. Oh yes, and he's deeply concerned, always has been, about the moral situation of scientists. Condemns Einstein for giving to Roosevelt the equation on which the atomic bomb was based. Says Einstein should have kept it to himself—and killed himself if necessary to keep the secret. Same with things like DDT. Komarov deplores the use of ideas, concepts and materials that have not been adequately tested, whose consequences are not predictable.'

I was still thinking about what Catto had said about the letter, and re-reading a copy. In the light of Catto's description of Komarov, some of those phrases seemed to imply reluctance and restraint. I said, 'Could he be in that situation himself?'

Catto turned to face me. 'I beg your pardon?'

'Are any of his ideas or theories the kind that could have serious, or unlooked-for consequences?'

'Oh, I see. No, I don't think . . . so.' He'd started to say it confidently enough, but he wasn't so sure at the end.

'Possible, though,' Mason rapped out.

Catto sat, thinking, for several moments, right upper canine tooth gnawing at his lower lip. Finally he said, 'I hardly think they'd be trying it. Komarov wouldn't want to, that's certain.'

Dawson said, 'He's either dead, or under some kind of arrest.'

'He'd never do it. He'd kill himself first.'

'Maybe they won't let him,' Mason said.

Catto stared at him, his frog face full of sadness.

'Komarov used to say it wouldn't happen until the 21st century, if then.'

Dawson asked very gently, 'What wouldn't?'

'The polar melt.'

CHAPTER NINE

I stared. We all stared. Every eye in the room was on James Catto. Since even I had heard of the potential hazards involved in melting the polar ice-pack, it was safe to assume that the rest of them were familiar with the question.

Mason spoke first. 'How and why? Can you tell us?'

'I can try. The oceans aren't my territory, so to speak. It might be better to ask your great oceanographer Columbus Iselin at Woods Hole Institute. He'll certainly be able to tell you more about what it would mean.'

Dawson said, 'We'll approach Iselin later, Doctor Catto. But we'd like to hear you.'

'Very well. The principle is very simple. The Arctic Ocean is very big. A huge proportion of the world's land mass borders it. All of Northern Canada, Northern Alaska, and all of Asia from North Cape to the Bering Strait. Most of that land is almost entirely useless, not because it is lacking in any of the fundamental properties, but because it is permanently frozen.

'The Arctic Ocean is also deep, safe water, as *Nautilus* and *Skate*, the nuclear submarines, discovered in voyages under the Polar ice in 1958. In poetic moments people have referred to an Arctic Ocean open to shipping as a northern Mediterranean.

'It is widely believed—no, it is known—that the Arctic

Ocean was not always ice-covered. But for many thousands of years there has been an accretion of ice. You will know that when water turns into ice its volume increases. Conversely, when ice turns to water, its volume decreases. The melting of the Polar pack should not, therefore, produce a greater volume of water. But—it is the accretion of ice that presents the problem. Water has gradually been turning into ice for thousands of years. If it melted, it would raise the level of the oceans a few inches, a foot, perhaps two. It would also open up all of Northern Russia to shipping, possibly even to production of foodstuffs.'

He paused. 'All clear?'

'We're right with you,' Mason said.

'All right. Remember that Russia has fewer good ports than any other major nation. In the West, only Murmansk remains ice-free the year round, and that's thanks to the Gulf Stream. Even the Baltic ports freeze in. In the east, well, Vladivostock and a few more, but they're all a devil of a distance from European Russia, and China's doing a lot of heavy breathing. If that vast northern coastline could be opened up to year-round shipping, the development of Soviet economic resources would get the biggest boost it is possible to imagine.'

Dawson came in smoothly. 'Doctor Catto, what would be the consequences?'

'For Russia, mainly very good. Ports would open up, as I say. They'd lose a certain amount of territory, of course—how much would depend upon the increase in global water levels—but they have a great deal more territory than anybody else, so they could afford it. It would certainly effect major changes in the map of the world. Quite large areas would be submerged, and low-lying territory would naturally be most vulnerable. Holland, of course, is the obvious example. Much of Holland might well be in danger. Canada, on the other hand, might benefit enormously.

He paused, frowning. 'The trouble is that it's all incalculable. We haven't really got the faintest idea what would happen. There's Greenland, you see.'

Mason said, 'What about Greenland?'

Catto looked at him. 'Fifteen hundred miles long, up to six hundred wide. A mile high, a lot of it. And solid ice. Supposing that a warmer Arctic Ocean began to melt the Greenland Icecap, and it could do that, gentlemen, it could do that!—well *then*, large areas of the world might well be inundated. An increase in the water level of the North Atlantic, for example, of three or four feet, maybe a lot more, would put London, Paris, New York under water. The main ports, capital cities and a tremendous amount of the land masses of Europe and the Eastern United States and Canada, would simply vanish.'

'Vanish?' Dawson said.

'Oh, completely. Heaven knows what would happen. One doesn't know how the ocean currents would carry the water away, or where they might distribute it. One doesn't know what the earth's rotation might do—it is, after all, a huge centrifuge.' Catto's voice was even, matter-of-fact, almost mild.

The rest of us just sat looking at him, our minds wrestling with mental pictures of a world in which the oceans rose to smother the cities; in which man was crowded into ever smaller land areas.

Mason broke the silence. 'I don't want to be rude, Doctor Catto, but would Komarov—or Iselin for that matter—know more than you?'

Catto said, 'Oh, infinitely more. This is their field, not mine.' He paused for a moment, then added, 'But neither of them could do more than guess at what would happen.'

'I see,' Dawson said slowly. 'Could the Russians do it?'

Catto spread his hands. 'It's engineering on a mammoth scale. Komarov has always believed it could be done, and the truth is, gentlemen, that the Russians know a great deal more about the oceans than the rest of us.'

'Why?' Mason asked.

'Simply because they have devoted infinitely more time and money to studying the ocean than the rest of us. The Soviet Union has always believed deeply in the fundamental importance of sea power—'

Dawson interrupted. 'Komarov!'

'Indeed, Komarov is, and has been for many years, one of the principal advocates of sea power. You see,' Catto said, 'they've been pursuing it hard for thirty years or more. Trawler fleets, submarines, shipping of all kinds, conducting surveys of the sea, mapping currents. Heaven knows what they haven't done! I don't think there can be any doubt at all that Russian knowledge of, for example, the topography of the ocean bed, the movements of currents, is greater than the West's by several magnitudes. There have been people in the United States who felt very strongly about the way you were falling behind. I remember Senator Magnusson telling

Congress ten years ago, "Russia has been winning the wet war with more and bigger ships; more, if not better, scientists; more, and in some instances superior, equipment; and more aggressive government encouragement and action." He also said that the outcome of the wet war may determine the fate of the human race. And there was the chap in charge of Research and Development for the US Navy, Admiral Hayward or some such name. He said years ago that Soviet effort in oceanography was designed to establish and demonstrate world leadership. You see?'

There was nothing I could contribute to this one; I simply sat and listened, aghast at the possibilities and wondering why nobody'd ever heard of the wet war.

'Yes, Doctor, I see very clearly,' Dawson said. 'But before we get too panicky about this, can you tell us the kind of means they might use?'

'Some of it, I suppose,' Catto said. 'There is, obviously, the possibility of thermo-nuclear explosions to destroy the ice. Another interesting idea is to dam the Bering Strait between Russia and Alaska. It's not too wide, you know. Then to set enormous pumps going to move warm water from the Pacific into the Arctic Ocean, and pump cold water back in its place. Huge operation, of course, and incredibly costly. And they'd need your co-operation to build the dam, so perhaps that's out. But I know Komarov had lots of ideas. One of the best—it sounds like a bit of science fiction but it is probably perfectly feasible, is the use of carbon powder.'

'How?' Mason asked.

'Well, it's simple really. Ice, as you will appreciate, resists the melting effect of heat by reflecting a lot of it. In the Arctic in the summer, the days are literally endless of course. But because the sun's rays are hitting a white ice mass, they just bounce off, or most of them do. But carbon is black, and black doesn't reflect. So if you coated the ice with powdered carbon, the sun's heat would be absorbed. Simple, isn't it?'

There was a still silence in the room. Everybody was thinking more or less the same thing, except Doctor Catto who had not been present earlier, and now looked mildly surprised at the effect his words had had. Mason got up and walked across to the big wall map and pointed with his finger.

'The shaded patches here, Doctor Catto, were transferred to this map from infra-red pictures taken by satellites.'

'Really? How recently?'

'The last few weeks.'

'Then they could be precisely what I'm talking about. Or not, you know. One doesn't want to leap to too many conclusions. In any case, they're quite small; I doubt whether they'd have any noticeable effect. Still it is interesting that they have appeared since daylight vanished up there. Most interesting.'

One of the men at the table stood. 'Excuse me, Lawrence. Something I'd like to check.'

'OK, Roger.'

Catto went on, 'But I know Komarov had a great many other ideas. Do you know about Pykrete?'

I didn't and the others looked blank, too.

'Marvellous stuff,' Catto said. 'Extraordinary properties.'

Dawson said, 'Tell us, Doctor Catto.'

'It was developed, oddly enough, in one of the London markets—Smithfield I think, where the meat is handled—by a team working under a chap called Pyke. Hence Pykrete of course. The idea is that you can strengthen ice enormously by mixing it with other things. Normally it's brittle and crystalline. But Pyke's mixture had enormously increased strength and insulated itself against heat. As a matter of fact, there was a plan to build vast ships of it. During the war, that was. I believe Churchill had a soup tureen of it brought into Roosevelt's room at the Quebec conference and invited him to pour a kettle of boiling water on it by way of demonstration. Just bounced off.' He looked round mildly. 'Anyone remember?'

Dawson said, 'A very distinct bell is ringing. Habbakuk, or something.'

'Habbakuk, that's right! That was the code name.' Catto laughed. 'It didn't really come to much, though one ship was built. In Canada I think, and it floated throughout the summer on a lake somewhere, barely melting at all.'

'Maybe I'm dim,' Mason said. 'I thought the point was that ice should melt?'

'I'm so sorry, I'm being obscure again.' Catto looked instantly contrite. 'But you see, Komarov was thinking of using it to build dams.'

'Where?' Dawson asked.

'Ah. I'm afraid that's the problem. They *do* know so much more than ourselves about the ocean currents, and a great deal of the time, if I may borrow an expression of yours, gentlemen, they ain't telling. In the last twenty years or so a great deal has been discovered about the ocean streams, and I rather fear they've discovered more than we know. As an example, there's the Cromwell Stream, which seems to originate near the Gilbert Islands and flows eight thousand miles, to the Galapagos. It's almost a hundred miles wide, carries three times as much water as the Gulf Stream, and it flows five hundred feet *below* the surface, along the equator. The Russians love that one, of course. It means their submarines can get to the US coast more quickly, like an aircraft with a tail wind.

'And there's another current, running in roughly the opposite direction to the Gulf Stream, but underneath it. There are currents of all kinds being discovered all over the place. Huge things.

'Komarov's idea is dam and divert. In a pattern, naturally, so that extremely favourable climatic conditions can be created. You can call it climatic engineering if you like. He wouldn't want to do it until he was sure nobody would be damaged. But you tell me he may have no choice . . .'

Catto looked round. 'I'm sorry, gentlemen. It's all very complex and unpredictable. I gather he planned to build vast Pykrete rafts. You know that most of an iceberg floats beneath the water? Well, just by spraying the top of a raft with supercooled water and sawdust, you'd gradually force it deeper and deeper until it hit the bottom. Then you'd have a dam. Well, there's one plan to build a dam between Siberia and the Russian island of Sakhalin, which is located between Northern Japan and the East Siberian coast. The dam will be thrown across the Tatar Straits, which are frozen over in the winter. Naturally, the Japanese are furious, because it would play hell with their climate.

'It goes like this. Southern Sakhalin is warmed by the Sea of Japan. Northern Sakhalin is surrounded by the cold Sea of Okhotsk. Every high tide a certain amount of warm water flows from South to North, then about turns smartly with the tide and flows back again. When the Russians build the dam, it will have big one-way gates in it, so the warm water will flow through *with* the tide, but the moment the tide turns, the gates will close and stop the flow back. Next high tide, more warm water.'

'Simple.' Dawson was looking at the map. 'I can see why the Japs wouldn't like it.'

'But the Russians will love it,' Catto said. 'At every tide the volume of warm water flowing through will be roughly four times the daily flow of the Volga, Don and Dnieper combined. And it will reach the northern coast of the island and the coast of mainland Siberia. It has been calculated that this could raise the temperature in Eastern Siberia by almost twenty degrees, and free the area of ice. Meanwhile the poor old Japanese would find the Kuroshio Stream, which benefits them, would move farther north because the Sea of Okhotsk became warmer. And the Russians *are* going to build the Sakhalin dam. They've announced plans. It will cost billions, of course, in concrete. That's why Komarov was playing with Pykrete.'

'I wouldn't call this playing,' Mason said.

Catto smiled apologetically. 'Just a figure of speech.'

'How much is feasible?' Dawson asked softly.

Catto spread his hands. 'The engineering techniques exist. It's largely a question of how much knowledge you have and how much you're prepared to spend. Or risk. You could trigger off a new Ice Age quite simply.'

I said, 'Jesus!' I couldn't help it. Neither could several others.

Catto grinned. 'Sorry, gentlemen. It may be happening already as a result of all our cars and factories. We're pouring carbon-dioxide into the air, you know, at a fantastic rate, and it's producing the so-called greenhouse effect. It admits the passage of warming radiation from the sun, but prevents the heat escaping back into space. So we're building up heat. Paradoxically, this is what could start a new Ice Age. If the Arctic Ocean melts, it will, of course, have the chance to evaporate. So you will get heavy snowfalls on the mainland glaciers. Well, a glacier's like a big piece of dough. Every snowfall increases the glacier's weight, which increases the pressure on it and in it, and makes it move in whichever direction resistance is least. So the glaciers would spread. Ice Age, you see.'

Mason said, 'Does that conflict with your point about melting the Greenland ice?'

'Yes and no,' Catto said. 'Sudden thawing would have sudden effects. Ice ages take a long time to get started. But all of this, you see, is why Komarov says we're simply too damn ignorant, at the moment, to begin tinkering.'

The door opened. 'Lawrence!' The man Dawson had called Roger hurried back into the room. 'Those black patches!'

'Well?' Dawson said.

'I thought I remembered something, so I went to check.

Do you remember a Russian plane crashed in Northern Greenland a couple of months back?'

'Vaguely,' Dawson said. 'On—' he sat up suddenly—'on Polar reconnaissance, wasn't it?'

'Right. The crew was killed. The bodies were recovered by a group of army engineers up at the Polar Research and Development place, Camp Hundred, on the icecap. The commander's a Colonel Chance. His report on it says the aircraft was rapidly being buried under blowing snow. But it appeared to be fitted with something that reminded him of crop-spraying equipment. And he found his boots were covered afterwards with black powder.'

Mason said, 'Carbon!'

'Chance's report says, "fine black powder of a carboniferous nature, which may have come from a fire of some kind, though there appeared to have been no fire on the aircraft". He also says that in the wrecked fuselage of the aircraft there were several large drums.'

'That seems to settle it,' Dawson said. 'Those black patches are carbon powder.'

I said, 'And Komarov tried to warn us.'

'He's trying to do much more than that, I think,' Catto said.

'What do you mean?' It was Mason.

'That letter. The second one. I've been thinking about it, and it puzzles me.'

'In what way?'

'That phraseology. May I see it again?'

Mason gave him a copy quickly, and Catto read it through. 'It's here, you see. "Over-eating is like over-work; one must be careful, and know the consequences of indulgence." Hm?' Catto looked round at us, questioningly. 'Then there's this one. The next sentence: "It is necessary sometimes to resist the pressures, stand back, and think before one becomes too carried away." '

'You think,' I said, 'that he's predicting his own arrest?'

'Dated March 14th,' Catto said. 'Not long before his disappearance or death. If pressure were on him, he could have known by then.'

I said, 'You're right. It goes on: "If we could work more closely together than the world now allows, I am sure the result would be productive." '

Mason said, 'And then: "I hope it will be possible for us to meet again one day." Doctor, it's possible to read anything into anything, but if you read this whole letter this way, there's a hell of a lot beneath the surface. This next sentence may be a direct reference to impending, well, restraint or arrest. Listen: "I am afraid that in my present physical situation, travel is difficult for me." '

'Did you hear from him after March 14th?' I asked Catto.

'No. My last letter was at New Year. Very cheerful. No hint.'

I said, 'Look. One thing bothers me about all this. Let's assume Komarov's being forced, against his will, to work on some gigantic project, involving the Polar ice plus anything else. He's disappeared. He writes regularly to Doctor Catto here, and off and on to Professor Ward. He sends this warning to Ward. But he sends it to Princeton.'

'Go on,' Dawson said.

'The next one doesn't go to Princeton at all. It comes to me. And why? Because it's addressed to Professor Edwards *at my address*. Why would Komarov do that?'

Catto said, 'Where do you live?'

'New York apartment block,' I said.

'Did Ward ever live there?'

I said, 'We'd better find out.'

I didn't know what it was; there was an idea lurking somewhere in the depths of my mind, but I couldn't get hold of it. The harder I tried to grab it, the further it receded.

I said, 'Can I use the phone?'

Mason pushed it towards me. 'Help yourself.'

'New York dial coding?'

Someone recited it and I dialled the property corporation's number.

'Sunlit Developments. Good morning.'

Dawson whispered, 'Mention the department's name. It helps.'

'This is the Central Intelligence Agency,' I said. 'I want to know whether a man called Edwin Ward ever lived in any of your apartments. Professor Edwin Ward.'

The girl on the other end took it in her stride. I envied her detachment. 'One moment please, sir.'

I waited. They must have had an efficient system: she came back in maybe a minute. 'We had a William Ward, sir, and a Henry Ward. And a Mrs Agnes Ward.'

'Professions?'

'William Ward was a lawyer, sir, and Henry Ward something to do with the theatre. Mrs Agnes Ward is a widow.'

'That's all?'

'That's all.'

I thanked her and hung up. Then I phoned Jane Macdonald at Princeton. 'Jane, John Edwards. Did he ever live in New York?'

'Professor Ward? No, I don't think so. I know he hated New York. Didn't even like going there to the AGA. He never stayed overnight if he could help it.'

'Fine.'

'Why?'

'I don't know,' I said. 'But thanks.'

I turned to them. 'He hated New York. Never lived in those apartments, or anywhere in New York as far as we know.'

Dawson said, 'We don't know if Komarov sent the message. If he didn't, it was sent on his behalf. An engineering paper with a reference to Komarov's temperature variation techniques.'

I said, 'So why me? And why did the KGB take the envelope?'

'What did the envelope say?' Mason said quickly.

'Wait a minute.' I remembered thinking there were three mistakes in it. I picked up a piece of paper and wrote the address as I remember it, then put it on the 3M projector so they could all see it.

PROFESSOR EDWARD, FAGS
60 E75th St, NEW YORK, USA.

Mason said, 'Look, if it had been done this way—' he wrote it out again and placed it on the machine:

Professor Ed WARD, FAGS,
60 E 75th St, NEW YORK, USA.

'—it wouldn't have been delivered to you.'

'So,' Dawson added, 'it would have been returned marked "not known at this address". In which case, the Post Office would have traced Professor Ed. Ward, FAGS. Right?'

'Standard practice,' Mason agreed. 'And the signpost's easy enough. The Geographical Association.'

I said, 'But the KGB took the envelope. Why? Listen—' I could feel it coming nearer, but I hadn't got it yet—'there's a message on the paper *inside* the envelope, and we've been concentrating on *that*! Is there another in the *address*? It's pretty precise after all.'

We all stared at the letters up there on the screen. You could hear the minds whirring.

Then Catto said, 'Perhaps it's because I'm a geographer. But it could be co-ordinates.'

We moved, in a body, over to the big map. 'Let's see,' Catto murmured. 'Sixty degrees east, and seventy-five . . . no, it's unlikely to be south, so seventy-five north brings us to—here!' He stood on tiptoe to place his thick finger on the map.

The lines or latitude and longitude crossed on the island of Novaya Zemlya in the Soviet Arctic.

CHAPTER TEN

Catto said, 'Novaya Zemlya used to be the nuclear proving ground until the test-ban treaty. They did pretty well all their atomic and hydrogen bomb tests there.'

'Yes,' Dawson said thoughtfully. 'They did, didn't they?'

Mason said, 'So now we have an unholy mix. We have Komarov, who's supposed to be dead, but isn't, sending information to help us, or warn us, in spite of the fact that he's a dedicated Communist. We have the KGB catching on to it and reacting desperately. Probably because it slipped through and they let it. We have all kinds of horrible things that *can* happen to the Polar Ice, the ocean currents and God knows what! We have the nuclear test centre and the dark patches, presumably of carbon dust. The only question is what it all means. And when we find *that* out, what the US and the West in general can do about it.'

Catto said, 'There's the rub, I'm afraid. Finding out. I suppose if you knew, all sorts of international pressure could be put on.'

'Pressure the like of which you've never seen,' Dawson said. 'This will go straight to the Director of the CIA and from him to the President, you can be sure of that.'

I walked away, back to the table. I wanted to read that letter of Komarov's again. There was a lot of talk going on; a lot of excited speculation; but the trouble was that it *was* only speculation, and something was nagging hard at my mind. I sat there, my mind shutting out the talk, trying to grasp what Komarov had been getting at. Komarov and Ward had talked during Komarov's visit to the United States. Then Komarov had sent that letter with its innocuous surface and its mass of veiled references. Then the paper. The purpose of the paper was to say that work had begun on temperature variation. The envelope said where. Was that all? Could it be all?

I read through the letter again, then got a piece of paper and copied it out, deleting the phrases that were only padding:

'My condition has been stabilized . . . over-work; one must be careful and know the consequences . . . necessary to resist pressures . . . carried away . . . the conversation we had . . . if we could work together more closely . . . the result would be for everyone's good . . . meet again . . . physical situation, travel is difficult.'

All that, I thought, was dated March 14th. Then, months later, the paper and the envelope.

So now one could add: 'Academician Komarov's work on temperature variation . . . Novaya Zemlya.'

It was a warning, certainly, sent to Ward in the only way possible. Because Ward would remember the conversation. 'Physical situation, travel is difficult' and 'if we could work again more closely.'

It hit me then, suddenly. The thought I'd been trying to grasp stopped eluding me and came knocking.

I got up, walked over to Catto and handed him the letter as I'd copied it out. He read it through, turned his big eyes on me, stared at me for a moment, then nodded. We moved across together to Dawson, and Catto gave him the sheet of paper. Dawson looked at it, too. 'Well?'

I said, 'He wants us to get him out.'

I still wonder whether Dawson was finally convinced. Or Mason. But I was, and Catto was, and the more we thought about it, the more convinced we became. Catto put it to Dawson like this:

'Komarov would seek to convey precise information. It is entirely uncharacteristic that he should talk much about himself. The fact that he does is critical. Look what he tells us. One, that he's resisting; two, that he's been "carried away"; three, that he's in Novaya Zemlya; four, that he would "like to work again more closely"; five, that he would like to "meet again", and six, that "travel is difficult".'

Dawson shook his head doubtfully. 'It's a hell of a conclusion to draw.'

'I should have seen it myself,' Catto said.

'Look, Mr Dawson,' I said urgently. 'If you read this stuff any other way, you're left wondering. You've got a warning they're up to something, but as Doctor Catto says, you haven't the faintest idea what! It could be any one of a dozen projects. Ward, if he'd been alive now, might have been able to help, but remember all this was addressed to Ward. Only one man knows what's happening. That's Komarov. And he wants to tell us. That's why he wants out.'

'Why else would he say where he is?' Mason said. I could have kissed him. 'There was no need for that address. If he'd wanted to warn you what was going on, he could have sent that paper to Ward at Princeton—'

I interrupted. 'That gamble with the efficiency of the US Mail was the only way of telling us where *he* is. The only way! He'd know Ward would be puzzled by the address, put two and two together.'

Dawson remained doubtful, but to give him the credit he deserved he wasn't the kind of doubter who tramples on things. He set up, and quickly, a large-scale analysis of everything that had happened in the previous year in the Soviet Arctic, and in Novaya Zemlya in particular. All over that building people must have been beavering away, going over logs of radio intercept traffic, interpreting photo reconnaissance pictures, checking whispers against rumours against hints. We waited, all of us, tensely; chaining down our impatience, going over and over again the phrases and the nuances of those letters. Mason, the crisp, unemotional Mason, was already half on our side, and in the waiting period, Catto and I won him over completely. It was strange that the two of us, amateurs among the pros, relying on instinct and knowledge of human behaviour, should be pushing a whole great agency of state.

Finally the answers came back. Photo reconnaissance had picked out one building, two storeys high, that had been built on top of a cliff on the island, during the short Arctic summer. Novaya Zemlya was one of the places where an increase in radio traffic had been detected. Not a huge increase, but an increase all the same. What made it more important was that the messages passed were in high-grade, mechanically generated ciphers that the computers hadn't been able to touch, and that the d/f bearings on those radio signals located that building clearly.

Dawson took the whole thing to the Director of the CIA.

Before he left, he looked at the three of us, at our strained, anxious faces. 'Don't worry,' he said. 'I won't sell you short.'

When he returned his face was grim. 'You'd better start thinking how, gentlemen. The Director is seeing the President in twenty minutes.'

So again we waited, looking at our watches, drinking coffee, wondering what was happening in that oval room in the White House; trying to put ourselves in the position of the man who sat there confronted by a new threat that threw another weight into the balance of terror, tipping its advantage away. Dawson's suggestion wasn't acted upon. Until the answer came, no one in the room could think of anything but the decision. Dawson paced silently up and down the conference room with one of the satellite pictures in his hand, pausing now and then to look across at Catto or me. I could imagine what he was thinking. Catto sat near me, his straight chair tilted back, his eyes on the ceiling. Once he leaned forward and said to me, 'The more I think, the more I'm sure. He'd want to die before . . . and they won't even let him do that.' Then he tilted the chair back again.

I was more puzzled than anything else. It was the first chance in days to think; the first time I had realized just how crazy it was that I should be here at all. A few nights ago my biggest problem had been a dull dinner in New York; after that the kaleidoscope of violence, pursuit and death, culminating in the presence of an obscure young surgeon at a conference upon whose conclusion the President of the United States was now ruling. I couldn't even imagine why they'd let me stay or let me talk or listened to me. I'd have kept pinching myself to make sure I wasn't dreaming if the wound in my leg and the dozen tense men in the room hadn't been there to remind me.

Time dragged by. Eventually, I think we must all have stopped thinking. I know I did. I'd been watching the electric clock on the wall so much that I gave in and just stared at it, gazing at the sweeping red second hand that revolved slowly round the face. When the phone rang I just about jumped clear of my shoes. Dawson picked it up, listened, and went out of the door on the run, returning a few minutes later with a piece of paper.

'Gentlemen,' he began, but a frog in his throat stopped him and he had to start again.

'Gentlemen, this order is from the President. It reads:

' "It is clear that the security of the United States and many of our allies faces a new threat. To know its general nature is not enough. It is imperative that we therefore seek, by all possible means, to learn the specific nature of the threat. This is a matter for several departments of state and for state agencies. They will be instructed as necessary.

' "I hereby instruct the Central Intelligence Agency to remove Academician Frol Ilyich Komarov from the territory of the USSR and to bring him to the United States.

' "I draw your attention to the fact that such a mission, carried out by United States service personnel, would constitute an overt act of war against the USSR. This is *not*, repeat *not*, permissible.

' "The personnel engaged in this venture must therefore be of several nationalities. I am consulting our allies urgently with a view to the provision of personnel.

' "All must be either civilians or, if they are service personnel, must be dismustered and discredited so that responsibility may be laid only at the doors of individuals and not of nations.

' "Within these conditions the Central Intelligence has freedom to act as it sees fit. Such action should take place as soon as suitable means have been devised.

' "Resources necessary will be provided by the United States."

'This letter is dated today,' Dawson said. 'A meeting will take place in this room, this afternoon, to discuss the means. Representatives of the equipment branches of the services will be present.'

They all broke for lunch then, and I knew that for me at least it was over. I stood looking round the conference room, still trying to digest my own astonishment, then I headed for the door. Mason was in the way.

I said, 'If you'll just sign me out of here, I'll go back to being a doctor again.'

He shook his head, grinning. I'd never seen him grin before and I've seen pleasanter sights. 'You're going nowhere, Doctor Edwards.'

'Don't be stupid,' I said. 'I've work to get back to.'

'Until this thing's through, you stay right here. In this building.'

I said angrily, 'Don't worry, I won't talk.'

'I don't believe you, Doctor. I can't afford to. I want to know where your mouth is every minute, and every word it says.'

I said 'Christ!' loudly and angrily, and stalked across to

Dawson. 'Mason says you're keeping me. It's damn well ridiculous. I must go back to New York.'

Dawson said, 'He's right. You're a hell of a security risk. Don't forget our friends in the KGB. They'll still be waiting in New York.'

He had a point. It was a reunion I could do without. Then I noticed Dawson was looking at me thoughtfully.

'What now?' I said.

'Read the letter again. The bit about his diet. Komarov's a diabetic.'

'So?' I said. I was puzzled. I must be very dumb.

'He'll need a doctor.'

Now I understood. 'No.'

'The fewer people who know about this, the better.'

'No.'

Mason strolled over. He was grinning again.

He said, 'We could keep you here for years.' Now Dawson was smiling. I never saw anything so humourless in my life. 'There's only one way you'll get any fresh air now, Doc.'

I said 'No' again, but it was beginning to seem pointless. It was.

Mason said, 'The United States will provide necessary resources. You're a necessary resource.'

'The President gave you to us,' Dawson said.

I was drafted.

CHAPTER ELEVEN

Once, in the days that followed, I asked Dawson why I'd been conscripted into the party. He just looked at me and said, 'Call it an Act of God. There's been a finger pointing your way since that letter was sent. We need a doctor, you're a doctor; we need a skier, you can ski; we need somebody who understands the importance of this mission, and you understand it. You're young and you're strong. You're going.'

They picked the man to lead the mission the same way, and if they played rough with me, what they did to Luke Chance was brutal. Maybe it was all logical enough: they wanted a guy with a lot of Arctic experience, and Chance's name was already on the table. He'd spent four years up there and what he didn't know about Arctic transportation wasn't worth knowing. His record showed he was a born leader, tough, hardy, brave and resourceful and with medals to prove it from the Pacific island-hopping in World War Two and from Korea.

That line in the President's memorandum caused all the trouble. Chance was a full colonel, a career soldier with twenty-seven years' fine service, and the instruction said specifically that if the mission were carried out by United States service personnel, then it constituted an overt act of war. The requirement was that the guys who went to get Komarov should appear, if captured, to be a bunch of private freebooters. That way the UN wouldn't ring with accusations.

So when I met Chance he was blazing mad and didn't care who knew it, and Luke Chance mad was a formidable sight. A huge guy; not just tall, though he was around six-four, but built to match all over; one of the people who reach forty-five about three times as tough as they were at twenty-five. Those years in isolation commanding Camp Hundred had made him independent, too, and his mind was as strong as his body. He wasn't even asked, or given the option, to volunteer. One minute he was commander at Hundred, the next he was ordered to Thule, where he ran straight into an escort of six officers who took him to a jet and flew him to Fort Belvoir, Virginia, where the Corps of Engineers is headquartered. There they confronted him with papers proving he'd been milking the accounts systematically for years and demanded his resignation. Chance said, 'The hell with you. Court-martial me.' They held a secret summary court-martial then and there by order of the Chief of Staff, sentenced him, dismissed the service, and slung him in the stockade for the night—which just doesn't happen to officers—to give the Press the opportunity to work over the story. Next morning he'd been on his way to see his Senator with a newspaper headed 'Arctic Hero dismissed Army for Theft, Fraud' tucked under his arm, when a couple of CIA men bundled him into a closed car, incurring contusions and abrasions at all points while doing so. Only then was Chance told what the hell it was all about. He had a right to be mad. He left none of us in any doubt that he thought the whole scheme cockeyed. Every time somebody came up with a plan, Chance kicked its legs away. If he didn't, somebody else did. We were free to draw on the whole resources of the

US army, navy and air force, plus those of some allies, and the mere thought of all those planes and tanks and submarines gave us a kind of wide-eyed optimism like kids in a toy shop.

Gradually, though, as we argued, the principles that must govern the trip became clear, and most of the heavy equipment was ruled out.

Firstly, we had to get in, and out, fast. Really fast. A man in his sixties, and a diabetic at that, isn't the ideal choice for Arctic shenanigans and Komarov's frozen corpse would be no use to anybody.

Secondly, the Russians must not know we were coming. We reasoned what had worried the KGB was Komarov's warning that work on temperature control was going ahead; they couldn't have understood the come-and-get-me part of it. Further, the West isn't in the habit of reaching into Russia and making grabs, because Soviet internal security is far too tightly-buttoned. That factor was on our side. They wouldn't be expecting a raid, especially in the Arctic, and the sheer weight of history argued that the station on Novaya Zemlya wouldn't be too heavily guarded. You don't guard places Mother Nature guards for you. We thought, at first, of using a nuclear sub for transportation, but it was abandoned for several reasons: it was a US warship, it might be picked up by underwater defence systems or attacked by a Russian hunter-killer sub beneath the ice.

Thirdly, we needed to play some pretty clever chess with Nature herself. She'd be putting plenty of obstacles in our way, and if there were a few advantages to be gained, then we should grab them.

A raid by air was out; raiding planes approaching the Soviet coastline would be knocked clear out of the sky by anything from night fighters to air-to-air and ground-to-air missiles. That left only a surface approach, and a surface raid needed darkness. Study of the tables showing the incidence of daylight in the area gave us a nasty shock. Not only was the only possible time frighteningly close at hand, but the time-slot in which a surface raid could have any possibility of success was terrifyingly narrow. In Spitzbergen and Novaya Zemlya there's continuous darkness through the winter. From February 1st on, twilight creeps in, which means the sun still can't stagger above the horizon, but the horizon is visible, and so are the stars. By February 16th there'd be three hours of twilight and if we hadn't gone then, the whole thing would have to be postponed until the end of the summer, by which time anything could have happened. We daren't delay beyond mid-February, because that was when old man sun climbed into the sky. By March 1st there'd be six hours or more of daylight in which hornets from the nest we intended to raid would be able to find us and sting us to death.

So then we checked how the moon would be behaving, praying it wouldn't be too bright. Luckily it wasn't. The new moon showed on February sixth and came to its first quarter on the 13th. Much more than a quarter moon would be too much for us. You can read your newspaper by a full moon on the ice, always provided the wind doesn't snatch it out of your frozen hands.

We were committed, therefore, to a few days between February 6th and 16th, when twilight varied from one to three hours and the moon from new to one quarter.

Chance snorted. 'Like everything else in this shindig, it's crazy. I wouldn't give a nickel for our chances of good enough weather at that period.'

'How good does the weather need to be?' I asked innocently.

He scowled at me. 'Ever heard of windchill?'

'No.'

'No. Naturally not. Well, I'll tell you. Windchill is what happens to flesh. Cold doesn't matter too much, on its own. But cold plus wind is a very quick killer. There are windchill tables that show how quickly exposed flesh will freeze solid. At minus forty degrees and forty knots of wind, windchill time's around a minute and a half. The weather up there ain't playing games.'

I could feel my stomach knotting with plain ordinary fear, and there were pictures in my mind, remembered from my childhood, of Peary and Scott, stories of fearful endurance. Until that moment, I don't think I'd really appreciated the gravity and the toughness of the thing to which we were committed.

Chance had faced most of it before. The weather, at any rate, was no novelty, and he could assess the hardship and danger in a way none of the rest of us could match.

I asked him soberly, 'What are the odds on pulling it off?' He slung his pencil on the table top.

'Listen,' he said. 'We're going to have to make the whole run, as I figure it, in one twenty-four hour period. Maybe we can kick off during twilight. We'll then have twenty-one, maybe twenty-two hours, before we're into the twilight again. In that time we're gonna have to get there, break in, get this guy Komarov out, and take him back to our pick-up point. So the question is where that pick-up point can be.'

'We've been running some checks,' Dawson said. 'We've got a pretty accurate picture of the defensive pattern.'

Chance said, 'Go on.'

'Well, to start with, along the whole northern coastline of Russia there's a radar chain comparable with our Distant Early Warning and Ballistic Missile Early Warning Systems. Plus the whole anti-missile-missile complex. But I think we can take it they won't be looking our way.'

'They will if we take any airplanes that way,' Chance said grimly.

Dawson shook his head. 'We know what happens. It's been tested often enough. As you know, there's a lot of air traffic round the Pole. The Russians don't seem to bother about it much until an aircraft gets within about two hundred miles of the coast, and that's a bit more than half way between Spitzbergen or Franz Joseph Land and Novaya Zemlya. At that point, they start to scramble.'

I said, 'So we start two hundred miles away?'

'Looks like it,' Dawson said.

Chance muttered 'Give me strength!' and turned again to the big map.

'If you allow yourselves three hours there, and remember there's the cliff to climb, and you've got a two hundred mile trip there and back, it means you've about nine hours for each trip,' Dawson said.

'Nine hours!' Chance turned to face him. 'The fastest things we've got are Polecats. They can do about thirty miles an hour on a favourable surface, but that—' he gestured at the great white ice area of the map—'how favourable is that going to be?'

'Seven hours flat out,' Dawson said soberly. 'It's not much margin.'

'It's no margin,' Chance said. 'You know what pack ice is like! Sure, it's flat enough most of the time, but where the ice has buckled and reformed you can get ridges ten, fifteen feet high. Polecats can get up a step or two, but they can't climb like that and we can't lift them. If we can't get nearer than two hundred miles, we haven't a hope.'

'Nearer than that and they'd be swarming out to investigate,' Dawson said.

'Then it's off!' Chance was standing very upright, his face set.

I stared at him. He was angry still, but this wasn't a product of anger; this was a high-grade operator's professional assessment.

Dawson was staring at him, too, face pale and eyes angry. 'That decision isn't yours to make, Chance.'

'*Colonel* Chance!'

Dawson said, 'Not any more.'

For a moment I thought they were going to start brawling, and maybe that's what gave me the nerve to sling in my two cents' worth. The winter before I'd spent a skiing holiday at Aspen, Colorado, and among the other pleasures of the place, there'd been the hours whooshing across the snow slopes in a Ski-doo.

So I said it. Quickly, while my nerve lasted. 'Why not go in Ski-doos?'

They both switched their wrath to me. As the angry eyes came round I felt as though I were looking down the barrels of a pair of shotguns. The silence may not have been long, but it was intense.

Then Chance said, 'They're toys.' His lip was curling in contempt.

I said, 'They're fast and they're light. We could manhandle them over the ridges.'

'Look, buster,' Chance said, 'I told you a few minutes ago about windchill. Even if a Ski-doo could make it, you'd be out in the air. You wouldn't last twenty minutes, in all the parkas in the world.'

I heard Dawson say, 'Maybe with heaters and cabins . . .?' I didn't look at him because Chance's eyes were fixed on mine and their grip was strong.

Chance did, though. He released me and focused on Dawson. 'They're toys,' he said. 'They're for carrying girls on sleigh rides.'

Dawson seemed to withdraw into himself, his manner stiff and formal. 'I recommend that you leave this whole matter of transportation to be investigated here while you go off and select your crew.'

Chance said, 'What's the point if we can't go?'

'If you can't go,' Dawson said coldly, 'the decision will be made when every possibility has been investigated. Not now.'

So we had to leave the problem unsolved to go to Alaska and pick the team. Selection, training and acclimatization were to happen simultaneously in Alaska. The spot assigned to us was an all-but abandoned camp that had been put up to accommodate construction crews while the BMEWS installation was being put in at Nome.

Chance and I drove out there in a Polecat from the air base, and he gave me a vivid demonstration of the cat's impressive capabilities, and also showed me precisely why it would not be his chosen chariot on the pack ice. It was a bumpy ride, but we finally made it, and they were all there waiting for us.

They came from all over the place; you name it and we had one. There were about fifty to begin with, red, white, brown and yellow, and most of them were staggering about with a chip weighing one shoulder down because they'd landed there through some unsubtle variation on the trick that had been played on Chance.

He had only a few days to weed them out, and the way he felt, he wasn't gentle about it. He was stuck with me, so I got away fairly lightly: just a few twenty-five-mile ski runs and some nasty nights of Arctic survival training. The rest of them went through hell, except that hell's hot and where we were was colder than charity. Chance knew his Arctic, knew what it could do, and made sure everybody else found out. Nobody actually lost a leg through gangrene, but everybody felt at least the first numbing touch of frostbite, and the agony when the frozen flesh warmed up. As our numbers thinned, he got up to little tricks like dumping us in the tundra forty miles from the base with only skis, a compass and enough food for one poor meal, just to see who made it back. One guy found himself fighting a hungry timber wolf with his ski-sticks. He won, too, eventually, but he'd had one hand bitten through to the bone which meant an outside possibility he could be incubating rabies, so he left.

Eventually, there were six of us, and when we assembled in that hut at Nome, you'd have thought it was a quorum of the United Nations: one American, one Englishman, one Scot, one Norwegian, one Canadian Indian and the biggest Japanese you've ever seen.

I'll tell you about Iain Meldrum first, those of you who haven't heard of him already. He came out of the Scottish motor racing tradition that produced Jim Clark, Jackie Stewart and plenty more. All racing motorists, of course, need to be pretty good mechanics, but Meldrum was a lot more than that; he could handle engines like nobody I ever saw. Meldrum could listen to an engine running on a test bench, and tell the guy who thought he'd just tuned it as high as it would go, 'That's running thirty revs retarded,' then put it right. He started out as an apprentice at Rolls-Royce, built his own five hundred out of his pocket money, and started winning races. He had the reflexes of a cat, too, and he could handle anything on wheels or tracks.

So he was our mechanic. At first Chance didn't want him because Meldrum, apart from being a little guy, had very little respect for authority, hair down to his shoulders and a tendency to wear purple velvet trousers in the evenings; also he came out less well than most on the tough, cross-country stuff. But nobody else came near him with motors, so he was included.

Then the Norwegian, Harald Ericson. He'd been slung out of their army about as kindly as Chance had been slung out of Uncle Sam's. He hadn't liked it, but he'd seen the necessity and took it all calmly. Ericson was tall and thin, and looked supercilious; six feet and maybe 160 pounds, put together tight and springy. He was the guy who came out best cross-country, and should have done because he'd done it in the Winter Olympics pentathlon. Ericson could keep going all day on those short, tricky running skis, floating over the miles with a rifle slung across his shoulders, and stopping every now and then to hit something with it at a thousand yards standing up. He came from Narvik, which is inside the Arctic Circle, and he had Antarctic experience too, hunting with his whaler-skipper father on the edge of the southern pack-ice. Ericson would have made a hell of a Mountie.

Which brings me to James Grey Smoke. It's a funny name at first, but it grows on you. He was a full-blooded Indian who'd spent all his life in the far north. He had grey eyes, set back in a complexion like brown shoe leather, and they always seemed to be looking somewhere beyond you. Horizon eyes, I've heard them called. James Grey Smoke spoke less than anyone else I ever met, and there was in him a capacity for stillness and silence that was uncanny. His speciality was survival in Arctic conditions, but he was clever in all sorts of ways; concealment was one. You could, and I've done it, be looking for him, be standing less than ten yards away, and not see him. Don't ask me how; he could do it, that's all. I reckon that if you set Ericson hunting Grey Smoke the whole thing would go on for ever, because Ericson would never stop hunting and Grey Smoke would never be found.

Which leaves Yamamoto, Satsumi Yamamoto. Everything the Japs are supposed not to be: big, gregarious, informal, generous. Of all the men I've ever met, the one I'd least like to tangle with physically. Cassius Clay would think a few times, and an entire football team might hesitate a little before taking him on. His co-ordination was like Meldrum's in some ways, but his sensitivity was toward men not machinery. Yamamoto was skilled in two of those uniquely Japanese sports: karate, which they have exported and everybody now knows, and kendo which hasn't been exported much, but consists of fighting with long poles like the old time quarter-staffs. It's fast, skilful and murderous. At karate he was a black belt of the third dan, which is about as high as you'd get; I don't know what his kendo-rating was, but I'd believe anything. He was an Alpinist, too, a rock-climber capable of tackling faces formally classified as 'of extreme severity', and if that wasn't enough, was an oceanographer from the Japanese Ocean Institute in Tokyo Bay. He'd done all that by the time he was thirty-two!

Among that crew, I felt like Little Lord Fauntleroy selected by accident for the Rose Bowl game.

CHAPTER TWELVE

Other people have effective security, too.

Dawson did manage to persuade Chieftain Oil to let us on to their North Slope drilling location, but even he was surprised by the tightness of the cordon. He must have been working other miracles, too, before he'd flown up to Alaska with the two adapted Ski-doo Invaders. Looking at them as they backed down the ramp of the transport plane, I could see what Chance meant. In the short time I'd been in Alaska, I too had become accustomed to the reassuring roar of heavy diesels, and the puttering 640 cc two strokes sounded tinny and fragile. If you've never seen a snowmobile, they're about seven feet long, and I suppose the nearest thing is a scooter. There's a metal frame with the motor mounted in it, and the thing is driven by a continuous belt, like a caterpillar track;

but made of rubber and nylon. Two short skis stick out of the front to do the steering and the passengers sit one behind the other in tandem like motor-cyclists.

Normally, of course, snowmobiles are open to the air. Dawson, however, had had cabins built on to them: made of low, riveted aluminium sheets and with armoured glass windows. There was also a heater passing air over the engine and into the cabin.

I'd suggested them, but as I stood there looking at those tiny bugs, bright amid the whites and greys all around, I realized just how puny they were for the task they faced.

Chance's lips were compressed, his eyes hard, as he looked at them and the others didn't look very happy either. Except Meldrum. He walked over towards them and patted one bonnet, grinning at the hollow sound, then put his thumb on the accelerator, pressed until the engine screamed, and kept it there for maybe half a minute. He kissed the tips of his gloved fingers and patted the Ski-doo's flank.

'Just like that?' Chance said.

'Deutsche two-strokes, lovely,' Meldrum said.

He put his hands against the metal and tilted the Doo. 'I reckon two of us could lift one of these.'

'Do you want to die?'

'No, no,' Meldrum said. 'First class machinery. Don't let it fool you.'

Chance said, 'It's not fooling me for one second. It's too light, too fragile, too amateurish.'

Chance lost. He didn't like losing, and in particular, he didn't like losing to Meldrum, but he was on Meldrum's territory. Doos aren't exactly complicated, and Meldrum had himself adapted to them in about fifteen seconds flat. He went skimming round the airfield, sliding the Doo hither and yon as he picked up the feel of it. When he stopped beside us, he got out grinning widely. 'Fun,' he said. 'An idiot could do it. Try her.'

Chance said, 'Thanks,' and climbed in. The little engine raced and off he went. It didn't take him long either, and watching the Doo whooshing across the field, spraying snow on the bends, I began to feel, for the first time, that it might work. Chance came up beside us, and Meldrum said, 'Well?'

'Fun, I'll grant you. But across the ice? We'd be mad!' Chance said.

Meldrum just looked at him soberly. 'What's a fair test?'

And that's how we got to the North Slope and watched

Chance and Meldrum howl off on to the frozen sea. A helicopter had laid down a pattern of small, battery-powered lights to make a roughly square lap of about ten miles, and we watched the Doos go into the darkness. Ice conditions could have been worse, but they weren't particularly good; there were a few narrow leads where water was visible between the icerafts, and three or four pressure ridges up to ten feet high.

Eventually the rest of us, plus Dawson, retired into a heated shed, leaving them to it, but Chance and Meldrum just kept going round that improvised track until the petrol-oil mixture in the tanks was running low. Then they came in. They'd made roughly six hundred miles in fourteen hours, and Chance was dog weary. Meldrum, on the other hand, was cheerful as a kid, chaffing Chance and looking for a party.

'OK, you win,' Chance growled. 'Now I'm going to bed.'

'Not yet, sport,' Meldrum said. 'First of all we're going to strip these engines down and see what's happened.'

What had happened was nothing. We watched Meldrum's miraculously deft fingers turning those motors into a pile of parts, shiny and smooth with oil, then putting the bits together again. He sieved the oil, looking for deposits, and it was clean and clear. At the end he smiled at Chance. 'Sleep well, my old cock-sparrow. They'll take you.'

I knew how Chance felt. There wasn't much he could say, but his doubts remained. I was in the same position myself.

Next morning we were back in Washington for final fitting out and then for briefing. Dawson conducted the briefing in that conference room of his with the maps and charts on the walls. It was warm and comfortable and it gave a wonderful sense of reassurance as long as you weren't thinking about the ice and the cold and the Russians. When we all walked in, another guy was there with Dawson and Mason and the first thing I noticed about him was his eyes: they were like James Grey Smoke's; horizon eyes that didn't seem to blink any too often and just sat there among the surrounding creases looking through you. He was wearing a dark blue suit that looked as though it had been built for someone else, and he kept pulling at his collar as though he weren't accustomed to wearing one.

We all exchanged puzzled glances, but there were no introductions until we were sitting round the big table.

Then Dawson said, 'I'd like you to meet Skipper Harry Hutton of the Hull trawler fleet from England.'

'Bluidy Sassenach,' Meldrum said, just so no one would forget.

A couple of wrinkles shifted position on Hutton's face. It could have been a grin, but I wouldn't have bet on it. 'Bastard Scot,' he said amiably. The vowels were short and flat and emphatic, the consonants bitten off. I looked at Meldrum and he was grinning, so I deduced that relations were reasonably friendly. You could have fooled me.

Dawson was smiling his silver, ambassadorial smile. 'Skipper Hutton comes originally from Whitby, like Captain Cook, whose descendant he is. He's a distant water fisherman who has skippered trawlers round Iceland, Spitzbergen and the White Sea for thirty years. He's won the Silver Cod for the season's top catch seven times, which no-one else ever has or ever will come near. He knows the ice and the Arctic seas, and he did his share of fighting against the Germans as commander of a destroyer on the Murmansk convoy run.'

Dawson paused and Hutton stopped picking at a button on his jacket with a horny nail, realized something was expected, and looked up. ' 'Ow do,' he said. I got the impression he didn't talk much.

'Bluidy Tyke,' Meldrum said.

Hutton's head turned slowly, the eyes lining up on Meldrum like cannon. One of them closed in a slow wink, but I got the impression it had been a near thing. Hutton looked hard and dangerous, one of those silent men who grow like granite. I was impressed, glad he was on our side. I think we all were. Why Meldrum was doing it was something I didn't understand, some ancient tribal rivalry still near the surface, presumably. But they seemed to understand one another.

'All right, gentlemen,' Dawson said. 'We've worked the plan out. Here's how it goes. The starting point is Thule Air Base, Greenland.'

'No escorts this time?' Chance asked bitterly.

Dawson took no notice. 'There the Ski-doos will be loaded into a Buffalo aircraft. Colonel Chance will know the Buffalo.'

Chance said, 'Built by de Haviland of Canada. Turbo-prop developed from the Caribou. Wheels and skis. Good aircraft.'

'Right,' Dawson said. 'In the Buffalo, you all fly with the Doos to Spitzbergen, where the Buffalo refuels, before flying on to land—'

I interrupted him. 'Wouldn't it be better if it didn't stop anywhere?'

'Much better,' Dawson said dryly. 'But no aircraft capable of landing on ice has the range for the round trip. So, the Buffalo refuels at Spitzbergen, then flies on to land you on the ice. Here.' He pointed to a small cross on the map. 'It's two hundred miles short of Novaya Zemlya and about four hundred miles from Spitzbergen. When you have disembarked, the Buffalo will take off again and fly direct to Thule. With luck, all the Russians will notice on their radar is that an aircraft came within two hundred miles, then turned back. It shouldn't worry them.'

Chance said, 'So how do we get back? Now that the Buffalo's back in Thule?'

'Later,' Dawson said. 'Bear with me, gentlemen. You will have roughly an hour of twilight in which to get going, after that it's moonlight. I appreciate the hazards, but—'

'Do you?' Chance said.

'I think so.'

'It's going to be a great moment,' Chance said. 'We stand there in the middle of the ocean watching the plane fly away. It's only sixty below, of course, and—'

'And you'll have to get moving,' Dawson said tightly.

I looked at him and then at Chance, wondering if it was always like this, sympathizing with both of them; one who had to make the plans and give the orders and do it efficiently and dispassionately; the other who had to take the orders and carry them out. One a cold man, the other not.

Dawson went on. 'I'm assuming now that the weather gives you the chance you need. From this point until the next twilight, you'll have around twenty-three hours, according to which day you go. There are six of you and there will be six Ski-doos. The Doos cannot take more than two people, but the margin allows for the breakdown of two machines. That's thirty-three and one third per cent and I'm told it's unlikely you'll have that high an incidence of breakdown in four hundred miles. The Doos are fitted with supplementary petrol tanks to give each machine fuel for roughly thirty hours. If any breakdowns occur, fuel can of course be transferred to other machines. All clear?'

We all nodded, even Chance, but he didn't look as though he wanted to nod.

'OK,' Dawson went on smoothly. 'Assuming, and we have

to assume something, that you make twenty-five miles an hour, and stop once to eat, you'll approach Novaya Zemlya around eight or nine p.m., which is maybe a bit early. But it gives you the chance to case the joint. You should go in, probably, between ten and eleven; and once inside it shouldn't take long. That is, *if* you're going to succeed.'

He paused and I felt suddenly cold. I hadn't, until now, been able to see any pictures in my mind's eye, but now I could: I could see men with guns; doors opening and bursts of bullets spattering out of them. My stomach churned. I looked round at the others and found I was alone: whatever they may have felt inside, they all looked pretty damned impassive outside. Except Meldrum. He looked like a sparrow with the bacon rind. He said, 'We'd be better crawling a bit on the way there. We want everybody in bed, not up and about.'

'You'll just have to see how it goes,' Dawson said. 'If you make good time early, then you can slow a bit. If you're held up at the beginning, you'll need all the time you can get.'

Chance said, 'If it's anything like Camp Hundred they'll go to bed early.'

Meldrum nodded.

'Getting in and getting out,' Dawson continued, 'it's up to you. Photo-interpretation suggests the cliff is around a hundred and fifty feet high and steep but not sheer. There are certainly what look like chimneys in it.'

Yamamoto said, 'Beginner's climb only, I think. If I must put pinions into rock, will they hear?'

'If you can help it, don't,' Dawson said. 'If there's seismological equipment there, it's bound to pick it up. Just in case, we've had some made with a rubber pad at the end to reduce the noise, but it's vibration rather than sound that's dangerous.'

'Understand,' Yamamoto said.

I thought that Yamamoto's idea of a beginner's climb was probably a bit different from mine, but I let it pass. The Jap looked big enough and strong enough to carry any three of us up with him.

'When you go in, you take protective clothing with you for Komarov; you get him dressed, and bring him out with you. You lower him down the cliff on a rescue stretcher, load him into one of the Doos, and away you go. He rides with Colonel Chance.'

I said, 'I don't think we're wrong, but what if we are?

What if he doesn't want to come?'

Dawson said, 'He goes with you. Period.'

'No choice?' Chance said.

'None. Now, the getaway. You head away from Novaya Zemlya on a course that takes you slightly south of your inward track. You're making for a point here.' Dawson marked a cross on the map. 'It's still roughly two hundred miles, I'm afraid, but there's no good way of getting closer unless a nuclear sub surfaces and that's out.'

Dawson nodded towards the trawlerman. 'That's where Skipper Hutton comes in.'

'Billy Muggins,' Hutton said.

'He's flying direct from here, after this meeting, to Keflavik, Iceland,' said Dawson. 'His trawler, the *Polar Star*, is there now, and aboard her, crated, are two things: one an Otter aircraft, and two, a hut constructed in sections. The hut is made of panels of expanded polystyrene faced with glass fibre. It's light and easy to erect. Skipper Hutton will take the *Polar Star* to the edge of the ice-pack, unload the hut, erect it, then the Otter will be unloaded, along with a pilot and a mechanic. The crew of the *Polar Star* will help assemble the aircraft and then the *Polar Star* will sail, leaving the aircraft assembled and ready to fly, in the hut. When you arrive, you transfer to the Otter, ditch the Ski-doos, and fly back to Thule. Once you're over the Greenland coast you'll be escorted by flights of jet fighters. OK?'

Chance said, 'Why can't an aircraft pick us up on the ice?'

'Because they'd track it in by radar. You'd never get clear. As soon as the plane landed the sky would be full of Migs.

'I see that,' Chance said. 'But just how do we find the aircraft? You know what happens to compasses up there.'

Dawson said, 'I know. That's why you'll be doing no navigation. There's a radio set built into each Ski-doo and while you're making your outward run, the mother ship of a fishing fleet, well out at sea, will steam towards you emitting for thirty seconds in every five minutes, a signal you can home on. You simply steer directly on to it.'

'OK.' Chance nodded. 'And if anything goes wrong?'

'Navigate,' Dawson said. 'Stars and compass. It's difficult but it should be feasible.'

'I meant with the Otter.'

'Your alternative is the *Polar Star* herself. In the event of anything being wrong with the aircraft, *Polar Star* will be riding five miles clear of the pack. She'll be on the beacon signal, too. You radio and she comes in to pick you up, then returns to the fishing fleet. Among eighty ships. she'll be safe.'

He paused and looked around. 'Any questions?'

Grey Smoke said, 'We need skis. If more than two Ski-Doos are damaged, the others can tow.'

'Snow boots need metal tips for climbing,' Yamamoto said. 'I show how.'

'Komarov's a diabetic,' I said. 'We don't know anything about his diet or anything else. Not even the kind of insulin he's on.'

'He speaks English,' Dawson said. 'That should help. Meanwhile take fifty-seven varieties in your little black bag.'

We were still talking, still working over and over the details, when Hutton rose monosyllabically to catch his plane for Keflavik. He walked to the door, ungainly, even scruffy in that cheap, tight suit, turned and half-raised a hand.

'Luck,' he said. The word brought it home, suddenly and sickeningly, that we were talking about solid and terrible realities. And that they were getting nearer all the time.

The talk was suddenly sober, intense.

CHAPTER THIRTEEN

The vast US Army Air Base at Thule, Greenland, has a weird incongruousness that is unique. Technology, fighting the conditions, has adapted to them, too. The business of running a base from which giant bombers can operate round the clock has involved housing thousands of men, feeding and entertaining them, providing a modern environment in a climate fit only for Eskimos and bears. We spent our few days waiting at the Officers' Club, which might have been built by Conrad Hilton at his most extravagant. Inside there were films and bars, fine food and squash courts, fresh vegetables and fruit, and fruit machines too, in serried ranks. At any door leading to the outside, windchill tables were displayed, and big notices reminded you to change into felt boots. It seemed hardly necessary if you were going only a couple of hundred yards, but in fact it was vital: leather communicated cold and a few hundred yards was enough for feet to freeze. There was a story, retold endlessly, of two new arrivals who had lost both feet through failing to change boots.

I was glad of those few days. The wound in my calf had healed cleanly, the new skin had grown over it and every day it became stronger. Persistent cold probes for weak spots, finds wounds remorselessly, and attacks there. When I was indoors I could no longer feel the wound. Out of doors I knew that it was there.

On the twelfth of February we heard that Hutton and his crew had succeeded in landing the Otter on the ice. The hut's sections had been unloaded and the hut itself erected, fastened to the ice with long expansion bolts, and inside it the Otter now waited. Its engine had been run for an hour, and all was well. Hutton had taken the *Polar Star* clear of the ice, leaving pilot and navigator alone with the Otter, cooped up in the hut. I didn't envy them. Those huts have unbelievable insulation properties and a small stove keeps them snug whatever the weather's like outside. But sitting and waiting on the ice wouldn't be fun.

It seemed Hutton had just got clear of the ice in time. Shortly afterwards a white-out had dropped, filling the air with minute ice crystals that brought visibility down to nothing and made radio reception freakish and unpredictable. According to the weather reconnaissance planes that monitored the area for us, it stayed there for thirty-six hours before it lifted.

Chance paced moodily about his room, stirring only when the weather reports came in. Thule itself was badly battened down by high winds and blowing snow, and though the aircraft were flying, getting up and getting down wasn't funny, even with the semi-automatic landing systems. On the fourteenth we could have gone; the weather where we were going was as near OK as we could reasonably expect, but conditions at Thule were such that taking off the Buffalo would be too hazardous: the wind was sixty miles an hour from the northwest, gusting sometimes to ninety, and the chance of crashing on take-off was high. We went to bed that night with the wind crashing about outside like a drunken banshee, our minds ful of weather forecasts, wind-chill tables and anxiety.

We were awakened at one a.m.

I felt as though I had been asleep about five minutes when the orderly came in and shook my shoulder. 'Time to get up, sir.'

I looked at my watch, sleepily, and said, 'What? Now?'

'Listen, sir.'

I listened. There was silence and for a moment I did not

appreciate what it meant. Then I did. I went to the window and pulled the curtain back, peering into the darkness outside. It was like a scene from a Christmas card; snow, deep, crisp and drifted against the sides of the buildings; glowing, golden patches beneath the yellow overhead lighting. It was absolutely still.

I splashed water over my face and dressed quickly, then hurried out to the waiting Polecat. James Grey Smoke and Yamamoto were in it already, Chance came immediately after me, then Ericson and finally Meldrum. The driver engaged the engine with the tracks and we were off to the hangar where the Buffalo waited. As we got out, a weather report was put into Chance's hand and he read it quickly, then more slowly.

'OK, listen. Conditions for the moment look good. At the touch-down point there's light snow blowing in a twenty-knot wind. Ground temperature estimated at ten Fahrenheit. The same conditions should prevail all the way. The forecast says so anyway, for what it's worth, though God knows what may be cooking in the weather kitchen in Siberia.' He screwed up the paper and tossed it into a waste bin. 'Let's go.'

The rear loading door beneath the upswept tail of the Buffalo was lowered to form a ramp, and the Ski-doos were already inside along with our equipment. We climbed in, sat down in the paratroop-style seats, facing inward from the cabin walls, and fastened our lap-straps. The two Pratt and Whitney turbo-props hummed, then began to whine and the Buffalo gave a little lurch as it moved slowly forward out of the hangar. We peered out of the windows into the darkness of the airfield, watching the lights moving laterally past as the Buffalo moved round the perimeter track. Then there were no more lights, just the grey-white of the snow, and the aircraft stopped, awaiting permission to take off. We sat there for a moment or two listening as the engines idled, then heard the whine grow louder as the throttles were opened and the air frame began to vibrate as the engines worked up to full power.

A little jerk told us the wheels were beginning to turn, and then we were buffeting down the runway in that rapid build-up of power and vibration that eases miraculously when the stick is pulled back and the aircraft leaves the ground and moves confidently into the element for which it was designed. Then came the little heart-stopping drop as the pilot throttled back, and the No Smoking and Fasten Seat Belts signs were switched off. Nobody lit cigarettes, but we all unfastened the clasps of the lap-straps and eased our bodies.

'Ten thousand feet.' The pilot's voice came back over the loudspeaker. 'I intend to fly to Spitzbergen at an altitude of twelve thousand. The cabin is not pressurized, but oxygen is available if you wish to use it. Masks are in the lockers above your heads.'

There was a click as he switched off and it seemed unnaturally loud in the cabin. No one talked. Chance and Yamamoto were already asleep and Grey Smoke might have been too. He sat motionless in his seat, eyes open and staring across at the cabin wall. I wondered what he was seeing, what those strange grey eyes were presenting on the screen of his mind. Ericson was removing bullets from his ammunition pouch and wiping them carefully with a lightly-oiled rag, cleaning them of every speck of dust. When he'd done that he began on his rifle, removing the bolt, examining, polishing, checking the breech mechanism. Iain Meldrum, hands clasped behind his head, whistled through his teeth, his felt-booted feet tapping a clumsy drum-beat on the cabin floor. He saw me looking at him and winked.

I couldn't quite bring myself to wink back and gave him the best smile I could muster. Gradually, for days, I had been becoming more and more aware of what we faced, but the mind has its protective mechanisms that head our thoughts away from the unknown and the frightening. It was still difficult to believe that in a few hours we would be out on the ice, but I was beginning to believe it.

I heard a movement and looked round. Meldrum got up and walked over to sit beside me. 'Hell, isn't it?'

I wondered: had it shown as much as that? I said, 'It'll be all right on the night.'

'I feel worse than you. Look.' Meldrum held up his hand and I could see it shaking. He laughed. 'Always like that.'

'Before a race?'

He nodded. 'And afterwards.'

'But not during.'

Meldrum laughed. 'I wouldn't be here to talk about it. It's being still and thinking that crams the pressure on. Once things start, everything stitches itself together nice and tight.' He looked at me. 'You'll be fine and dandy, anyway.'

'What makes you so sure?'

'Nice white face. Meldrum's first law. If you're white-faced and frightened you'll hold together well. If you're red-faced and frightened, you'll fail. I've seen it a dozen times in motor racing. You see these chaps flushed and sweating and you might just as well phone for the undertaker.'

I felt myself flush. Meldrum laughed. 'You've spoiled it, old boy.'

Behind him a voice said, 'Where do I get one of those pale faces, Paleface?'

I looked round Meldrum. James Grey Smoke's leather skin was creased by a little smile.

'Medicine man,' Meldrum said, grinning.

'Sorry,' I said. 'Not this one.'

'White man speak with forked tongue,' Grey Smoke's smile broadened.

'Shut up and sleep!' We looked across. Chance was awake and glaring across. 'Cut out the vaudeville and sleep. You'll need it. That's an order!'

Melrum tore off an elaborate salute and returned to his seat. Grey Smoke shrugged and resumed his contemplation of the infinite.

I closed my eyes obediently and tried to sleep, but this was one of the times when it wasn't allowed. It wasn't that my mind was too busy, racing with thoughts. In fact the opposite was true. Everything seemed set, somehow, forever: still and calm and lazy. I turned and looked out of the window, at the moonlit surface of the Greenland Icecap six or seven thousand feet below. It, too, looked calm, peaceful and eternal. From up there you couldn't see the cruelty or feel the cold. 'Greenland's icy mountains,' I thought. What was it next? 'India's coral strand.' I wished I were on India's coral strand right that minute. The snatch of the children's hymn book took me back to my boyhood among the English lakes.

I must have fallen asleep as soon as I stopped trying. The popping in my ears awakened me as pressure increased in the cabin and I held my nose tightly and breathed against it, equalizing the pressure to ease the discomfort. My limbs felt stiff and I stretched deliberately for a while, watching the rest of them stir and come awake. Looking out of the cabin window again I could see the islands of Spitzbergen below us: north of them the white line of the edge of the Arctic ice, to the south the dark silver of the sea under the new moon. The line between them might have been drawn with a ruler.

We didn't even get out of the aircraft at the airfield at Spitzbergen. Someone handed in a container of hot food and the latest weather report.

Chance read it and said, 'Unchanged. We're lucky. So far, we're lucky.' Then he opened the container and began to pass round plates of thick beef stew. When that was done there was a heavy sweet pudding made with treacle, which I didn't want, but forced down for the sake of the fuel it contained. Finally there came a mug of thick, sticky liquid that didn't so much flow round the cup as ooze round it. Whatever it was, I didn't like the looks of it.

'What's this?' I demanded.

'Cocoa,' Ericson said. 'Very good.'

I've always hated cocoa or chocolate drinks. 'No thanks.'

'Seaman's cocoa,' Ericson said. 'Drink. It keeps out the cold.'

It was like drinking syrup, but I saw what he meant. When the meal was over my stomach contained a cannonball made of solid carbohydrate and protein. I felt like a python that has eaten a cow : ready to coil up and go on digesting for a month.

As soon as we took off from Spitzbergen, Chance rose.

'OK,' he said. 'Let's get dressed.'

The Buffalo made just short of three hundred miles an hour, which meant we had maybe ninety minutes to get ready. It was too long and we all knew it, but as the time approached it seemed better to do anything than do nothing. Like the others I was already wearing the long, fleecy underpants and vest, and the woollen trousers and field jacket. Now I put on Grenfell cloth windproof trousers and jacket, the big white felt boots and the fur hat, and put my parka over the top. They were magnificent garments, all of them, particularly the boots. The idea of these boots is that thick felt keeps the cold out like nothing else, so the whole boot is about a quarter of an inch thick. The sole is maybe an inch thick, and with just a thin layer of rubber on the bottom to take the wear. The only thing is, you must not get them wet; if you do, the cold will freeze the boots and then your feet before you know it. So if you get them covered in powdered snow, it's essential to kick it off before you go anywhere warm. For this trip we were going one better and wore sealskin overboots too. The fur hats were wolverine, and so were the fur rims round the parka hoods; of all furs, that's the one that resists cold and damp best. We couldn't have been much better equipped for the Arctic if we'd been polar bears.

Meldrum had dressed quickly and was giving the Ski-doos a final once-over. They were white-painted now, to blend with the snow, and looking for them would be like looking for needles in about a million square miles of haystack. I didn't much like the idea of trying to find them if any of us became detached from the group, either.

I checked my own medical kit. I'd brought dressings, splints, bandages, morphine, benzedrine and insulin in several forms: long-acting and immediate absorption, plus some of the tablet kind that only certain diabetics can take. There was also the usual range of emergency stuff, but this little black bag—in fact it was a green fibreglass case—contained no obstetrical gadgetry. Any polar bears or seals could get on with their own midwifery.

We were all standing, patting ourselves and checking the equipment of the Ski-doos when we realized the angle of the cabin floor had changed. The Buffalo was coming down. I turned and looked out of the window at the ice three thousand feet below. I couldn't see far, but wherever I looked there was only ice, clear to the horizon, marked here and there by pressure ridges and small polynyas: gaps in the ice caused by cracking and shifting. In them the dark sea waited to freeze.

The Seat Belts light came on and we strapped ourselves in, waiting, listening to the changed pitch of the engines as our airspeed slowed. We came down slowly, steadily, evenly, while somebody banged a big bass drum hard somewhere in my chest and a muscle in my arm went into a mild nervous spasm.

The pilot must have been good, and he must have had his spot picked out from way back. We drifted down towards the ice, then turned into the wind and began the approach. With my head turned to the window I watched the ice coming up to meet us, a coating of snow smooth on the surface. We dropped towards it, then it was skimming quickly by the windows. A moment later we began to bounce as the skis touched and slid along the ice. I prayed that there was no hidden trough or ridge in the way . . .

Then we were down and the engines were throttled right back. As we halted, Chance unfastened his belt and rose. We all followed suit.

A whining sound, followed by a sudden blast of bitterly cold air made us all turn. The ramp that formed part of the tail section was being lowered, and the Arctic night was in among us. I gasped and decided, as the icy air filled my lungs, that gasping wasn't wise.

Already, as the end of the ramp bumped down on to the ice, Iain Meldrum had the engine started on the first Ski-doo. Chance got in quickly and drove it along the cabin floor and down the ramp. As Meldrum started each engine and got out again, each of us climbed into his machine and drove it carefully out of the aircraft and on to the ice. Once out we opened the throttles to heat the engines quickly. Chance left his Ski-doo and returned to the aircraft to make a final check on our position. He came out and walked from machine to machine, shouting instructions. When he came to me he pointed to a star that gleamed brightly in the Southern sky.

'That's our direction,' he shouted, and slammed the door of the Ski-doo.

I sat there waiting for the signal to move and watched the Buffalo. The hydraulics lifted the ramp back into position, and then I saw the propellers revolving faster and faster. An arm waved from the cockpit, and then the Buffalo began to move, picking up speed fast now that it was lighter. In a few moments the tail lowered a little, then the skis lifted and it roared away into the night.

I looked around. Already the Buffalo was just a light in the sky. The Ski-doos were small, white humps nearby, wisps of steam puffing from their exhausts.

We were alone on the Polar Sea.

CHAPTER FOURTEEN

Through the windscreen, the scene in front of me looked like one of those photographic prints that has had only half its proper time in the developer: big areas of white with coal black shadows. From the infant moon came a thin light, enough to show the snowflakes as flying traces against the dark sky.

The single headlight on Chance's Doo flashed, then flashed again, and Meldrum eased slowly away from the line, turning to face that star, then moving slowly forward. Meldrum was to lead. Because every yard of the journey must be over a totally unknown surface, and because the speed at which we would be going was too great for safety, it was essential to have cat-quick reflexes at the head of the little column. The stopping power of snowmobiles is remarkable, and with a gap of about ten yards between the Doos, it ought to be possible to avoid collisions.

One by one we fell in behind, Yamamoto in two, myself in three, Chance in four and Ericson and Grey Smoke in five and six respectively, running abreast at the rear. It increased the hazard for both because neither was riding, like the rest of us, in Meldum's track. Instead, five feet apart, they ran on either side of the trail, over virgin snow. On the other hand it was unthinkable that one man, any man, should be last in line. Grey Smoke and Ericson would watch each other; if one got into trouble, at least the other would know.

It was strange, sitting there in the Doo, following Yamamoto, catching occasional glimpses of Meldrum up ahead. The little 640 cc Rotax two-stroke roared healthily and the snow and ice outside swished softly, but there was no other sound. The wiper moved steadily back and forth across the screen, and through the quadrant it cleared I watched the two white bugs ahead of me as they picked up speed, scampering across the ice-pack.

Meldrum, up ahead, was almost feeling his way, if you can call it that at twenty miles an hour. His hands and the remarkable seat of his pants, still obviously sensitive beneath the layers of clothing, were learning about the surface beneath. He was picking up speed steadily as his confidence grew and communicated itself back along the line. My gloved hands on the handlebars simply had to steer straight at the rear of Yamamoto's Doo, and my thumb on the throttle button had to increase its pressure, revving the engine higher, to keep up.

The snow surface was surprisingly smooth beneath us. The Doo bumped occasionally, and tilted a little as the tracks went over small mounds and hollows in the ice, but it was no worse than driving the MG over rough country roads.

By the time we had covered five miles the cabin was uncomfortably warm and I was sweating. I pushed in the knob of the heater control and zipped the front of the parka down. I'd have liked to have taken it off, but that would have meant stopping and to stop was impossible. But it was important not to sweat too much, particularly in the feet. Sweat is, after all, largely water, and it could dampen the felt of the boots dangerously effectively. I didn't want to get out, when the time came, and find my feet freezing.

After forty minutes the sky began to lighten, at first almost imperceptibly, but then quite quickly. The short Arctic twilight was beginning. It became easier to follow Yamamoto's Doo as it coursed through the snow up ahead. I realized suddenly that the air was no longer full of snowflakes, and switched off the wiper. I was over-optimistic. The wind caught the snow that flew from the flying tracks of Meldrum's and Yamamoto's Doos and plastered it over the screen. I reached and switched the wiper on, and after a couple of rather ineffectual passes it cleared the screen reasonably quickly. I had learned the lesson and wouldn't switch it off again: the warmth from the inside of the cabin was melting the flakes as they hit the Plexiglass and the wind was turning them into ice. If the blade stopped working for any length of time, I would be driving blind.

Already Yamamoto's Doo had gained on me. The gap between us was now almost a hundred yards, and I opened the throttle to catch up, listening as the engine roared happily and feeling the back of the Doo dip as the tracks bit harder into the snow. It was like aqua-planing as the speed increased. I seemed to be floating along, the momentum absorbing the occasional bumps. It was uncanny, somehow: a weird feeling as though one were in a speed-boat tearing across a vast, lonely lake without a shore.

Meldrum was using the increased light to push ahead as fast as he could. Every mile we covered was a mile in hand, better done than to be done. Occasionally he would swing wide to avoid some projection, some small ridge rising from the ice, and we would follow obediently in his tracks as he skirted it, then swing back on to course. Every few minutes I would half turn on the seat to glance out of the rear window at Chance's Doo, barely distinguishable in the plumes of flying snow behind me.

We were making the better part of forty miles an hour, now, steadily and consistently, eating up the miles easily and almost casually, roaring towards the flat, unchanging horizon that receded endlessly in front of us. Now, at least, we could see the horizon and see it clearly: the Arctic twilight is brighter by far than the twilights of more temperate latitudes, and the light on the ice was reflected so efficiently that it would have been easy to read a newspaper. We made the most of it. All too soon it would be gone and there would be twenty hours and more of darkness to plough through, when danger would multiply and progress slow.

We had been going two and a half hours, and had the

better part of eighty miles behind us, when something seemed to happen to the horizon. The flat line began to show traces of unevenness, that became the jagged spikes of a big pressure ridge as we raced nearer. Meldrum swung first left, then right, and I could sense how he must be staring out through his screen, looking for a break in it.

But there was no break. He stopped beneath the great rearing wall and we all pulled up in a group beside him, fastened our parkas, put on goggles, tightened the draw-strings of our hoods and climbed out.

The wind hit us. Cocooned inside the cabins, we had felt nothing of the bitter cold; it had been like riding in a limousine. Here, even under the shelter of the ridge, it was unpleasant; fine particles of snow scoured from the pack were blasting at us, driving like flying sand against our parkas.

We stared at the ridge. It was thirty feet high, rising almost sheer in our path. A Doo can climb a slope of forty-five degrees if it has a half-way decent run at it, but it was impossible to try that here: it would be like driving into a wall. Unbidden Yamamoto walked forward, mountainous in his layers of clothing, looked at the ice face for a moment, then began to climb upward. Perhaps, for him, it wasn't a difficult climb, but it looked frightening. He went up like a fly on a wall and seemed to stumble momentarily at the top as he hoisted himself clear of the protection the ridge offered against the wind, but he regained his balance, edged forward to examine the other side, then came back, holding his arm outstretched with the thumb of his gauntlet turned down. We waited until he climbed down again, then Chance shouted, 'What's it like?'

Yamamoto's head shook from side to side inside the parka. 'Other side like this.'

'Does it look any better anywhere else?'

'Perhaps. Is difficult to tell. Both sides two, three miles ridge flattens.' Yamamoto shrugged. 'May be eye effect only.'

Chance walked over to his own Ski-doo and returned with a pair of hand walkie-talkie sets. 'You, Doc, come with me and Grey Smoke. We'll go left. Meldrum, Ericson and Yamamoto go right. Everybody stay close to the ridge. See if we can find a place to cross.'

Ericson took the handset. 'Why these, not radio?'

Chance said, 'There's only twenty miles range in these things. Enough but not too much.'

I went back to the Doo and climbed in, pulled the heater

knob and felt the warm air flow in. I listened to the engine with affection. That little cylinder block and the few moving parts that a two-stroke has were all we had in the way of protection. I was happy that it sounded so noisily sweet, was prepared to pray for its continued good health.

Chance's Ski-doo swung away to the left, along the base of the ice wall, and I followed, turning to make sure Grey Smoke was doing the same. We hadn't much more than half an hour of twilight left and if we were going to have to haul the Doos over the ridge, we needed light to do it.

We chugged along, Chance cautiously keeping the speed down. Anything could have happened to the ice in the region of the ridge and he wasn't taking any chances. Beside us the wall was continuous, unbroken except for changing craggy shapes on its top that ranged like battlements as far as we could see. It was awe-inspiring, frightening, to think of the monstrous pressure that had brought two great rafts of ice together with enough power to crumple them like that. After two miles, after three, it was still the same: there was not one place where it was conceivable that the Doos could cross, even be carried up and over.

Then Chance stopped and turned, heading back the way we had come, waving for us to follow. I swung the Doo about and went after him. He made better speed this time; travelling over ice we'd crossed before, we could at least be sure of the surface. After ten minutes we passed the spot where we had first stopped, where the Doos' tracks led away across the ice, and headed in the direction Meldrum had taken. But still the great ridge continued. On our left it rose sheer, rearing anything from twenty to forty feet above the ice. And the light was beginning to go, now. Soon the short twilight would be over and we would be back in the dark.

I wondered what Meldrum's group had found, but there was no way of knowing. Chance had the walkie-talkie and there was no point in his stopping to tell us. Obviously, though, something had been discovered. I hoped it was the end of the ridge.

It wasn't. When we came up to them in the last of the twilight, the three Doos were stationary beside a gap in the ridge maybe forty feet long. As we approached all I could see was what looked like a collection of ice boulders scattered about the surface. I stopped the Doo and got out to join the others, clambering over the clumps of outcrop ice. What I saw turned my guts over.

A narrow polynya was open in the ice. Six, perhaps seven, feet of water filling a gap in the ice. At either end the ridge was sheer, stretching off into the distance.

Chance gave it one look and turned away. 'We'll just have to look further along.'

Meldrum caught his arm. 'I've been further along. There's no gap there.'

'How far did you go?'

'A mile, perhaps more. This bloody ridge goes on for ever.'

Chance said, 'So?' But he knew. I knew too; knew what Iain Meldrum had in mind.

Meldrum didn't answer. He walked over to his Doo, came back with a pick, and began hacking the ice beside the polynya.

'You're crazy,' Chance said.

Meldrum shook his head. 'I want to live. If we can get a run at it, the Doos can make the jump.'

'Too far.' Chance shook his head.

Meldrum said, 'A London bus once jumped a five foot gap on Tower Bridge with fifty people aboard. What we need is a good take off.'

'And good landing,' Yamamoto said. He went for the pick from his own Doo, then marched off towards the ridge and climbed across it.

I grabbed my own pick and followed him.

'OK,' Chance growled. He fetched his pick and Ericson and Grey Smoke got theirs, and began to chip away at the ice. It took us nearly an hour to get a narrow path cut through to the edges of the polynya, and it was a heck of a rough surface, but they were ramps of a kind. Sweat poured off us and, when the narrow ramps were cleared, we stood looking at them doubtfully while the sweat froze on our brows.

Meldrum grinned and spat on his hands and I wondered whether they were shaking. He went back to his Doo, closed the door and drove off into the darkness for about a hundred and fifty yards. I watched the faint outline of the little machine as it turned and began to move towards us. He must have had the throttle wide open from the start, and the engine was screaming as the Doo accelerated towards us, throwing low waves of snow to each side.

He must have been doing about forty when he hit the ramp and the Doo rose into the air like something in a fairground, flashed across the gap, and landed in an awkward, slewing sideways skid on the other side. He must have been correcting in the air, balancing the Doo with his own weight as he landed. I thought for a terrifying moment that it would turn over, but he held it, raced clear of the ramp, pulled over to one side, stopped and got out. He'd cleared the gap by a good six feet, but it had been a wicked moment, and my palms were clammy inside my gloves.

Meldrum advanced to the edge of the polynya and Chance went to meet him. 'Too risky,' he shouted.

'It's all right,' Meldrum bawled. 'At least I'm over!'

'You nearly broke your neck!'

Meldrum shouted, 'I'll do them all, if you're scared.' It was a stupid thing to say. Chance was thinking of the mission, not his own skin. But he wasn't the man to resist the taunt.

Chance turned and strode towards his own Ski-doo, climbed in and followed Meldrum's route away from the polynya, turning a hundred and fifty yards away and roaring for the ramp.

I don't know what happened exactly; it was all too quick. But he must have been off centre as he hit the ramp, and the Ski-doo half turned on its side in the air and fell with a dreadful crash on the far edge. The motor stopped instantly and there was a tearing, clacking noise as something gave in the track mechanism. Not much more than half the Doo was actually on the ice; the rest hung out over the water, and some movement of Chance's body inside was enough to start it sliding back. I watched, horrified as it moved, infinitely slowly it seemed, back towards the black water that waited in the gap. It was already pivoting beyond the centre of balance, and in a second it would be in the water, and Chance would be dead from shock.

It seemed to be happening in slow motion, but inexorably too. Then I realized the pick was still in my hand. I launched myself forward, driving the head of the ice pick through the thin metal sheeting of the Doo's nose, and leaned back, half-sitting, bracing my weight and strength to hold it. It didn't stop it though. My arms felt as if they were being pulled out and I could feel my boots being dragged along the surface, a millimetre at a time. Suddenly something hit my shoulder, almost knocking the handle of the pick out of my hands. I slipped and fell but the blow had come from Yamamoto as he dashed up to grab the handle. Now he had it firmly and I joined my grip to his. Together we held it, then bent our knees and straightened them, heaving backwards, with all the strength we had. It was Chance's weight that had been against us. The impact must have thrown his body back into the rear of the Doo. But now he climbed forward and there was a bump as the centre of gravity moved our way and the Doo came level on the ice. It was easy now, and Yamamoto and I dragged it clear quickly, then waited for Chance to get out.

He couldn't, though. The impact must have buckled the metal of the door and the frame it hung in. Whichever it was, Chance couldn't open it with the handle, and finally had to kick it out. He climbed out holding his arm.

'You hurt?' I asked.

'Just a bruise, a bang,' he said. He stared angrily at the crippled Doo with its door flapping in the wind and the head of my ice pick still sticking into the metal. Meldrum was already unclipping the engine cover, and he pulled the pick head clear before raising it, then turned to me.

'Bloody good shot,' he said. 'Hit the carburettor smack dead centre.'

Chance said, 'Spares?'

'Not a spare carb,' Meldrum said.

'So we're one down. A quarter the way and we've lost a Doo already.' Chance's voice was bitter.

I said, 'We nearly lost a man, too.'

'I didn't thank you, did I?' Chance said. 'Thanks now. And to you.' He nodded at Yamamoto. 'Now—we've either got to get one back over there and find another way over the ridge, or we've got to get the other four across.'

CHAPTER FIFTEEN

What we needed, and what we hadn't got, was anything that could be used as a bridge. Chance didn't want any more polynya-jumping, and I didn't blame him, but a few minutes of casting around showed clearly there was no other way. We had four pairs of skis, but even if they were tightly lashed together, it was doubtful whether they'd bear the weight of a Doo and we daren't risk damaging the skis. There was also the little folding mountain rescue stretcher, but the same argument applied to that.

So finally Yamamoto helped Meldrum to climb back across the side of the ridge, and he went first to my own Doo, handling it the way he'd done before. He vanished back on to the far ice until we'd almost lost sight of him, until he was just a moving outline in the snow; then he roared towards us, hit the ramp true and centre, and brought the Doo down straight and level on my side of the water. How he did it I'll never know; he was virtually flying the thing, holding it in balance as it made the jump, then letting it down, admittedly with a tremendous thump, but beautifully-balanced all the same, on the other side. Then he went back for the next one.

I'm damned if he didn't do it better each time. I wouldn't have tried that jump for all the scotch in Scotland, and the only other guy who'd tried it had written off the machine, but Meldrum brought all four of them across without the suggestion of a mis-jump. The last of them barely even shuddered. Somehow he'd worked out how to keep the back end down and the nose in the air, and it sailed across like a glider, landing neatly on the rear of the revolving tracks, and just carried on ploughing forward in a straight line.

We were over; it was unbelievable, but we were over. We were also down to five Doos, which meant somebody had to double up.

Chance walked across to Meldrum, said, 'I'm safer with you, chauffeur,' and climbed in behind him.

The stars were out again now, and Meldrum ran to his left for three miles, under the bulk of the ridge, then headed off again on course, with the rest of us following. We'd lost the better part of an hour, but we'd been doing so well before we hit the pressure ridge that it didn't matter too much. My watch told me it was just after four o'clock, which left us with about a hundred and twenty miles to go in something approaching five or six hours. Skimming along behind the Doo in which Meldrum and Chance were riding, I began to think we ought to make it easily.

Several times we encountered other ridges, but they were either much smaller and therefore quite readily negotiable, or there were gaps to get through. Then we hit an area of choppy, chunky ice maybe a hundred yards across that looked like those photographs of tank traps Hitler built in the Western Wall. We followed the same practice we'd followed before, splitting the party and heading off both sides to see if there was a way through. There wasn't. At some time in the past, two giant ice rafts had rubbed together at this point, grinding chunks off one another and letting them drop in the sea between. When the sea had frozen over, what was left was this incredibly rough stretch of ice. It looked like a piece of coarse glasspaper magnified a million times, and it was obvious the Doos wouldn't make it across under power. The jagged ice teeth would have tipped them over a hundred times.

There was only one thing for it. The six of us would have to carry the Doos across, one by one. We picked Number One, Meldrum's, up first, and staggered forward among the spiky ice. We staggered not so much because the Doo was desperately heavy, as because our feet seemed to have no solid purchase on the ice. At any given moment it seemed as though four men were slithering and sliding while two were taking the strain of the sudden lurches and swings of weight. About two-thirds of the way across, my feet slid suddenly from under me and I sat down with a thump. I'd hung on to the Doo instinctively to try to break my fall, and because several others seemed to slip at the same time, I found myself staring up at the Doo, poised above me, with only Ericson at one corner and Grey Smoke at the back, to take the weight. I could hear them grunting as they struggled, exerting every ounce of strength they had. I tried desperately to struggle to my feet, and take some of the weight before it crashed down on me. It must have been like a scene from an old silent movie as I tried to get up, my feet and hands slipping in all directions while I struggled, and Ericson and Grey Smoke standing there like two pillars holding up a swaying roof, sweating in the icy cold.

Yamamoto had better luck in getting to his feet, and his massive strength took some of the weight. Then Chance was up and helping, and Meldrum. In the end I had to crawl away a few feet before I could manage to get up and edge over to join the others. After that we took it very slowly.

As soon as we lowered the Doo on to the ice on the other side, Meldrum was in the cabin like a rat up a rope, punching the starter. The engine roared splendidly to life and we all let out a sigh of relief. To carry the Doos across that ice it was necessary to kill the engine each time, and that carried the danger that they wouldn't restart. Bombadiers, the French-Canadians who manufacture these snowmobiles in Quebec, fit an electric starter that works well in sub-zero temperatures, but there isn't a starter motor on earth I'd like to trust my life to, and that was precisely what was involved here.

Leaving the engine running, we went back for the next machine.

Half an hour later, we were on our way again. This time we ran for a bit more than an hour, more slowly, over rougher surfaces that handed out nasty jars and jolts occasionally. We were making twenty, or maybe twenty-five, miles an hour, and were well up to schedule, thanks to the fast run we'd had through the early twilight.

About six, the Doo in front of me slowed. We all pulled up beside it and Chance got out, walking along the line. I opened the door inquiringly and shuddered as the icy wind howled in, dissipating in a second the comfortable warmth of the cabin. 'Better eat now,' he yelled above the roar of the engine.

I nodded, closed the door and reached behind me for the insulated pack of food. We still had about eighty miles to go and reasonably decent progress ought to bring us in under the cliffs more or less when we wanted to be there. I sat there chewing on the heavy beef stew and swigging cocoa. I had no appetite for either, but was conscious that it might be many hours before the chance to eat would come again and I forced it down. The engine ticked over cheerfully and the cabin was warm. If I closed my eyes it was possible to believe I was sitting in a car somewhere, but as soon as I opened them again, as soon as I looked out through the quadrant the wiper made on the windscreen, the illusion was swiftly dispelled. Ahead of me the pale silver of the ice stretched away until it blended with the dark sky. It was a menacing kind of silver, too, that the thin crescent moon shed. This was one of the world's most bleak and hostile places, an environment intolerable unless man was properly equipped. I finished the food and stuffed the box away again in the back. I was ready to go again and peered out at the others, looking from one to the other of the little Doos as they stood throbbing on the ice. Yamamoto was out of his, leaning on Number One, talking to Chance. I glanced back at his machine, and noticed suddenly that it was the exception; it wasn't throbbing at all.

I opened the door and got out, moving quickly across to the Doo. Sure enough it was silent. I wondered how long ago it had happened, how long ago Yamamoto had left it, and what had caused the stoppage. I dashed across to Number One, and tapped Yamamoto on the shoulder.

'Your engine's cut,' I yelled. He turned, face anxious.

'Stopped?' Meldrum's voice. He came out of that cabin like a spring and dashed across to the dead Doo.

He tried the starter first. It turned over, yagg-yagg-yagg, but the engine didn't fire. In a flash the front was up and Meldrum was peering at the engine, whipping off the lead.

'Someone turn the starter!' Yamamoto slid into the seat and did so. Meldrum nodded to himself, opened the toolbox and whipped out the bar spanner. I'm a surgeon and I reckoned my hands are neat and quick, but Meldrum's deftness was astonishing. He was wearing thick, heavy gloves and working in them with the dexterity of those girls who solder micro circuits into television sets. The plug was out and replaced in a flash, the lead re-connected.

'Try it now!' Yagg-yagg-yagg. The engine spun several times and I had visions of the new plug oiling up too. That's the only trouble with two-strokes: the way the petrol/oil mixture can coat a plug. But then it fired, coughed for a second or two, and ticked on healthily. Meldrum, however, was taking no chances. The screwdriver was out and he was adjusting the carburettor setting, raising the tick-over rate a little. He stepped round to the door.

'How's your fuel?'

'Twenty-two gallons,' Yamamoto said.

'You'll be OK.' Meldrum put the spanner and screwdriver away, closed the cover with a snap, and hurried back to Number One. It must be nice to approach a carb with that kind of confidence. My MG has two of them and tuning is something I leave strictly to the experts and pay twenty bucks a month for.

We moved forward, steadily, without real difficulty. After a while the snow began to blow again, more heavily this time, and it piled up at the sides of the screen, but the wiper seemed to handle it happily enough.

Ahead there was still no horizon, just the dull sheen of the ice moving away until it blended with the sky, and the stars shining brightly. Our star was still dead in front. We might be a little bit out when we got there, but I reckoned we had travelled pretty straight, and I kept wondering what it would be like when we arrived. I cast my mind back to the model that had been made in the CIA building from the satellite reconnaissance photographs.

The two main islands of Novaya Zemlya are really a continuation of the high and rugged Northern Urals. The ocean has cut them off from mainland Siberia, but they are part of the same geological structure: mountainous, glacier-topped, and more than six hundred miles long, the land curving in a crescent out into the Arctic Ocean and separating the Barents Sea from the Kara Sea. The new building of the Arctic research station stood high on a cape in the North Island; a cape that hooked out into the ocean. Our course approached the North Island at an angle, and would run about parallel to the coastline over the last miles.

As we moved steadily ahead it was difficult not to think of the Russians on the island ahead: to wonder what equipment was in use, what monitoring was being done, how strongly the islands were guarded. In the days of the development of the hydrogen bomb, when the islands had been the principal proving grounds, the whole place would have seethed with scientific and military personnel, but the test-ban treaty had presumably changed all that and it seemed unlikely that the Russians would maintain, unnecessarily, large and pointless installations.

All the same, with less than fifty miles to go now, we were running into the area of potential discovery. It was unlikely that the massive radar chain would be directed at the ice surface, and in any case the Doos were so small that they might well remain undetected. The bigger problem was super-sensitive seismological equipment that would almost certainly pick up the vibrations in the ice caused by our movement across it; the more so because ice itself is crystalline and a nearly perfect conductor of vibration. On the other hand, the constant movement, the breaking and cracking and grinding of the ice which never stopped, was bound to create a vibrational pattern, a threshold of noise. It wasn't as though we were introducing noise and vibration into stillness, we were simply adding to the existing volume. In Washington somebody had compared it with a drum and it was an image that was easy to appreciate. Imagine, he'd said, that you have a big drum, and half a dozen drummers are doing a steady drum roll on it, then somebody else slides a fine, wire brush lightly across the surface. The sound would be there, and audible, but would the instruments separate it, and if they did, would any of the operators notice?

From this time on, as we approached Soviet territory, an armed and fast-moving party, there could be no question what we were, no possibility that we were about any lawful business; for nobody had lawful business here, except perhaps the occasional, almost stationary, drift research station. If we were picked up, by radar, seismograph or anything else, we'd be tracked in and a hot reception would be waiting. All we could do was go ahead boldly. And pray. I prayed.

I don't know about the others, but I know how I was feeling. With the moon climbing the sky now, visibility was perhaps three miles across the dull gleam of the ice. My eyes switched constantly from the back of Number One Doo to the limit of our night visibility; the point where ice and night sky blended. It retreated, seemingly endlessly, in front of us, but soon that retreat would end; soon the sheets of ice would run against land rising sharply from the surface, and when it did, we would have to identify our position from the shape of the mountains before us, find the building on its cliff, and attack.

Novaya Zemlya loomed out of the Arctic night at eight thirty-six p.m.

CHAPTER SIXTEEN

The feeling is difficult to describe, but I shall always remember its curious clarity. The Doos were stopped in a little circle, engines running. As soon as the massive grey shape of the land became visible, Number One turned back the way we had come and ran for perhaps half a mile until the land was lost behind us. We stood out in the bitter night, listening to Chance, but turning occasionally, in involuntary reflex, to stare across the ice. The wind was about twenty knots, but for the moment there was no snow.

Chance said, 'We've been lucky so far. I got the shape of that ridge. We're about three miles north of where we ought to be and the time situation is good. Now here's what we do . . .'

We climbed back into the Doos and went south in a wide arc, moving slowly, stopping frequently, and generally trying to behave like a family of polar bears out seal-hunting. It took us an hour to come to a position from which the promontory was visible. We couldn't yet see the building.

Then Meldrum went round the Doos, slipping the special silence collars over the flanges on the exhaust pipes. Those collars cut the performance down by more than sixty per cent; when they were in position, the Doos could do no more than ten miles an hour, but they moved as silently as Rolls-Royces, and there weren't any clocks to tick. It didn't take him long, and when he'd finished he slid swiftly back to the driving seat in Number One.

I shall never forget our approach to Novaya Zemlya. The little column creeping forward in the stillness, the bulk of the island lifting dark and menacing out of the ice sheet, its mountain tops gradually looming in grim silhouette in the night sky. We moved, the wind moved, but nothing else. As we came closer, details of the land became clearer; we could see the cliffs, climbing sharply from the ice.

Then, dimly, I saw it; the concrete a different white from the snow into which it snuggled; a squat, square two-storey building, standing sightless on the cliff top, facing out over the frozen ocean. Every moment I expected things to start happening, lights to flare, tracer to flash through the dark. My heart was thumping and I thought seismographs would pick it up in Tokyo, let alone half a mile away. We edged gently forward, feeling horribly exposed, like little white mice creeping towards some great, crouching cat that would, any second, spring to violent, lethal life in front of us.

Now I could see the cliff, no longer solid, its grey-black marked with deep black lines and cracks running up and down its face. The building sat pale and still above the skirts of its cliffs, and as we came nearer I saw the outlines of shutters, menacingly like the gun-port covers in an old man-o'-war. In my mind's eye I imagined them lifting threateningly on the grey snouts of guns rolled forward, but they remained blindly closed.

There was a quarter-mile to go, then three hundred, two hundred yards. Had anyone been watching, we must have been seen : little white humps sliding, with our tiny plumes of exhaust vapour, across the last open apron of ice. I realized my hands were so tight on the steering handlebar that muscles and tendons were beginning to ache, and deliberately loosened my grip. It was easy, at that moment, staring at the implacable cliffs, the white of the snow, to think of the slave camps of Vorkuta, on the Soviet mainland behind Novaya Zemlya, where millions had died, worked to death and frozen to death, in expiation of imagined counter-revolutionary activity. This was the world of Stalin, and across the years the cruelty reached out at me and I shivered.

The building was high above us now, beginning to be

hidden from sight as we slid under the lee of the cliffs and brought the Doos to rest in a line, a few yards from the rocky face. Here, in the short Arctic summer, murderous storms must fling their waves against those cliffs, but now the water was tamed by the iron grip of cold and ran, smooth almost as a rink, to the base of the granite wall. Beneath it, we were almost invisible.

It was ten o'clock.

Time to attack.

We checked our equipment. I remember looking at my clumsy white felt boots as I peeled off the sealskin overboots, and wondering whether they were really adequate for the climb before us, then grinning nervously at the thought.

Yamamoto was already standing at the foot of the cliff, staring upward at the hard stone with its veining of gleaming ice in every crack, its crusts of frozen snow on every ledge. My harness felt tight, the belt constraining my waist, as I moved forward to join him, pulling at the straps, feeling the long coil of nylon line bumping at my hip. Beside me, Chance had the stretcher folded on his back in a small, awkward, aluminium and canvas pack. Grey Smoke and Ericson had ropes too, and each of us wore a carbine slung across his back and a pistol at his belt.

Behind us, Meldrum was pacing up and down the line of Doos, the only one left behind; the man whose job was to keep the engines running, to make sure that our only possible means of escape remained open to us. Soon he would be left behind in the night, waiting. I didn't envy him.

Satsumi Yamamoto knotted the rope carefully to the loop in his climbing belt and looked across at Chance, who nodded. In a few moments, Yamamoto had hoisted himself five or six feet to a nook in the rock; he looked ahead, before moving on. The aerial photographs had suggested an easy climb, but though the cliffs were not vertical, they must have been steeper than he had thought. This was no beginner's climb; just watching him made that apparent. It wasn't that he made it look difficult because he didn't; he went up easily and expertly, but the fact that expertise was so obviously necessary was hardly good news for the rest of us. I watched him nervously and admiringly, knowing I must soon venture up on to that face myself without reserves of skill and experience; knowing that every scrap of strength and balance I had would be tested.

I felt a slap on my shoulder and moved to the rope, fastening it to the harness, my clumsy fingers wrestling with the knot. Yamamoto was forty feet above us now, belayed into a crack, feet braced to take the strain, to haul me, if necessary, towards him.

Our order on the rope was dictated by the lack of skill of the weakest: Yamamoto first, the expert, carrying the whole burden, backed not by another skilled climber who knew rope technique, but by a novice he must get to the top. Behind me was Ericson who, though not in the Jap's class, could climb well; then Chance, not quite a novice, but not skilled; and finally Grey Smoke, a man of the Arctic who did everything well.

I looked up at Yamamoto, and felt the rope tug at my belt as he tightened it, taking a loop across his shoulders. My feet moved off the ice and on to rock. Then I was feeling with my hands for the first hold and finding it and, with my toes, testing each hold before I committed my weight. Slowly I moved upwards, trying to obey the instruction not to use knees and elbows, instead to keep my body clear of the rock and climb with hands and feet. It sounds easy, but isn't. The temptation to get as close to the rock as you can, to grip it with everything you have, including your teeth, is almost overwhelming, and it increases as you get higher. Always, and with wonderful reassurance, the rope remained tight and through it I could feel Yamamoto helping me. He wasn't lifting me up the cliff, but the strength was there when it was needed, when my balance might betray me. I crawled precariously upward, concentrating always on the next yard, the next hand-hold, the next ledge for my toes. About twenty feet up I came thankfully on to a hard ledge about a foot wide and paused for a moment, but two swift tugs on the rope told me that time was not to be wasted, and I climbed on, the stone wall a foot from my face, until I was ten feet or so below Yamamoto, in another safe, wide gap in the upward crack. Looking down, I saw Ericson already moving up towards me, looped the rope round my shoulders, and braced myself hard back in the crack, taking the strain until he reached the ledge below me. Then another tug on my rope told me to get moving. I saw Ericson already established, back against the rock, with Chance climbing slowly towards him, and below there was the dark face of Grey Smoke, still waiting to begin. On the ice Iain Meldrum was already patrolling from Doo to Doo, keeping vigil on the engines.

I turned to face the cliff again, looking upward for Yamamoto, and my heart gave a desperate thud as I failed to see him, but another tug, and a glimpse of the rope running upward, told me he was merely out of sight, hidden in the rock. Again I concentrated on the rock itself, feeling ice slip beneath my fingers as I searched for hand-holds, taking a kind of desperate care that there should always be one hand or foot anchored firmly before the next hold was sought.

It didn't feel like a hundred and fifty feet, it felt like a hundred and fifty miles; the strain and tension were gradually getting at the tendons in my hands, the muscles in my calves, as I went higher, with the rope taut above me.

Yamamoto was climbing silently somewhere above, and Ericson coming towards me up the rope with Chance out of my sight and Grey Smoke moving towards him, when it happened. How, I don't know, but something must have given under Chance's feet and I saw him topple, very slowly it seemed, like a slow-motion film, arms and legs flying. I could see the rope between him and Ericson snapping taut and knew instantly that in a second Ericson would be plucked off the cliff and that I alone could never hold their combined weight. As they fell, they would drag me off, then the tension would pass to Yamamoto and he would tumble, too. I was standing on a boulder that was wedged into the chimney, and I did the only thing I could do, jumping off on the other side, praying that there was enough loose rope above me not to jerk Yamamoto off the face above.

As my body fell, the sudden tightening of the thin nylon line, with the weight of three men on the other end, felt as though it would cut me in half. I fell a few feet; I don't know how many, then there was another terrific jerk on my belt. I saw the wall of stone hurtling towards me and felt a tremendous crack on the head . . .

Yamamoto must have been incredibly quick, coming down the face. Dimly I felt myself being lifted, my belt slackened and the terrible pressure on my chest relaxing. My head was a great ball of pain and I clutched it, moaning, while Yamamoto secured the line and the three below scrambled to new hand- and toe-holds on the stone.

When the pain subsided a little and I had enough control to open my eyes, I saw Yamamoto braced against the cliff, a turn of the rope round the rock from which I had jumped, easing them up. I crawled forward and looked over at the white face of Harald Ericson twenty feet below. He looked uninjured. Chance clung to the cliff beneath him and Grey

Smoke stood cleanly on a ledge. My head was aching desperately and my body felt as though it had been put through a mangle, but the rest, as far as I could see, were all right.

'Quick, we must hurry,' Yamamoto hissed urgently. 'I climb.' He gestured upwards and hoisted himself back on to the rocks as I forced my bruised arms to take the weight of the rope and Ericson moved towards me.

A few minutes later we were back in pattern, working our way steadily up the cliff in the sequence we had used when we started out. I wondered whether any of us had cried out in the desperation of the fall; to have done so would have been natural. Had I let out a shout as I jumped? I tried to think and couldn't remember; things had happened just too quickly and the crack on the head that had knocked me out had drowned, for all my senses, anything that had been going on around me. But it was important. I peered upward to where Yamamoto was climbing, expecting every second to see lights shining down the cliff face. If anybody at all had been out of doors up there, something must have been heard.

I strained my ears, but there was no sound except the hiss of the wind, which seemed to get colder with every foot I climbed. When it came again to my turn to stand and hold the rope, I looked down to where Meldrum was maintaining his icy vigil among the muffled Doos, walking endlessly up and down the line, checking those vital engines. Then I was climbing again, the cold gradually penetrating my clothing; my hands growing numb, even through the gloves, from contact with the icy rock. When I looked up, the lip of the cliff seemed to grow nearer with dreadful slowness and I decided not to look at it again, to think instead only of the next cranny, the next tiny ledge.

It seemed to take hours, alternately climbing, then pausing while others climbed, then climbing again. The reality, I suppose, was that we made the climb, apart from that one desperate slip, quickly and efficiently considering the level of our climbing skill. I was surprised, suddenly, to find myself staring at Yamamoto's boots, then his thighs, and being hauled up to stand beside him on a shelf a few feet from the top. We hauled the others up behind us, and stood waiting there.

Now Yamamoto edged upward again, a few inches at a time, climbing silently until his head was just below the lip, then pausing for a long moment before raising it to look cautiously over the top. I watched his head move from side to side while his eyes searched the night in front of him.

Beside me I could hear the hissing breath of the others, see the steam of their breath whipped away by the wind as we stood staring upward at the black silhouette of Yamamoto outlined against the sky.

He looked down and gestured with his hand for us to follow. This time Chance went first: the soldier's eye was needed now. I watched him climb, heavy but strong, until he was level with Yamamoto; until he too could see above the lip. Then Ericson followed, lean and easy, and between them he and Grey Smoke got me up there, too.

Cautiously I raised my head and looked over.

CHAPTER SEVENTEEN

The building stood ten yards or so back from the edge, anchored firmly to the rock. The windows were still shuttered and I thought it unlikely that they were much used except in the brief summer. In any case, they were now only dark outlines in the forty-yard-long concrete wall. At the far end, the building was hard against a great rock outcrop and behind it the ground rose fairly sharply towards the mountains. Round the end of the building nearest to us, a dark diagonal suggested an outdoor staircase rising to the upper storey. It looked the bleakest, loneliest place in the world.

We stayed there, clinging to the cliff, gasping, for perhaps a minute, examining the scene before us, listening, nerves taut to detect any movement, anything that might indicate guards, but the Arctic silence was only broken by the wind, which seemed stronger here, high above the ice surface.

A sound to my right made me jerk my aching head round. It was Chance, scrambling over the edge, then falling softly to his belly in the snow. Quickly we all followed and lay beside him, hearts thumping, slipping our automatic pistols from their holsters.

A minute passed, then Chance began to crawl forward on his stomach towards the wall, his body ploughing a channel through the snow. We watched tensely, wondering what lay beneath the snow; whether the Russians, with their obsessive need for security, had stretched trip wires or planted mines. It seemed unlikely, but we were, I realized suddenly and sickeningly, actually *in* Russia, now, in a world none of us knew.

Chance reached the wall, paused, then crawled towards the corner in its shelter. He looked round it cautiously and waved, and we crawled after him, swiftly, to form a tight, crouching group under the concrete face of the building.

Chance turned to whisper softly: 'There's a radio antenna on the hill behind.'

Grey Smoke nodded, and moved past us, round the corner, and melted into the snow. The rest of us waited while Chance watched him. It seemed likely that all communication with this God-forsaken spot would be by radio; likely too that the channel would be kept open most of the time. To cut that channel might carry its own risks, but it would be far more dangerous to leave it open.

Five minutes passed, minutes in which the cold seemed to be eating into our bones, numbing our limbs, cramping us in our stiff, crouched postures. Then Grey Smoke reappeared —it almost seemed as though he materialized—back among us. He was extraordinary: absent one moment, there the next, defeating sight and hearing by some strange subtlety of movement.

'Cable is cut,' he said. 'No sign of other radio or radar installation here.'

Chance murmured: 'There may be another aerial up in the mountain.'

'We'd never find a cable underneath the snow,' Grey Smoke whispered.

'What's round there?'

'Almost nothing,' Grey Smoke said. 'The stair leads to a door on top. Wooden, I think. The stair is metal. Behind the building there seems to be nothing but a rubbish dump and a parking bay of some kind. Nothing in it and no tracks.'

'It has probably been there since the place was built,' Chance said softly. 'You're sure there are no other entrances?'

Grey Smoke shook his head. 'Couldn't see anything.'

Chance nodded. I knew what he was thinking because we were all thinking it: the only way in was that door at the head of the steel staircase. So far we had been lucky: we'd got this far undetected, undamaged except for the loss of Chance's Ski-doo. But now—now, any sound on that stair would be heard inside. The door might be locked; might lead anywhere. And if anybody had heard us on the stair, we might go through that door to face men armed and ready and in a position of great advantage. Preparations and equipment had now brought us as far as they could. From this moment we were five men on our own.

We moved stealthily round the corner of the building, our feet making almost no sound in the hard snow, and looked at the ladder: sixteen rungs of steel without risers, all coated with ice and treacherous as hell. There was a tubular metal handrail on the side of the staircase away from the building At the top was a narrow square platform on which three men might possibly stand, but not if the door, as it probably did, opened outwards.

Chance inched forward, pistol at the ready in his left hand, and put his right on the handrail, then put his weight carefully on the first step and moved up. Ericson followed. The rest of us covered them with our carbines, praying we would not have to use them. Slowly, carefully, Chance climbed the ice-covered staircase to the platform, and began to examine the door. In a moment or two the cautious Ericson had joined him and we watched them both take off their outer gloves and begin to feel the woodwork. Then Ericson bent for a moment and I saw a movement of his shoulders inside his parka that could only be a shrug. They exchanged a few whispered words, and Ericson began a slow careful descent of the staircase. At the bottom he waved us towards him.

'There is no handle on the outside,' he said, 'and the door opens so that only one man can stand on the platform as it swings. Here is what we do. You, Yamamoto, climb the stairs, cross the platform and climb the rail. You flatten yourself against the wall on the far side. Colonel Chance will be on the stairs, also flattened against the wall, and you—' he pointed to Grey Smoke—'behind him on the stairs.'

'Me?' I whispered.

'Behind Grey Smoke.' Well, I wasn't there for my abilities in a roughhouse; I didn't mind.

Ericson went on: 'I stand on the platform and bang on the door, then turn away so that when they open it, they see only my hood. But I have my carbine in my hands so that when I turn . . .' he left the sentence unfinished.

We were all in position quickly, anxious for any kind of movement in the crippling cold. We stood there, barely breathing, as Yamamoto threw a leg over the handrail and stepped over the side to balance in space, with one foot and one arm unsupported, in the dark beyond the platform.

Ericson glanced at Chance. There was a little pause. Then Chance nodded. Ericson stepped forward and banged on the door, hard, five times, spacing the bangs a second apart. I knew why: no prowling animal approaching the door would bang it in that way. He stepped back to the door. His left hand was on the rail, fully mittened. On his right he wore only the silk underglove, and in the moonlight the metal of the carbine glinted dully.

For a few seconds nothing happened and I watched Ericson start to turn towards the door again, but then we heard a voice from inside, grumbling interrogatively but indistinguishably. A shouted question. Ericson glanced at Chance, then shouted an unintelligible reply. I heard the sound of a bolt being drawn, a key turning, and the voice grumbled again. Then, staring up, past Grey Smoke and past Chance, as they stood flat against the stair wall, I saw the dark shape of the door swinging outwards and the fishtail of light, at top and bottom, shining out into the night.

Ericson still stood, shoulders hunched, apparently staring out into the darkness. I heard the voice grunt a question, then its owner stepped forward. Beneath the door I saw his boots as he stepped on to the platform, then a hand reached forward to tap Ericson on the shoulder.

There was a thud that could only have been Yamamoto hitting him and Ericson spun round to grab the man as he fell.

As the door swung wide and came to rest against the wall, Yamamoto and Ericson stood on the platform, the unconscious Russian between them, looking dazzled in the rectangle of light. There were no shots, no other sounds. Chance stepped quickly up to join them, then vanished through the door with Yamamoto and Ericson at his heels. James Grey Smoke and I clambered quickly up after them. We had entered a small room that looked as army guardrooms must look in every country in the world. A plain table, with a telephone on it, two upright wooden chairs behind it; a plain wooden floor. Fire extinguishers on the walls, a notice board and another board on which several tasselled keys hung. Apart from the door by which we had entered, there were two others. One, in the wall behind the desk, looked as though it might lead to storeroom or lavatory. I looked outside and there was no opening in the concrete wall; no window or vent. I didn't know the Russian sanitary arrangements, but anybody who builds lavatories without adequate ventilation is a fool. I changed my mind:

that door probably led to a staircase.

I slammed the main door and rattled the bolt a bit in case anyone might be listening, then we waited a moment. Ericson, with unlikely humour and real nerve, whistled a few notes of *Kalinka* and gave the chair a little scrape across the floor. Chance grinned tightly and gave him a little nod of approval, then moved to the door, removed his mittens and let them hang on his neck straps. He unfastened the hood of his parka and pushed it back and laid his ear against the door. Quickly I went across to the other one and did the same. I could hear nothing and shook my head. Chance waved me across and we all flattened ourselves against the walls on either side of the door. Chance gripped the handle carefully, and began to turn it silently. I watched his wrist turn and then the little pull as he tried to open it. The door did not move; it must be locked on the other side. He pulled harder, making sure, but still it didn't move.

A little groan brought all our heads swivelling round. The Russian Yamamoto had clobbered was regaining consciousness where he lay propped against the far wall. Chance stepped across to him, carbine at the ready. When the Russian's eyes opened it was the first thing he saw and they widened in fear. Chance put his fingers to his lips and waggled the carbine threateningly, then pointed first to the door, then to the key board. The Russian shook his head, then nodded quickly as the carbine moved close to his eye. Yamamoto crossed to the board and began pointing to each key in turn, the Russian shaking his head until the Jap's hand came to the right one, then nodding violently.

Swiftly Grey Smoke tied him up and gagged him with a fur hat from the clothes peg on the wall. When he had finished, Chance slid the key cautiously into the lock and the tiny scraping sound rasped in our ears. The key turned slowly, and at the end there was a click as the tumblers fell: a sharp, noisy click that sounded thunderous to my ears.

He opened the door, gently at first, just a crack, then peered round the edge. After a moment he opened it wide and passed through, and we followed him into a corridor which stretched the length of the building. Dim lights burned in the ceiling, but there was no other light. The walls on either side were only partitions, wood to waist height and reeded glass above, and all the rooms were in darkness. We tried the doors, but all were locked. The rooms looked like, and probably were, offices, workshops and laboratories. We turned and filed quietly out of the corridor, back into the guardroom, and across to the other door. It opened easily as Chance turned the handle and led, as I had thought, on to a concrete staircase, lit again by one of those dim roof lights. Somewhere we could hear an engine running, a diesel; probably the source of the power-supply.

Chance stepped through, the carbine ready in his hands, and began to tiptoe down the concrete stairs, stopping two or three steps down, then waving for us to follow. The stairs turned back on themselves half-way, and went on down, and at the bottom was a door. The felt boots might be clumsy, but the inch of felt with the rubber beneath it made them totally silent, and we went almost noiselessly down the stairs except for the soft rustle of the parkas.

I hoped this door wasn't locked; that we didn't have to go back to the guardroom and prise from the Russian up there the identity of the key. The tense wait seemed endless as Chance listened at the door. Behind it, unless the Russian had been the building's only occupant, were other Russians. When that door came open, we'd be in action.

Chance's hand went to the handle and began to turn it, slowly, through a ninety-degree arc. When it would turn no more he pushed gently, opening it a fraction, his eye narrow at the gap; then he looked at us and nodded. It was the signal.

He flung the door open and sprang through, Ericson at his shoulder. As they passed the door each stepped to the side and Yamamoto came between them, and the three of them stood with their carbines covering the room.

We interrupted a film show. There was a screen to the left of the room and a projector on the right. Between the two, men sat or lay on beds and it was astonishing how slowly they reacted. Perhaps film has some hypnotic quality, I don't know. One or two heads turned quickly towards us, and mouths dropped open, but the rest took their time even to be surprised. The whole process was as easy as shelling peas. I squeezed past and hunted for the light switch, found it, and dismissed the gloom.

The language of the levelled carbine is one of the truly international media, and when the men had finally taken in the fact that intruders with guns were covering them, they got up and shuffled, muttering and puzzled, in the direction the carbines indicated. Ericson and Yamamoto watched them while Chance moved the other way to herd the man who was operating the projector out to join them. Apart from the noise of the door opening, there hadn't been a sound above normal conversational level.

The whirring of the projector died and the sound track died with it, and we looked carefully round the big room. Obviously it served for eating, as a dormitory and as a recreation room. The walls were lined with lockers and small chests of drawers; clothes pegs supported outdoor clothing. The atmosphere had the heavy taste that characterizes rooms in which too many people spend too much time, an atmosphere with sweat in it, and staleness and too much heat and tobacco smoke.

Chance, Grey Smoke and I crossed to a door in the far wall and went through it quickly, peremptorily. The shape and structure of the building told us there could be only one or two small rooms there. This was where the building butted up against the rock outcrop outside. It was square, about ten feet by ten, sparely furnished. Just a chest of drawers, a wardrobe, a table and a couple of chairs, a few books, a washbasin and a narrow, metal bed. In the bed a man was sleeping, face turned to the wall. But his hair was grey.

I walked over to him and tapped his shoulder. There was no response. Another, harder tap, had no effect either. I held his shoulder in my free hand and pulled it towards me, rolling him on his back.

There was no mistaking Frol Ilyich Komarov.

'Waken him quickly,' Chance said. As I bent over the old man I heard him shout to Yamamoto and Ericson in the other room: 'I want those guys stripped and their clothes piled in the middle of the room,' and grinned to myself in the confidence of the moment, wondering how the other two would translate the order into Russian.

I shook Komarov's shoulder without effect, then tried again, harder. His pulse was all right. He must have taken some kind of sleeping drug and with a film blasting away in the next room, I could understand why. I put down my carbine and pulled back the lid of his left eye. He was certainly drugged.

Chance said, 'What's wrong?'

'He's taken sleeping tablets, I think,' I said.

'Can you waken him?'

'I can't with any of the equipment I've brought with me. In any case, it's not a good idea.'

'Take him like that, you mean?'

I turned. I started to say, 'Why not?' but the words died before I could speak them.

The woman was smiling grimly. She had a revolver and it was aimed at my chest. She said, 'Don't move. Don't anyone move.'

Chance and Grey Smoke started to spin round towards her, their carbines ready to fire. One or other of them would probably have got her. But they couldn't see what I saw. The revolver wasn't pointing at Chance or Grey Smoke. It wasn't even pointing at me. Now it had moved.

It was pointing at Komarov. And it was very steady in her hand.

'No,' I shouted. 'Don't shoot!'

CHAPTER EIGHTEEN

In the excitement of finding Komarov, we hadn't noticed the other door; the one through which she had come. Behind her, as she stood framed in the doorway, I could see a bed in it, but there wouldn't be room for much else.

She said, in good English, 'You will move back against the wall.' The revolver was still pointed at the head of the sleeping Komarov.

I raised my hands and shuffled back towards the wall, staring at her. I don't know which surprised me more: the suddenness with which our advantage had been lost, or the appearance of a blue-eyed blonde in a place like this. She was attractive, too; tall and athletically built.

'Place your guns on the floor.' Her voice was quiet but cold and the blue eyes watched us closely. Out of the corner of my eye I saw Chance and Grey Smoke bend to obey. From where she was standing she was in complete control, able to cover Komarov, us and the door behind us that led into the main room. None of us said anything. There was nothing to say. But they must have been thinking, as I was, of Ericson and Yamamoto in the other room. She would know there was somebody there, because she'd have heard Chance shout to them, but she wouldn't know how many there were.

Chance said, 'You speak English?'

Her eyes snapped at him. 'No talking!' The revolver followed the eyes and she gestured with it, indicating that we should move round to our right towards the door through which she'd come. She was going to herd us into the little room, and once in there we were finished. We had to do something, but it was difficult to see what, short of a concerted rush, we could do. And one of us, maybe two, would die in that rush. Somehow, one of us must attract the attention of Yamamoto or Ericson. But how? Chance went past the open door that led back into the dormitory with his hands high in the air and Grey Smoke followed the same way. There were continuing subdued shuffling noises from the dormitory and I assumed the Russians in there were removing their clothing as ordered. I moved sideways towards the door, wondering whether I could make a dash backward through it but there wasn't a chance; that gun barrel covered me every inch of the way, her watchful eyes mainly on me, but flicking back and forth to the other two. In another moment we would be in there, then she'd go out and get the drop on the other two and our little venture would be all over.

It was vital that we should stay in Komarov's room and that we should somehow convey the fact of our capture to the others.

I said loudly, 'He's very ill.'

She looked at me grimly, silently, merely motioning with the gun barrel.

'See for yourself,' I said, raising my voice as high as I dared. 'He's sweating. Do you know what that means?'

Her eyes flicked briefly towards the sleeping Komarov, then back to me. She shook her head.

I said, 'Not his face, you fool. His hair and his clothes are wet with sweat. He's hypoglycaemic!' I was trying to get concern into my voice and it wasn't difficult.

She half-turned again to look at him. I shouted, 'What fool gave him too much insulin? Did you? He'll go into convulsions soon.'

She wasn't sure whether to believe me. She wanted to look at him closely, but not to relax her control. She backed cautiously towards the bed, still facing us, her left hand reaching behind her. It was awkward for her because the head of the bed was in the corner of the room.

'Look at him, woman,' I shouted angrily.

The revolver pointed at me unwaveringly as her fingers sought his face. Once she touched it, touched the dry hair, we were done.

Out of the corner of my eye I saw a movement in the

big room and Ericson came into view. I kept my eyes off him and stared at the woman, at the revolver. 'How long ago did he have the injection?' I demanded, taking half a pace forward.

She pushed the revolver threateningly forward and in that second it spun out of her hand and she was clutching her fingers. The shot was very loud in the confined space and the bullet ricocheted several times off the concrete walls as we flung ourselves to the floor. I heard a grunt of pain.

Ericson appeared grim-faced in the doorway, working the bolt of his rifle, a thin plume of smoke rising from the muzzle. He bent and picked up the carbine from the floor.

'Thanks, Harald,' Chance said. He hadn't got up: at least, not far. He was kneeling, clutching his right thigh.

I said, 'What happened?'

'The bullet got me in the thigh.'

'Let me see.'

He grinned. 'Not in front of the lady.'

'In there,' I said.

She backed away towards the door, still holding her fingers. The shot hadn't hit her; it had taken the revolver cleanly out of her hand, but the impact must have given her fingers a hell of a bang. Ericson followed her out of sight.

The wound wasn't bad; Ericson's bullet must have been almost spent when it struck, but it had penetrated Chance's clothing, and was stuck in the flesh, badly distorted. I pulled it out, opened my kit and bathed the wound. It was bleeding fairly heavily. I sprinkled penicillin powder on some gauze and jammed it into the hole in his thigh, then bandaged it tightly.

'You'll suffer a bit but it's not mortal,' I said.

'Thanks, Doc.'

'If it starts to hurt too much, I'll give you morphine,' I said.

'Not now, Ericson!'

Harald came out with the girl walking in front of him, and we moved together into the dormitory. The fifteen Russians were standing naked at the far end by the screen, with Yamamoto standing well clear, positioned so that his carbine covered the entire room.

Chance slid the stretcher pack off his back. 'Get him dressed and fastened to this,' he said.

I took Grey Smoke with me, went back into the bedroom and pulled back the blankets. Komarov was wearing silk pyjamas, and as we stripped them off him I saw a Macy's label and wished I were back there, browsing among the haberdashery. Dressing an unconscious man is a trick and I'd mastered it a long time ago. There was a set of Arctic clothing in the wardrobe and we had him in it quickly, and fastened the buttons and straps of the rescue stretcher. He must have taken a tremendous jolt of pheno-barbitone, or something similar, to be so far under. I wouldn't let any diabetic patient of mine do it: the risks of staying under and going into coma are considerable.

When Komarov was secured in the stretcher, lying like a green canvas parcel on the floor, I went out again.

Chance and the girl were having an argument.

'—then I come, too,' she was saying.

I said, 'What's happening?'

Chance looked at me. 'She says she's his nurse. Won't leave her patient. All that jazz.'

She turned to me. 'I'm his assistant. I have been given nursing training because of his condition, but I work with him. If you are taking him away, I must go, too. I have his supplies, his insulin.'

I said, 'We're taking him out of Russia.'

'I know. We got a message out. I didn't believe anybody could help him.'

'So why the revolver?' Chance said.

She flared. 'How did I know who you were? You could have been KGB. Anybody. Wouldn't you try to protect him?'

'And if we had been KGB,' I said. 'What then?'

'Taking him away at gunpoint like that? I'd have killed you. And him, too, before I'd let them take him to a labour camp.' There was a deep urgency in her tone. 'I would not let that happen to him.'

'It's impossible,' Chance said. 'We can't take you.'

'Please.' Her eyes glistened. 'Oh, please, please take me. It is *so* important. Academician Komarov needs me. I have helped him for a long time.'

Vaguely I remembered Dr Catto talking about a dedicated assistant Komarov had. Catto had thought she might have sent the message.

I said: 'How did the message get out?'

'I posted it,' she said. 'We were taken back to Moscow for some meetings. He was watched, but I posted it there. We did not know if it would get through.' The intensity softened and she smiled. 'Oh, I am so glad you have come for him.'

This was Chance's decision. 'Do you want to go with us? Back to America?'

'Oh, yes! I do!' She gestured towards the doorway to where Komarov lay trussed like a turkey on the stretcher. 'He is a wonderful man. I would not want to leave him.'

I said, 'You may die. We may all die. It's a dangerous journey and we might not make it.'

There were tears in her eyes. 'You do not understand. It is an honour to work with a man like that. More important than—than nationality, than politics.'

'They'd call you a traitor. What about your family?'

I looked at my watch. It was eleven-thirty.

She said, 'I have no family.'

'Have you Arctic clothing?' Chance asked.

'Oh, yes!' she said eagerly. 'In my room.'

'Ericson will go with you,' Chance said.

'Thank you, thank you!' She seemed overwhelmed.

I suppose women have followed their men to the ends of the earth for so long that it's second nature, but I couldn't think of anybody I valued enough to follow them behind the Iron Curtain. I wouldn't do that if they gave me the surgery department of the Kremlin and de Bakey and Shumway as assistants.

Ericson followed her out in his thin, alert, purposeful way. A cold guy, that. And hard.

'Top of the stairs, Yamamoto,' Chance ordered briskly. 'Cover them coming up.'

Yamamoto headed for the staircase, carbine ready in his hands, and Grey Smoke followed. We listened as footsteps sounded on the steps.

'OK?' Chance called after him.

'OK.'

Chance moved towards the Russians. 'Pick up your clothes,' he said.

They stared at him.

'One of you understands,' Chance said. His carbine gestured at the heap of clothing. 'Pick them up.'

Still nobody moved. He walked forward, Grey Smoke covering him, picked up a bundle of clothes and thrust them at the nearest man, then signalled the rest of them to follow suit. They comprehended then, and we herded them towards the stairs, marching the lot of them up in a line. In the guard-room Chance said, 'I want every bit of clothing dumped over the cliff.'

We made the Russians go back down again to get the rest and bring it back up, and they obeyed, scared and slightly ridiculous as naked people always feel.

A few minutes later all the clothing, all the boots, were outside and Yamamoto was dragging the stuff to the cliff edge and kicking it over. We herded the Russians down to the girl's room, smashed the bulb and locked them in. Ericson stayed with them, his gun trained on the door, while Grey Smoke and I carried the rescue stretcher up the stair, then carefully down the outside iron stair to the edge of the cliff. The girl stayed with us, her hand never leaving the stretcher, steadying it through the sways and jolts.

Yamamoto grinned at me. 'Not go far here if no trousers.'

'No,' I said. 'It should keep them quiet for a bit.'

We anchored two ropes to the iron rung of the staircase and began to lower the stretcher on one, Yamamoto moving with it, down the other, easing its passage over the rocks on the descent. Below us, Iain Meldrum still paced backward and forward from one Doo to another.

It took perhaps ten minutes to get him down, and it was done without mishap. When Yamamoto climbed down on to the ice, we saw Meldrum having to help him.

Grey Smoke went to get Ericson, and he came out quickly, glad to be clear of that little room in which fifteen hostile men waited fuming in the darkness.

Looking down, I watched Meldrum drag the stretcher over to the Doos, while Yamamoto came up the rope like a squirrel.

'Have you got the insulin?' I asked the girl.

She held up a small canvas satchel and her eyes smiled inside the fur hood. I was glad we had the stuff he was used to; I don't know a thing about Russian pharmaceutical products, and was obviously better not to make any changes at this stage.

Chance came across. 'Can you climb?'

She shook her head, and he signalled to Meldrum to send the stretcher up again. It would be quicker that way than trying to ease her down on a rope.

Half an hour later we were all at the bottom and Komarov was secured, still sleeping heavily, in the back of a Doo. All around us on the ice, and scattered at various points on the cliff, was the Russians' clothing. They'd freeze to death before they could get near it. For once I was thankful for the knifing wind and the bitter, Arctic cold. It probably wouldn't take them long to get out of the downstairs room, but unless there was a radio transmitter apart from the two Ericson had carefully smashed, it would be a while before they got a signal out.

Meldrum had done a superb policing job on the Doos. Twice during his lonely vigil, engines had died; two-strokes aren't meant to be kept on tick-over for an hour or more. Each time he'd got it started again quickly. So all five remained serviceable.

In a few minutes we were off. We had to change order a bit. Now Meldrum was alone again in the leading Doo and Chance rode next, carrying Komarov propped in the back, so that the scientist was in the middle of a protective sandwich, with Yamamoto in the following Doo. Behind them Grey Smoke and I drove side by side, the girl in the back of my snowmobile.

The two directional receivers were mounted in Meldrum's and Chance's machines. It was risky, in a way; if disaster struck the leading Doo, we'd be left with only one and wouldn't dare keep it at the head of the column. It was the only way, though. The man in the lead needed the radio and it was important both that Chance should have one, and that the rest of us should be behind, shepherding.

I sat in the warmth of the cabin, following Yamamoto, feeling a sense of elation. We hadn't got clear yet, but I found it difficult to believe we'd got as far as this without more trouble. My head had even stopped aching from the crack it had taken on the climb up the cliff. Behind me as we slid slowly over the first few miles, the girl sat in silence and I wasn't sorry. There are times to talk to girls and times to concentrate on other things. This was one of those.

We were making about eight miles an hour, the heavy silencers still muffling the engines. They would not come off, Chance had ordered, until we'd made ten miles, and anxious as we all were to get a move on, it became irritating to go so slowly. The ice beneath us was roughish and I worried a bit about the sleeping Komarov bumping about in the back of Chance's Doo. He was held only by a seat harness round his waist and the danger was that his head would bang against the cabin walls. There wasn't much we could do about it, though; the little Doos hadn't been designed to carry sleeping men.

I kept glancing behind, both to check on the girl and to see if anything was happening on the land. The girl sat quietly in the back, smiling a little, and the island of Novaya Zemlya was vanishing into the dark. I wasn't sorry when finally I turned and the scene behind consisted entirely of ice and darkness.

After an hour and a quarter I saw the two Doos in front of me slowing and stopping. I pulled up too, got out, and saw Meldrum bending at the rear of his own machine. He straightened with the silencer in his hand and flung it out across the ice, then went on to Chance's machine and did the same again. When he came to me he banged me on the shoulder. 'Great stuff, eh, Doc?'

I smiled at him. 'So far, so good.'

'Don't be depressing.' He went on his knees, reaching beneath the Doo to unfasten the collar, and the engine roared, suddenly three times as loud. Meldrum straightened. 'Sounds happier, doesn't it, laddie?'

The girl's voice said, 'What is he doing?'

I turned. She'd slid forward on the seat and was looking out. I said, 'Stay inside. You'll freeze to death.'

Obediently she moved back and I climbed in again and blipped the throttle, listening with pleasure to the healthy liveliness of the little Rotax engine.

'He was getting rid of the silencers,' I said. 'We can move faster without them.'

'I see.' She remained silent for a little, then said, 'I am Natalya Tukhachevsky.'

'John Edwards,' I said.

Meldrum moved past us at a run and climbed back into Number One. A moment later we were going again, picking up speed as the unblanked engines spat their exhaust fumes freely into the night. Meldrum seemed in no doubt where he was going and the Doo headed confidently into the softly moonlit night. Snow began to fall more heavily, blowing in dazzling patterns in front of us. I ached to switch on the light, but didn't dare; it was unlikely anybody was out looking for us yet, but if the Russians had aircraft out, a column of light would lead them straight to us.

I glanced at the luminous dial of my watch. It was one-twenty in the morning, and with twilight about nine hours away we'd need to average twenty miles an hour, which meant thirty or so allowing for any halts. I settled myself more comfortably in the seat, eased my parka open at the neck, and concentrated on my driving.

Even moving blind, Meldrum was setting a good pace. The capacity for fierce concentration over a prolonged period that he had learned on the motor racing circuits was a tremendous blessing to us all. The two Doos ahead of me ran easily along into the night, weaving occasionally as Meldrum saw the outline of some hazard looming up.

Then we hit another patch of really rough ice. It was like the one we'd met coming in, but a bit narrower. We'd learned that the only answer was to carry the Doos across and I climbed out reluctantly. Meldrum's went first, then Chance's, with Komarov still heavily asleep, in the back. It was quite a struggle and I wished he'd wake; even if he'd dosed himself heavily, the passage across the ice ought to waken him soon. I made a mental note to ask the girl what he'd taken.

Then we picked up Yamamoto's Doo and started across. We'd gone perhaps sixty yards when there was an explosion behind us.

CHAPTER NINETEEN

We looked at one another in a sudden access of tension. Chance said slowly, whispering each word, 'What . . . the . . . hell . . . was . . . that?'

We waited, with the wind blasting around us and the frozen snow pattering like light hail on our clothing, feeling the cold eating into us. But there was no other sound. After a minute we finished carrying the Doo across and listened as Meldrum re-started the engine, then went back across the band of rough ice.

'You'll have to get out, I'm afraid,' I told Natalya, then realized she might know something about the explosion.

'Did you hear a bang just now?'

She shook her head. 'No, but—' and hesitated. 'What sort of explosion?'

'Short and sharp,' I said. 'A cracking sort of sound.'

She nodded. 'Sometimes the ice does this. When a big sheet of ice breaks it sounds like explosions.'

'Not explosions,' I said. 'Just one.'

'It could be a seismic charge,' she said. 'They are let off quite often, to make recordings of the vibrations. A pattern of them, on timing mechanisms. Volyov's work.'

'Volyov?'

'He wears steel glasses. You may not have noticed him.'

'What else could it be?'

Her eyes widened and she thought for a moment.

'Nothing else, I think. Either ice or a seismic charge.'

I told Chance about the conversation as we carried the Doo across. I think we felt equally relieved.

We got the remaining Doos over relatively quickly and again there was no trouble re-starting the engines. But time was ticking by and the pressure was on; we weren't behind the clock yet, but running in the dark, and without the lights which had been so useful on the inward journey, we needed all the speed we could get. Meldrum pressed ahead, pushing the column along as fast as he dared. I could imagine him sitting there in Number One, leaning back as he always did, steady eyes and relaxed posture disguising the instant reflexes, the cat-like wariness as his senses felt the surface ahead. He'd be wearing a smile, a small one, but it would be there.

We were making a good pace now; thirty-five at least, tucking the miles away behind us, and I began to relax too. I almost relaxed too much. My eyes had been focused on the tail of Yamamoto's Doo for so long I must have been semi-hypnotized, the way you get when you've been driving too long on a turnpike. When Yamamoto's Doo suddenly swerved, bucked and crashed down on its side, I was almost too late. I twisted the handlebar desperately and missed him by a whisker, braked and stopped, then got out and hurried back.

The Jap was bruised but all right and we got him out. The thickness of his clothing had saved him. The Doo was a write-off. One of the steering skis must have hit some projection in the ice, snapped and gone underneath the track. Anyway, the track itself was almost severed. Without effective steering and with one track bound to snap in a few miles, the Doo had had it.

I looked at it regretfully. 'We'll have to leave it for the polar bears.'

'Or the Russians,' Chance said. 'Look, we'll have to reorganize. Yamamoto!'

'Yes.'

'You OK?'

The big Jap grinned. 'A little sore. But I am very fit man. Am OK.'

Chance nodded. 'You go with Meldrum. And let's pray we don't lose another, or somebody'll have to take to skis.'

I turned to face the wind. It was brutally cold and I offered my back to it immediately. We weren't heading into it, but the cold was intense. Anybody who had to take to skis was in for a rough time.

I said, 'Fuel. Is everybody OK?'

'OK or not,' Chance said, 'we're going to siphon a few gallons into each of them. It could make all the difference.'

The siphoning took no more than five minutes, and most of that was spent manoeuvring the machines together. At four gallons each it meant the better part of three hours extra running. If we needed it . . .

We pushed on again. More time lost and only four snow-mobiles now: the minimum necessary to get us all warm to the rendezvous. Now we had to move: we'd still put fewer than forty miles between ourselves and Novaya Zemlya and it simply wasn't enough. I'd checked the time before we moved off again and it was three-thirty. With a hundred and fifty miles, plus one or two, to go in seven hours, we couldn't afford more trouble.

I was glad I wasn't Meldrum. Everything now depended on his skill and I tried to imagine what it must be like to sit up there in front, streaking into the blowing snow, eyes alert for faults in the surface ahead, knowing that nobody else could do the job he was doing; that without him we would have to slow; knowing too that this imposed an impossible level of watchfulness which would have to be maintained hour after hour. My eyes switched mechanically from the windscreen in front of me to the side window on my right where Grey Smoke and Ericson's Ski-doo ran beside ours.

We streaked on and I was praying that we wouldn't have to cross another polynya or meet another big ridge. In the next two hours we met two small ridges and had to get out and manhandle the Doos across, but in both cases it was possible to do it under power and in minutes. They lost us a bit of time so Meldrum in front piled on the speed, going faster and faster into increasingly heavy snow.

In front of me the Rotax two-stroke revved happily. There's a great deal to be said for two-strokes when there's a lot of simple, unsophisticated work to be done. No broken con-rods, no problems with oil; you just open the throttle and they flog away.

In these two hours we covered sixty miles, homing on to that beacon signal, whipping across the ice-pack like speed skaters, and after a while the snow began to lighten again. It wasn't any less risky, charging into it like that, but it felt less risky and that was reassuring in itself. I suppose I was beginning to feel a lot better all round: we'd five and a half hours of darkness before the twilight came and only a hundred miles or so to go; we were bucketing along merrily; we were a hundred miles from Novaya Zemlya or any other Russian territory, zipping along in white Doos on white ice in dim moonlight. All we had to do was keep going in the right direction.

But life doesn't like people to think like that. It's when your footsteps get most confident and your head's high, that you tend to put your heel where the dog has been.

Around five-thirty I said to Natalya, 'There's a flask in the back there. Pour it for both of us.' We'd stopped to have a cup of coffee, which was a pretty elegant gesture considering we were a hundred miles from anywhere on the Arctic ice-pack. I sat sipping it cheerfully, then, when it was finished, got out to walk forward to Chance's Doo and have a look at my patient. Komarov was still sleeping soundly, even in his cramped position in the back of the Doo. He couldn't have been very comfortable with his legs straddling the fore-and-aft seat and his body in a sort of semi-sitting position. I'd have thought aching back muscles, if nothing else, would have broken through the drugs. In any case, the drugs themselves were bound to begin to wear off quite soon. I checked him over as best I could, and he seemed normal enough: there was no sweating, no sign of diabetic coma; his breath was all right with none of the acetone smell that means danger in a diabetic. When I straightened and backed out of the cabin, the girl was standing anxiously waiting.

'How is he, Doctor?'

I said, 'Does he always sleep as deeply as this?'

She hesitated. 'I think he often takes more tablets than he should.'

'Why?'

'Because—' she gave a sad little smile—'because he wants to escape. To get away. Do you understand?'

I thought of him marooned for months in that concrete barracks back there with the same faces day after day. The colleagues who were also gaolers. 'I understand.'

She said, 'I have to shake him quite hard to waken him.'

'And the insulin?'

'When he has eaten. He usually injects himself, in his office. Academician Komarov does not like being a diabetic and he hates anybody to be there to see it.'

'What time?'

'He eats at nine and injects himself about ten-thirty. And again before he goes to bed. About ten in the evening.'

I nodded. It was a typical enough pattern. Good news, too. An hour doesn't matter too much with diabetic injections and what Natalya said meant there was no need to shove insulin into him while we were out on the ice.

We climbed back into the Doo and I shut the door. 'How long since his diet was last stabilized?'

'Two months.'

'Good,' I said. And good I meant. In so far as any diabetic's in a safe condition, a guy who'd been stabilized two months before might be said to be.

I looked out of the windscreen, saw Chance signal to Meldrum to move off then move after him. I glanced across to my right where Grey Smoke and Ericson were ready to roll along with me, and pressed the button. We slid forward for about a yard, then there was a horrible metallic clanging, crunching noise from underneath and we stopped.

All the cheerfulness drained out of me. I knew, as soon as I heard the noise, that it was disaster. I hoped, but I knew. I flashed the warning lights twice to warn the others, and sat waiting till they turned and came back, then got out and Meldrum and Chance walked across.

'What happened, Doc?' Meldrum looked tired.

'I don't know. Something in the tracks, I think.'

'Give me a hand. Tilt it.' Chance and I leaned our weight against the Doo, raising the right-hand track clear of the ice, and Meldrum dropped to his knees, peering underneath with a pencil torch.

I couldn't see what he was doing, but he was pulling and wrenching at something with increasing force, grunting with the strain. Finally he backed out and straightened.

'You bloody fool!' he said. His face was grim and angry.

I stared at him. 'What's wrong?'

'Your bloody ice axe. That's what's wrong.'

'My ice axe?' I repeated stupidly. 'It's here.' I reached for the rack on the side of the Doo's cabin, where the axe was supposed to hang in a metal loop. No point in looking there.

Meldrum said savagely, 'It's embedded in the back roller mechanism. And nothing will shift it. There's bent metal all round it.'

I said, 'How the hell—'

'I'll tell you how the hell,' Meldrum said. 'As some bloody fool got out of the cabin, he knocked it off the rack. Then he kicked it with his bloody great feet. Into the track mechanism.'

'But I didn't—'

'No?' He was furious. 'Bloody carelessness. Just don't ever operate on me, Doc. You're the kind who leaves the forceps inside!' He turned and walked away, then came back. 'I hope you enjoy your bloody ski ride.'

I flushed guiltily, trying to think how it could have happened. I'm not naturally clumsy, and racking my brains I couldn't think how I could have done it.

'I'll go on skis,' I said to Chance.

'Two men have to ski,' he said. He didn't look as though he liked me any more than Meldrum did.

'One is me,' I said. 'I'm OK on skis.'

'You're too precious,' Chance's voice was harshly sardonic. 'We can't afford to lose the doctor.'

'Look,' I said. 'I did it. I ought to pay.'

'You should,' he answered bitterly. 'But you won't. But just so you won't forget, the two guys who go on skis have a first-class chance of freezing to death.'

'Let me do it,' I said. It would be intolerable to ride in a warm cabin while two men hung on to ropes behind in forty degrees of frost.

'The best skiers are Yamamoto and Ericson,' Chance said implacably. 'They ski.' He walked back to Number One to give Yamamoto the bad news, but the big Japanese must have guessed already and was already bending to the fastenings of his skis. The nylon towing lines were broken out of the Doos and clipped in position.

Jim Grey Smoke went forward to join Meldrum in the leading Doo and the girl and I climbed into the remaining one. 'I'll tow Ericson,' Chance growled. 'You take Yamamoto. At the back of the line.'

'Abreast, surely,' I said. 'Not in line.'

'In line,' he said. 'Is that clear, Doctor Edwards?'

I said, 'But it's a hell of a lot less safe for the end man.'

His voice was level, but anger throbbed somewhere just beneath the flat tone. 'It's not men I'm thinking of, Doctor.

We've got too many already. But we can't afford to lose another Doo. So get this straight: I follow in Meldrum's tracks and you follow in mine. Like a bloodhound. You don't deviate one inch. Right?'

'Right,' I said miserably. I climbed into the Doo.

Behind me, Natalya said, 'It could have been me.'

'What do you mean?'

'When we got out, I stumbled. Do you remember?'

I remembered. Her heel had slipped on the ice and she had fallen against the side of the Doo.

'Did you touch the ice axe?' I turned in the seat to look at her and there were tears in her eyes.

'I don't know. I don't *think* so. I just tried to stop myself falling. Oh, I'm sorry. So very *sorry*! It must have been my fault!'

I looked at her, remembering the moment. I had climbed out first, then stood clear to let her out. As she came upright, she slipped and I reached out to grab her as she fell. She hadn't been anywhere near the ice axe. But I had! I'd been right beside it! I felt my face flush with guilt. The axe must have caught on a loop or the tape that held my mittens, something like that. And I wouldn't have heard it fall on to the snow.

'Look,' I said. 'However the hell it happened, Yamamoto's out there on skis as a result. So you turn and watch him out of the rear window. Face the back and don't take your eyes off him. If anything happens, anything at all, I want to know instantly!'

She nodded soberly and turned round on the seat, straddling it the other way. 'I am ready.'

In front of me I saw Chance's arm wave. Meldrum was already moving. The rope tightened and Ericson slid forward, knees flexed, body leaning back, mittened hands gripping the tow bar. I eased the Doo forward cautiously. 'Is he all right?'

'Yes,' she said. I glanced back and through the rear window I could see poor Yamamoto out at the end of the tow line.

Ahead of me, Ericson swung easily behind Chance and I dropped back a bit, allowing about twenty yards between my snowmobile and the man on skis. His position was dangerous enough without the additional hazard of being run over if he fell.

Meldrum increased speed steadily, but it was obvious that forty miles an hour was out of the question now. In good conditions and on good snow, in daylight, a really expert skier might hold that speed for a while, but to expect Ericson and Yamamoto to do so in the desperate cold and on a surface of ice would be to expect too much. Meldrum got us up to twenty-five and then settled to maintain steadiness.

Every minute or so I said, 'Okay?' and Natalya said yes. While she watched Yamamoto, I kept my eyes on Ericson, floating along in front of me. Chance couldn't watch him and Komarov was still unconscious in the back of Chance's vehicle. My responsibility for this situation sat on me like lead. It was my fault the two of them were out there and it was my burden to make sure nothing happened to them.

'OK, Natalya?'

'Yes.'

Another minute.

'OK, Natalya?'

'Yes.'

Sometimes I glanced back, too, to where the bulky figure of Yamamoto bobbed on the end of the line that strung behind me, then turned to the front again to watch Ericson and to make sure that the Ski-doo followed with precision in the tracks of the Norwegian's skis. Increasingly, though, I found it difficult to concentrate.

Weariness was beginning to settle on me, too. I felt deadly tired. Calculating quickly, I reckoned we had been awake now for twenty-eight hours. A fit and healthy man should be able to manage that easily enough. But the tension and the concentration sapped one's energy.

'Okay, Natalya?'

'Yes.'

My eyes kept slipping out of focus and it became more and more an effort of will to focus them on Ericson, to ask Natalya about Yamamoto. By the time an hour had gone I knew my reactions were getting slow. I found myself looking not at Ericson but at the windscreen itself, my eyes hypnotically following the metronomic beat of the screen wiper; I forced my gaze forward to Ericson and then, when I knew he was still there, to Yamamoto. If we had hit something suddenly, we'd have been finished. I seemed to feel hot then cold in turn.

'Okay, Natalya?'

'Yes.'

I wondered how Meldrum was managing up front, whether even his remarkable concentration and reflexes were proof against this terrible, numbing tiredness, this endless peering through the windshield quadrant at the unchanging scene ahead, which seemed increasingly to be happening in a tunnel. Such a cold tunnel. I found the door was open. My elbow must have moved the catch.

Out of the fog of weariness a thought came to me: benzedrine! I had it in my kit. I stretched out my hand to the light switch, flashed the headlamp twice and watched the two Ski-doos ahead slow and stop, and Ericson glide in to stop beside Chance.

'Benzedrine will help, Natalya,' I said. There was no reply.

'Natalya!' I said sharply, then turned, panicking, shouting, 'Natalya!'

She stirred from her doze.

I threw open the door of the cabin and stepped out into the blast of icy wind, looking for Yamamoto. The line still hung from the back of the Doo, but limply. I picked it up and walked along it. The towing handle came up from the ice into my hand.

There was no sign of Yamamoto.

CHAPTER TWENTY

Our tracks led back across the ice, narrowing gradually until they vanished into the darkness. He was somewhere back there; he had to be. I began to follow them, looking for him, calling his name into the bitter wind that tore my parka. I suppose I must have had enough sense to tighten the drawstrings on the hood, but I have no recollection of doing so; just a confused memory of blundering on, back along the tracks, shouting, searching . . .

Then there was a roaring sound, and the roaring stopped and I was gripped by strong hands that prevented me from going on. I struggled and tried to free myself, and then pain exploded in my face as something struck me.

Then my eyes began to focus and I found myself looking at Chance.

'Get in that Doo,' he said.

'Yamamoto. He's . . .'

'Grey Smoke's gone back. On skis.'

I said, 'The girl was watching him, but she must have gone to sleep.'

'Like you,' Chance snarled. I think he wanted to kill me then.

'I'm sorry. God, I'm sorry. I don't know how it happened. I don't think I was actually asleep. It was just . . .'

'It was just that you've lost Yamamoto,' Chance snarled. 'You forced him out there, and now you've killed him, you bastard. As soon as I saw your lights flash, I knew . . . I damn well knew!'

My mind was fogged by confusion and grief. 'It wasn't that,' I mumbled. 'Benzedrine. I've got some benzedrine.'

His hands left my shoulders and fell in disgust to his sides. He said softly, venomously, 'You'd better go look at your patient.'

I staggered back to the Doo and got my kit, fumbling in it for the benzedrine bottle. I found two tablets and swallowed them, then crossed to Chance's snowmobile. Natalya was bending over the unconscious Komarov and I looked down at her. There was no point in blaming her. The fault was mine, nobody else's.

'How is he?'

She looked up at me, blue eyes clouded in concern. 'Still sleeping.'

'Still? Let me see.'

I examined him as well as I could. His pulse was steady and his condition seemed normal. All the same, he shouldn't have been unconscious as long as this. By now the benzedrine was taking effect, and my mind was clearing. But I was puzzled. Pulse, temperature, breath: everything was normal; everything as it should be. Komarov's system wouldn't even be expecting food for another two hours or so, or insulin for three.

'Come on,' I said. 'Get back in the Doo. He's all right.'

She straightened and walked with me, then climbed back into the cabin. I closed the door, leaving her to it, and made my way back to stand beside Chance as he stared unwaveringly in the direction Grey Smoke had headed.

I said, 'Couldn't we take a Doo to look?'

He rounded on me. 'The Doos are going the other way. They're not going back. And a man's eyes, especially Grey Smoke's, will see more the way he's going.'

'But the lights!'

'We're not shining lights,' he said. 'Or risking Doos.'

Ten minutes, fifteen, twenty dragged by, but we didn't move. My mind was almost unnaturally clear now that the benzedrine was in my bloodstream and I could feel the deadly chill of ice and wind getting to my bones; knew my feet and hands were growing numb. I glanced at Chance, standing there like a boulder, staring in the direction Grey Smoke had taken. He wouldn't have wanted sympathy, but I was glad command was his. Because he was Chance he wouldn't move until he knew; but because he was in command, he would not go back.

So we waited. And waited. Until a movement in the silver-grey distance told us something was alive out there. The movement became an outline, then a man, skiing towards us.

It was James Grey Smoke, ski-running fast.

Chance stepped forward to meet him. 'Well?'

'Dead.' Grey Smoke's dark face was impassive but his eyes were hard. 'Must have tripped. Fallen.'

'You're sure?' I said.

Grey Smoke's eyes stared through me. 'He's dead. The cold.'

There was a ski slung diagonally across his back and he pulled it off. 'Look.'

I looked. So did Chance. Then we looked at one another. Across the sole of Yamamoto's ski, the wood was heavily scored and the edges of the deep scratch were splintered.

'How?' I asked.

Grey Smoke shook his head. 'Who knows? I buried him in the snow.' He paused and the strange eyes rested briefly, chillingly, on my face. 'He was a man, that one.'

Chance said harshly, 'Let's move!'

I stumbled back to the Doo, thinking about Yamamoto's body back there on the ice: the man who had died because I had been careless, criminally careless. Neither Chance nor Grey Smoke said a word to me. They didn't have to. Contempt radiated from them.

As I climbed in, Natalya asked softly, 'What happened?' She said it very gently.

'He's dead,' I muttered, turning to look at her. 'I killed him.'

She said gently, 'No. It was an accident. You were weary. Do not blame yourself.'

I grunted something. The blame was mine. Everybody knew it, including me. It lay on me like a great, crushing weight.

In a minute the Doos were moving again and I watched Ericson swinging on the end of the tow line, wondering how he felt. An hour and twenty miles had been sufficient to kill Yamamoto who was the strongest among us, and we still had almost seventy miles to go : seventy miles in which he could freeze and stumble and die; seventy miles in which the Doos could break down. So far we had lost three in a little more than three hundred miles : one during the outward journey, two in a hundred and thirty miles coming back. The odds against us were increasing.

I looked at my watch. Seven-fifty. In a little less than three hours twilight would be here and we still had seventy miles to go. That means averaging twenty-five miles an hour and there was no margin for accident, breakdown or hold-up. Nor was there any doubt in my mind that by now the search would be on. The Russians we had left behind on Novaya Zemlya would, by now, have got some kind of signal out, and the fact that we were theoretically in international waters, or rather on international ice, wouldn't help us. As soon as the light improved they'd be looking for us and looking hard, and the twilight lengthens rapidly in these latitudes. If we didn't get there in the dark, the Russians would have nearly three hours of twilight in which to search.

But how would they begin looking for us? I wondered what was happening back there; how they were organizing themselves. There had been blowing snow almost all the way; never very heavy, but probably enough to fill in the tracks the Doos had made. If the tracks were visible from the air, I realized, all a plane need do was fly along them, straight to us. Even a fairly slow aircraft would be able to reach us in about half an hour. And the signal, that steady, regular signal Meldrum was homing on, would be picked up by Russian radio operators. At first they'd just note it, then they'd be puzzled by it, then they'd take the d/f bearings and wonder. Then they'd act . . .

My eyes never left Ericson, the slender, gallant whipcord figure twenty yards ahead, clinging grimly to the rope, being dragged through the Arctic cold and dark. He seemed to grow until he filled my eyes. But it was Yamamoto who filled my mind. It was as though a loop of film were being projected endlessly on a screen in my brain : the lonely skier whisking through the night, attached to life only by a twenty-foot line and the fading watchfulness of weary people; then he tripped and fell and the line was jerked from his hands and he lay there on the ice watching life race away. Perhaps he rose and struggled on, with a ski that would no longer slide properly because something had gouged a great lateral scratch on its sole.

Suddenly I felt the hair prickle on the back of my neck. That scratch! I remembered Grey Smoke holding the ski, remembering the look of that deep score along the hard timber sole.

I forced my mind back, thinking about the things that had happened since we left the base of the cliff, about the explosion, the loss of Yamamoto's Doo, then the wrecking, the stupid careless wrecking, of my own vehicle and the ice axe that had somehow fallen and been kicked underneath it. Then the fatal fall of Yamamoto himself. I was still thinking about them when the little column began to slow. I stopped the Doo and got out, walking ahead to join the others. The ice seemed to stretch ahead in an unbroken line, but as I came closer, a break appeared in it: another polynya, long and narrow, like a four-foot ditch in the middle of the ice.

We looked to left and right, but the crack ran almost ruler-straight as far as the eye could see and in it the water lay dippling blackly in the wind, ten feet below.

Chance's mouth was set in a frustrated, angry line. He was staring at Meldrum.

'I said, we jump it.'

Meldrum shook his head. 'We should go round. If there's one more mishap of any kind—'

Chance interrupted him. 'It's easy. The lips are level. We can step across.'

'*We* can,' Meldrum said, 'but look at it. If any of the Doos miss, it's straight down into the water.'

I looked down the sheer faces of the two ice walls that dropped into the icy sea.

Chance said, 'We jump.'

'Look,' Meldrum said, 'if we lose one. If anything happens, anything at all—to the engines, the runners, the steering, then we'll have three skiers and two Doos. Somebody will die. We'd never get three skiers all the way back.'

I left them to it; they wouldn't want to hear anything I had to say. I walked over to Meldrum's Doo, where Grey Smoke sat huddled in the back. As I opened the door I could feel his eyes on me, cold and appraising and distant.

'That ski,' I said.

He continued to look at me.

'The scratch on the sole. What could have done it?'

Grey Smoke's eyes never left mine. His head moved fractionally from side to side, but those eyes stayed steady, staring at me.

'Could ice make a mark like that?' I shouted at him.

He shook his head again, minimally. Then he hoisted himself forward, off the seat, slid easily out of the door on to the snow, and walked round to the rear of the Doo, to the rack that held the tools. The ice axes were there, and the hammer, but when we had set off, that rack had also held pitons, and two grappling hooks in case we needed them on the cliff. Two grappling hooks were missing.

'My God!' I said.

Grey Smoke laid a hand on my arm. 'We go on. We are careful, but we go on. This is not the time.'

Meldrum stalked up to the Doo. 'Out of the way,' he growled. He climbed in, slamming the door, and turned the Doo away from the polynya. This time he did not take a long run at it; he seemed, indeed, to be going too slowly, and as I watched the little vehicle approaching that black, deep gap in the ice, my heart was in my mouth. He was over, somehow, almost imperceptibly; it was as though the tracks had never left the ice. There was no bump, no bang, just a clean and continuous forward motion.

I moved across to where Chance stood on the lip of the crack. Meldrum stopped the Doo on the other side, and came back towards us. He stopped for a moment; looking down into the polynya, and Chance stretched out his arm. Four feet, if you measure it out on the carpet, doesn't seem much, but I knew how Meldrum felt. He reached forward and gripped Chance's arm, then jumped.

I could see, instantly, that he wasn't going to make it. Maybe it was weariness; maybe his heel slipped, maybe he just didn't like the idea of the jump and his mind defeated him, but a second later he was dangling in the gap, held only by Chance's arm. Chance fell to his knees, grunting, and I threw myself flat on the ice, reaching down, trying to grab the other arm that waved frantically above Meldrum's scared, white face. He reached desperately for it, but his hand succeeded only in dragging off my mitten.

Chance, too, now lay flat on the ice, reaching down with his other hand.

'I can't hold him,' he ground out, 'I've only got half a grip and it's slipping.'

Meldrum gave a tortured gasp as their hands slid apart, and there was a jerk as the mitten straps tightened on the side of my neck. It was like a noose tightened, and I felt my body begin to slide forward on the slippery ice.

Below me, Meldrum clung to that one mitten, staring up at me. I tried to hook my toes in the ice, but I was sliding rapidly to the edge. In a second I would be over.

Then a weight crashed down on my legs and my knees and ankles were suddenly alive with pain at the pressure on the joints. But at least the slide had stopped.

We stayed like that, it seemed, for eternity. The pressure on the side of my neck was colossal and I could feel myself beginning to black out. I braced my neck muscles as hard as I could and concentrated on Meldrum's face, as it swayed from side to side below me. He was clinging on, but he couldn't possibly do so for long, and even as I looked, I saw his hands begin to slip.

The whole thing, from Meldrum's first slip, couldn't have taken more than ten seconds and in a couple more his grip would go and he would drop into the water and die. The human body can rarely stand the sudden hundred-degree change in temperature that immersion in unfrozen Arctic water involves.

Then there was a thud on the ice beside me, and other hands reached down beside mine, scrabbling for a grip on Meldrum's wrist. Grey Smoke's. But they couldn't reach. Meldrum was too far down.

Dimly, through the hammering of the blood in my brain as the harness slowly strangled me, I heard Grey Smoke shout:

'Get my ankles. Quickly, for God's sake!'

Then he grunted and slid forward, easing the upper part of his body out over the abyss, leaning down, reaching, reaching . . . The girl's voice said, 'Help, quickly. I can't hold him!'

I heard a ghastly crack and a thud and Grey Smoke gave a thin, agonized moan.

Suddenly, miraculously, the pressure was off my neck and I was being dragged backwards by the ankles. As soon as my chest was on the ice, I scrambled dizzily to my feet.

Grey Smoke's legs were on the ice but the rest of him, from the thighs down, was tilted over in the gap, holding the swaying Meldrum. Two things stopped him going over: one was the girl, hanging on grimly to his feet. The other was Ericson. The Norwegian's skis were across Grey Smoke's calves and his whole weight bore down on them.

Now Chance dived to help, flinging himself flat on the ice and pulling at Grey Smoke's parka, dragging him back. A second later I joined him.

Inch by inch Meldrum came up towards us until finally Chance and I could reach over and grasp his hands. As we did so, Grey Smoke released them with a grunt of relief which turned suddenly to a scream of agony. I turned awkwardly, still hanging on to Meldrum, to see the girl holding Grey Smoke by the ankles, trying to drag him clear.

'Don't pull,' I shouted. 'Just hold him.'

'Stand clear,' Chance grunted, and Ericson stepped away, awkwardly in the skis.

A minute later five of us were standing on the ice, strained and shaken. The sixth wasn't. Grey Smoke had passed out. He lay on his stomach, face in the snow, and his legs looked strange.

Ericson said, 'There was no time. He was sliding forward. I could not take off the skis. I had to jump.' I bent quickly, turning Grey Smoke's head gently so that the hood of his parka pillowed it on the snow. Then I took off the remaining mitten and felt gently at his legs.

'Well?' Chance demanded.

'Broken,' I said. 'Both of them. Below the knees.'

CHAPTER TWENTY-ONE

Meldrum turned away without speaking, hurrying across to Chance's Doo. He got in, revved the engine and brought it round towards the gap, and over it. A moment later he'd left the cabin and was standing on the other side.

'Well,' he said, 'isn't anyone going to give me a hand?'

This time he came across smoothly, in one step, with Chance hanging on to his hand like grim death. I think that four-foot step was the bravest thing I ever saw. Immediately Meldrum headed across to my own Doo, the last in the little line.

'No.' I stopped him sharply.

He turned, came across. 'Why not?'

I nodded at Grey Smoke. 'You'll have a passenger. We couldn't get him across any other way.'

Meldrum looked down at me, then at Grey Smoke. 'Christ,' he said, 'I can't—!' Then he had himself under control. 'All right,' he said. 'I'll wait.'

Ericson had his skis off now and between us we carried

Grey Smoke back to the Doo. I got my kit out, found the little telescopic splints, and bound them to his legs. There was no bleeding; no bone through the skin; the bones had stayed almost straight as they were crushed and snapped, but I shuddered to think what the fractures would be like.

I got the morphia and gave him enough to numb an elephant. When he came round he was going to need all the help he could get to live with the pain in those legs.

Finally I backed out of the little cabin with the bottle of benzedrine tablets.

'Here.'

Chance looked at them as they lay on my palm.

I said, 'Benzedrine. We all need it.'

'I'm OK.'

'Take it,' I said. 'Orders.'

Ericson and the girl took them without a murmur.

Meldrum refused absolutely. He stood there, sagging with fatigue, his hands shaking inside the mittens, his eyes red and weary.

'Go on,' I said, pushing them towards him.

He said softly, 'I've never driven drunk or drugged in my life, I'm better like this.'

I nodded. Maybe he was. Sometimes you just have to let the patient know best.

We wedged Grey Smoke in the back as comfortably as possible, then Meldrum climbed in and the Doo went over the polynya like a glider on a summer day.

My watch told me it was nine-fifteen. Any time now, Komarov must be coming round. We crossed the polynya roped together, just in case, and made it without trouble, then I untied myself from the rope and hurried to look at Komarov.

He was lying there in the back of the snowmobile, still fast asleep. I checked pulse and breathing and there was nothing wrong. But nobody, surely, could spend eleven hours asleep in these cramped conditions without stirring! The effects of the pheno-barbitone would have worn off well before this and the normal diabetic pattern would be for him to be awake and hungry. I was puzzled, but not especially worried: you don't worry too much about patients with strong heartbeats and steady breathing, and in any case it was useful that Komarov remained asleep. We were a rickety enough crew already without the problems of an elderly, scared passenger.

Behind me Chance said, 'OK?'

I straightened. 'He seems all right. Ought to be awakening soon.'

Chance looked at me. 'He should be awake now. Right?'

I nodded. 'Should be. But isn't. But he's OK. Physically, I mean. What worries me more is—'

He cut me off. 'We all have our problems. Get back there and let's get moving. It'll be twilight in not much more than an hour.'

'Are we all right for direction?' I looked down at the beacon dial on the dash in front of him.

Chance stared at me. 'If we're not, we'll all be as dead as Yamamoto. Get moving.'

The door slammed and I faced the wind, hurrying back to the Doo.

We had between forty-five and fifty miles to go, now, and with our speed limited to twenty-five miles an hour, we were inevitably going to be out in the twilight for an hour or more. I watched Meldrum move away with the injured Grey Smoke in the back, and Chance move in behind him. Ericson sat low on his skis as the rope straightened, then rose as it took the strain. A moment later I followed him. We were in bad shape now: Grey Smoke out of action completely, Meldrum weary to death, Chance with that wound in the thigh, which, though it didn't seem to be bothering him much, must still be weakening him.

We went on steadily, though, Meldrum still picking his way across the ice with cool efficiency, making things easy for the rest of us. Even following him was difficult enough; what it must have been like to be the trail blazer was beyond imagining. For nearly twenty-four hours now the little Scot had been leading us across the ice, avoiding ridges and projections, hillocks and hollows with unbelievable skill, and still he was required to do it; still the rest of us were depending on his judgment.

We made ground well in the last of the darkness. I watched Ericson lying back on the tow line, knees flexed, as the speed was pushed up to twenty, to twenty-five, to thirty, and the little convoy dashed across the ice.

Behind me the girl seemed to have gone to sleep. She had not spoken a word since the near-disaster at the polynya, and when I glanced back her eyes were closed and her head rested on the cabin wall.

Light began to spread across the ice at ten-forty and when it happened it happened rapidly, the transformation from dim moonlight to a light by which you could read a book, taking no more than a couple of minutes.

Promptly Meldrum began to pick up speed again. I knew how he felt, but I wasn't sure about his wisdom. Ericson had now spent nearly five hours on the end of the tow line and accustomed though he might be to long exposure through endless ski-running, his reserves of strength must now be sinking fast. But there was no let-up as he streaked across the ice. Another forty minutes, another thirty-five, another thirty ought to see us there.

I found myself staring ahead, looking for the prefabricated shed that Skipper Hutton's crew from the *Polar Star* had deposited on the ice. Every minute that passed brought it nearer and the temptation to scan what I could see of the horizon, rather than watch Ericson's flying figure in front of me was almost overwhelming. Once I nearly ran him down and that sobered me. I'd let Meldrum see it first; he'd earned it. My job was just to follow. I concentrated on following, on keeping well back from Ericson, on keeping the Doo on the track.

The minutes tramped slowly by. It was twilight, formally, but there are industrial towns where light is never better than our light was then. The horizon was clearly visible, flat and unchanging, receding before us.

Twenty minutes became fifteen, fifteen became ten. Any time now that shed should come over the horizon, beckoning to us with its promise of an aircraft with seats in it, seats into which we could strap ourselves and sleep. I felt that I would sleep for a week, a month even.

We raced on, past the time at which it should have become visible. Maybe my timings and calculations had been out and we still weren't quite there. I cursed: the need to see that hut ached inside me, tightening my nerves until my whole body felt tense and sensitive. Where was it? Where *was* it?

Forty yards ahead, Meldrum's Doo began to slow, then stopped, and I braked and brought my little snowmobile in behind the other two. What the hell was he stopping for? I wrenched open the door of the cabin and walked forward. Chance and Meldrum were already outside on the ice, and with a sick, sinking feeling deep inside me, I saw why they had stopped. Two miles ahead the shed was visible, a white hump on the ice.

Just two miles. But it might as well have been a million!

The ice on which it stood was part of a huge floe that had cracked clear of the main pack and was floating out on the grey-black water.

Meldrum said, a little desperately, 'Could we get at it from the other side?'

Chance shook his head. 'Not a hope in hell.'

I turned, scanning the sky and the ice behind us. Nothing moved except the little exhaust plumes rising from the Doos as they waited.

Chance walked heavily back towards his Doo. He was limping now, I noticed, and his face was grey and tired. He reached inside and switched on the radio.

'Chance to Hutton. Chance to Hutton.'

There was a pause and a lot of static. Chance reached inside, adjusting the set. 'Chance to Hutton. Over.'

We waited.

'Chance to Hutton. Chance to Hutton. Over.'

The seconds dragged by. I glanced round at the floe that floated so tantalizingly out there.

There was a crackle. 'Hutton to Chance.'

'Chance to Hutton. It's broken away on a floe. Come and get us.'

'Wilco. Am lying ten miles clear of the pack. Will make all speed. Over and out.'

Chance said, 'We'll make as much ground towards you as we can. Out.'

I said, 'Hutton told us he can make about twelve knots. That's nearly an hour.'

'I know it.' He stared at the shed away on the huge floe, swearing loudly and continuously.

I walked back to my own Doo and got the flask, poured coffee and drank it greedily, staring at the sky, at the ice. Out of the corner of my eye I caught a movement, and the girl came out from behind a small rise in the snow. I stared at her.

'Where have you been?'

She smiled. 'You should not ask.'

'I'm sorry.' I screwed the cup back on to the flask and walked back to Chance's Doo.

'Is he awake?'

'No,' Chance said. 'See for yourself.'

I bent, took his wrist and felt his pulse. It was strong enough. His face was turned away, hidden inside his hood. I leaned across to turn it, laid my hand on his brow, and thought his temperature seemed normal. Nor was there any clamminess on the skin. I lifted an eyelid, but there seemed to be nothing wrong. It was crazy. Why the hell was he still asleep when his body must by now be crying out for food? I slapped his cheek gently, but there was no response. I slapped it again, a little harder, with the same result. Again I leaned over him, feeling the strain of my bent, awkward position.

And then I felt something else. I looked at the tip of the fingers where the tiny sensation was, and backed out of the Doo. Standing up, I looked at it again, then transferred it to my mouth. The tiny crystal disintegrated against my teeth and momentarily my taste buds picked up sweetness.

Sugar! Quickly I went back to Komarov, forcing his mouth open. There were sugar crystals there, too. Somebody had opened his mouth and put sugar in, maybe with a drop or two of water to help it dissolve. It was a hell of a risky thing to do; a crazy thing, in fact. Komarov could easily have inhaled the sugar and choked. Not only that, but the whole business of feeding sugar to a diabetic who was beginning to need insulin, was highly dangerous. The sugar was probably enough to turn drugged sleep into a diabetic coma; at the very least it would expose Komarov's system to dangerous shock.

I felt the nape of my neck prickle. Somebody didn't mind if Komarov died. Indeed, somebody seemed to want him dead. The sugar had two chances of killing him.

Slithering out of the Doo, I marched across to Chance. 'Did you give Komarov sugar?' I demanded.

'No.' He turned to look at me. 'Do you think I'm—'

'Somebody did,' I said. 'And the ice axe that wrecked my Doo.'

He said, 'Yeah.'

'Don't be a bloody fool,' I said. 'It wasn't me. Somebody else wants us dead. Yamamoto. Komarov. Grey Smoke . . .' A thought struck me as I raced across to the Doo where Grey Smoke lay. I crawled in.

'Jim! Jim!'

His eyes opened, but they weren't focusing. I'd given him too much morphine for any clarity of mind to remain. I had to try, though. I slapped his face, hard, and a spasm of pain crossed his face.

'That ski,' I said. 'That scratch was done by metal, wasn't it?'

I slapped him again, 'Wasn't it, Jim?'

He stirred, blinking slowly, stupidly. He was away on the kind of trip junkies only dream about. 'Jim,' I said urgently. 'The ski!'

His lips moved, muttering something, and I leaned close, trying to hear. Suddenly he spoke clearly, loudly, almost shouting.

'Don't push!' he yelled. 'Hold me. Don't push!'

'All right, take it easy,' I said soothingly, easing him back into a more comfortable position.

I climbed out. Chance was angry. 'What the hell did you hit him for?'

'The girl,' I said. 'She tried to kill him. And God knows what else. She's trying to wreck us.'

He was staring at me. 'She saved Grey Smoke's life when she grabbed his ankles.'

'Didn't you hear him just now?' I said furiously. 'Hold me, don't push! It was Ericson who saved him.'

'You're right, Doctor.'

We both turned swiftly. She was standing on the other side of the Doo.

'You're right,' she said. 'If it gives you any satisfaction.'

She was holding a carbine in her hands.

CHAPTER TWENTY-TWO

She went from Doo to Doo, taking out the carbines and throwing them far into the snow. She had the drop on all of us and we knew it. There wasn't any point in trying anything because all of us, apart from Grey Smoke, were out in the open, and he was too doped to know anything about anything. What's more, the girl knew how to use a carbine; it was obvious from the way it was cuddled in to her, purposefully. She held it good and steady.

'The devoted assistant,' I said.

She looked at me. 'You might say that. But I'm not the devoted assistant you're talking about. She's safely held in Moscow. Or somewhere.'

'And you?'

'Be quiet.' She raised her voice. 'Come closer, all of you. I want you in a line, here, in front of me.'

We moved as directed by the muzzle of the carbine, and

stood there in front of her.

'Sit down.'

We sat.

I could have wept. We were so near, so bloody near, and we were going to lose.

Chance said, 'Look, lady, who *are* you?'

'KGB,' I said.

'Very clever, Doctor.' She stood looking down at us, completely calm, completely in control.

'So why did she want to come with us?'

'Go on,' she said. 'Explain.'

I said, 'She's Komarov's assistant, all right. But she was planted on him by the KGB to keep an eye on him. When we got him she had to come with us.'

'Why?'

'To kill him—if we looked like getting away with it. To bring him back alive if she could.'

'And I can,' she said. 'In fact it is certain. Soon a helicopter will join us. So be patient.'

'Helicopter?' I said.

She smiled. She was attractive, almost beautiful, but the smile wasn't. It was cold and hard as the ice we sat on. 'Your delicacy was charming but foolish,' she said.

'When you were over there?'

'I have a small radio. I was using it. You even apologized. Fool.'

I said, 'Why did you give him sugar?'

'Because I thought at the time you would succeed. But thank you for reminding me, Doctor. Insulin is necessary now.' The muzzle of the carbine moved. 'Stand up.'

'To hell with you,' I said. 'Let him die. We'll all be better off.'

She said, 'I shall count three, then I shall put a bullet through your thigh. One, two—'

I rose.

She unslung her medical kit from her shoulder and threw it to me. 'Two cubic centimetres. Until he has food it will counteract the sugar.'

I opened the bag. Inside was a small bottle of insulin and a stainless steel case with a hypodermic inside. There was also another bottle, a brown one, with tablets in it. I held it up.

'Phenol-barbitone?'

'You wondered why he remained asleep. That is why.

Now, Doctor, the insulin. Two ccs.'

As I walked across to the snowmobile where Komarov lay, she circled round behind me, changing her position to maintain her cover over all of us.

What the hell could we do? As my hands went through the mechanical routine of taking insulin into the hypodermic, then ejecting all but two ccs, my mind was racing, seeking desperately to find some answer, some way of regaining the advantage. A glance over my shoulder showed me how hopeless it was: the girl stood fifteen yards back from the line of Ski-doos, and the others were half-way between her and the vehicles. She had only to move the catch to Automatic Firing, and press the trigger. We hadn't even the slightest chance.

Dismally, I climbed into the Doo beside Komarov, and began to take off my gloves. At least it was warm in there. My nerves tingled! It was warm because the engine was running, and the engine, though small, was at least a bulk of solid metal in the nose of the little machine. It was a thin chance, but a chance all the same. I looked out at the rest of them. Chance, Meldrum and Ericson were sitting disconsolately on the ice with their hands on their heads, but they'd react quickly enough. The question was how long she'd delay shooting for fear of hitting Komarov. I slid down as far as I could in the space between the Doo's wall and the fore and aft seat, then reached up and pressed the throttle button with my thumb.

The Doo leapt forward and I twisted the handlebar violently with my left hand, spinning the little machine round to the right. The Doo spun sharply on its tracks and hurtled across the ice. If she didn't knock the engine out, I aimed to get the machine between her and the other three, then turn at her. There was no way of knowing whether she was firing: my head was low, close to the roaring engine; but I wrenched on to the handlebar again and lifted my head to glance out. Beside it a tiny hole appeared in the starred glass and I ducked again, spinning the handlebar to the left. I lifted my head again, quickly, and saw the three of them hurling themselves aside as the Doo slewed round towards her and I spun the handlebar to the right again. She was backing away, the carbine trained on the flying Doo as it hurtled towards her and it wasn't difficult to guess what was flashing through her mind. A burst of fire would kill both me and Komarov, and while there was a chance of bringing him back, she didn't want to do it. As I flashed past, she slid aside like a bullfighter and I brought the Doo round in a tight, spinning turn, slammed in reverse and went at her backwards, using Komarov's body as a shield.

Still she hesitated, turning slowly, wanting to get a shot at my head. I wrenched the handlebar right over, and pressed the throttle hard and the Doo spun on its tracks, going at her like a spinning top. There was a tremendous bang and I felt myself being hurled forward and upward, into the windscreen . . .

I came to a moment or two later, lying on the ice, with Meldrum bending over me. I ached in every bone and muscle, but the grin on his face helped.

'What happened?'

'You hooked the wrong way as she veronica'd,' he said. 'Knocked her cold.'

I dragged myself to my feet. The girl was still unconscious, stretched out on the ice, and the Doo lay on its side behind me. Chance and Ericson were lifting Komarov gently out of it, and the old man was groaning.

I staggered over towards them. 'Watch the girl,' I told Ericson. 'I'll look at him.'

Risking the wind and cold, I pulled back the hood of his wind-proof and felt his head, hoping it hadn't cracked too hard against anything. Lumps rise quickly on the head, and he hadn't any. I put the hood back and tested his limbs. They flexed easily enough, but he groaned like mad when I tried his right shoulder. It was probably dislocated, I thought.

I didn't worry any more. There wasn't time. While Chance and I struggled to carry Komarov across to the remaining Doo, Ericson yelled a warning. I looked up and saw the dot in the distance. We stuffed the old man inside without ceremony and raced for our carbines.

'Here,' I shouted, tossing one to Ericson.

He ignored it. His rifle was already in his hands. He dived behind the overturned Doo.

The roar of the helicopter came nearer. It was a great orange-painted thing flitting like a giant dragonfly across the pack. It didn't seem to have seen us, yet, judging from the way it flew in little jerks from side to side, then forward again. But suddenly the engine note steadied and it flew directly towards us.

It stopped, maybe a hundred yards from us, and hovered

at around a hundred and fifty feet. I could see the pilot, sitting forward in his seat, staring down.

Slowly Ericson raised the rifle. Probably the pilot hadn't seen us yet, and was still trying to understand why no one was standing out there waving to him, and why a body lay spreadeagled on the ice.

Then he decided to come down and find out. A door in the fuselage slid back and a couple of soldiers appeared in the doorway, guns at the ready. If they got down on to the ice, we'd really had it.

'Now,' Chance ordered softly. I glanced at Ericson, watched his finger squeeze the trigger then flick to the bolt and fire again. Nothing happened for a few moments. Then the helicopter seemed to jerk and the rotors tilted forward. The two soldiers in the doorway clung on desperately, one-handed, and opened fire and the bullets smashed into the ice a few yards away from us. Suddenly the nose of the helicopter tilted up and the long boom of the tail dropped and it fell out of the sky like a stone, smashing down on to the ice with a tremendous crash.

It burst instantly into flames; a great roaring wall of fire came up as the petrol caught and I felt a wave of heat wash over us. A series of little explosions came as the ammunition exploded, then there was the roar of another explosion. Whether it was another petrol tank, or explosives or bombs I don't know, but the remains of the helicopter simply disintegrated and there was nothing left but a pile of burning wreckage and a pool of flame, spreading across the ice towards the two Ski-doos.

Meldrum and I raced across to them, holding our hands before our faces to ward off the intense heat. I leapt into the cabin, slammed the Doo into reverse, and backed away swiftly.

Fifty yards back, we stopped and got out. The flames had stopped moving and the fire was dying down. Chance came across, limping a little, pointing.

'Look!'

Four or five miles out to sea, the *Polar Star* was heading towards us at maximum speed, the white of her creaming bow-wave shining in the dark sea. That's what sailors mean when they say a ship has a bone in its teeth.

I looked around us at the devastation, at the still-burning wreckage of the helicopter, at the overturned Doo, and at Ericson, standing by the girl, watching calmly and impassively as she struggled to rise. She got to her feet, stared at the wreckage for a long moment, then saw us and swayed across to where we stood.

Chance grinned at her and she looked at him strangely. There was no defeat in her face. Just hate and the beginnings of something else.

'Look,' Chance said, pointing to the speeding *Polar Star*.

She turned and saw it, then faced him again. Her expression was triumphant now, almost contemptuous.

'The helicopter was from the *Lenin*,' she said, and pointed away to the south-west.

Our eyes followed her pointing hand.

Away on the horizon, just distinguishable against the twi-lit sky, was a ship. A big ship.

She laughed. 'Yes. The *Lenin*. You know about the *Lenin*, don't you? The finest ship in the Arctic. Four knots through twenty-foot ice. Nuclear engines. A thousand men and marines.'

She stopped and looked at us triumphantly.

'Do you think you can escape her now?'

CHAPTER TWENTY-THREE

Even at that distance, almost fifteen miles away, the *Lenin* looked menacing: a squat, dark silhouette cutting the silver line of horizon. This ship had long been the spearhead of Russia's drive to liberate its Arctic north from the iron grip of winter: the first, and for many years the only, nuclear-powered icebreaker. It was rumoured that she was capable of smashing a hundred-foot-wide channel clear to the Pole.

Chance said softly, glancing quickly from her to the speeding *Polar Star*, 'The question is: is she in ice, there, or on clear water?'

I said, 'How much difference does it make?'

'She can make four knots plus through the ice. Fifteen in open water.'

I looked at the two ships, trying to estimate distances and speeds, but it wasn't possible.

Chance walked across to the Doo and switched on the radio.

'Chance to Hutton. Do you read?'

'Hutton to Chance. Loud and clear. Should be alongside in

ten or twelve minutes. Over.'

Chance said, 'We've got company.'

'More?' Hutton sounded aggrieved. 'I saw you knock out the helicopter.'

'It came from the *Lenin*.' Chance depressed the button on the hand mike, but there was no reply for a few seconds.

'Did it, by God!' Hutton spoke slowly, his voice low.

'And she's with us,' Chance said.

'Where away?'

'Port of you. To the south.'

There was a pause, then a short, hard laugh. 'Got her. I didn't need binoculars, did I?'

'Sheer off,' Chance said. 'We can lose her in the dark.' We couldn't, and he knew it. With only two Doos left and the injuries we had accumulated, it was doubtful whether the whole party could even move off successfully. But I knew what Chance was thinking: if the *Lenin* bottled the *Polar Star* up with us, nobody had a chance. One man, with Komarov, might be able to use the Doo's speed to get clear and be picked up elsewhere.

'Am coming in,' Hutton said. 'Stand by.'

'You'll never make it out,' Chance said.

Meldrum took the mike from Chance's hand, and when he spoke it was with a thick Scots accent I could barely comprehend. 'Ye bastard tyke. Can ye no' get yon wee tin pail oot o' second gear?'

There was a grating laugh. 'Poison dwarf's still wi' ye, eh? I'll gut you like a bloody haddie, me lad.'

Meldrum put the mike down, grinning, and we watched the water creaming as the *Polar Star* surged towards us. As she hurried nearer through the choppy black sea I could see through the binoculars a duffle-coated figure standing at the bow. The water was clotted with floating ice, from tiny chunks to fair sized growlers; they wouldn't bother the *Lenin* at all, but collision with them would cripple or sink the *Polar Star*.

'Look.' It was the silent Ericson, pointing toward the *Lenin*.

'Christ, she's turning,' I groaned. Part of her side was visible now, where before only her bow could be seen. There was no mistaking what the manoeuvre meant: the big icebreaker was heading out of the ice into open water to use her speed. And while we watched, a small, dark object detached itself from her and lifted into the air. Another helicopter!

There was a little rattle beside me as Ericson unslung his rifle from his shoulder. It was no more than a gesture, for the helicopter was still miles away.

'OK,' Chance said. 'Let's get towards the edge of the ice.' There was maybe a quarter of a mile to go.

Meldrum took over my Doo, with Grey Smoke in the back, and Chance drove Komarov. Ericson hesitated before picking up the tow line.

'Don't worry,' I said. 'I'll bring her.' As they moved off, I turned to the girl. 'Get moving.'

'I stay,' she said.

'Like hell you do!'

'Shoot me then.'

'Don't think I wouldn't.' I tried not to think of Yamamoto and to think instead of the Hippocratic oath, but it didn't stop my trigger finger itching.

She stood facing me, feet apart, defiant.

'Move.'

She didn't. The look in her eyes said she didn't believe I'd shoot.

The bullet whanged off the ice about an inch from her toe. She stared at me for a moment, then turned to follow the Doos. Moving six feet behind her, I kept the carbine pointing at the small of her back. She trudged along terribly slowly, stopping, turning to look at the rapidly approaching helicopter, and nothing I did could hurry her.

'It's getting nearer,' she said, tauntingly, every few yards, and soon, sure enough, I could hear the sound of the motor. After a while she kept her head turned and glanced only occasionally at the ice in front of her.

Chance and Meldrum had already reached the edge of the pack, and beyond the girl I could see them waving to me to hurry and pointing at the helicopter, but still I marched on, the roaring getting louder and louder. She stumbled, fell on to the ice, and stayed on her knees as though unable to rise. I glanced to my left. The helicopter was perhaps two hundred yards away, and low. In the doorway stood a soldier with a rifle.

I swung the carbine round and loosed off a burst from the hip. There wasn't a hope of hitting the helicopter in any vital spot, but it might keep it away.

In that moment she hit me from the side, her shoulder taking the side of my knee like a hard tackle from a pro footballer, and as I fell she was all over me, her knees and boots hacking at me, one hand clawing at my face, the other reaching for the rifle. And she knew what she was about.

There was a hard, penetrating, numbing pain in my thigh as her knee drove into the sciatic nerve, then her thumb was under my nostrils ramming upward. I struck downward fiercely with the butt of the carbine, then again, and heard her grunt with the impact. She didn't give up, though. Pivoting her body on the ice she swung her boot at my face. I jammed the carbine in the way, but the kick knocked it from my hands, then the boot swung again, catching me a tremendous glancing crack on top of my head.

She was all hands, arms and knees, striking at me from every angle. I punched desperately upward, but her parka must have absorbed the strength of the blow, and in a second her thumbs were driving for my eyes. I flung my body away to one side, but her weight was half-pinning me and I couldn't make it. Rolling back I saw her raise herself, hands held like hatchets, sideways, for karate chops.

For a moment my left leg came free and I drew it up, then kicked forward with every ounce of strength I had. It caught her on the shoulder and she spun back on to the ice, but as I struggled up she was coming at me again. My right leg was still numb from that blow on the nerve, but I braced myself on my left leg and started an uppercut from ground level, straight up. It was the sort of thing boxers try when they're nearly done and it doesn't often work. But she was already committed, off balance and hurtling forward and hadn't a chance. It caught her squarely on the point of the chin.

Her eyes glazed and her knees buckled and she went down. I'd never hit a woman before. Probably I never shall again. But that one time I enjoyed it. I grabbed the carbine and looked up at the helicopter. From away on my right a sharp crack came to me on the wind, and I saw Ericson, down on one knee, firing at the helicopter.

Prudently, it moved back, hovering clear of rifle range for a moment or two, then came circling back towards me. I bent and picked up the unconscious girl in a fireman's lift, hoping they wouldn't fire at me for fear of hitting her.

I wouldn't be a fireman. By the time I'd carried her twenty yards she was getting heavy on my shoulders and my thigh threatened to give way under me. I stopped looking at the others because they seemed too far away ever to be reached, and concentrated on putting one foot in front of another, counting the paces out to myself. At fifty I was ready to drop; at a hundred I knew I'd never make it, but I had to get as near as I could.

I glanced up awkwardly at the hovering helicopter, saw the soldier in the doorway sighting down his carbine and stumbled on for a few more steps, staring at him like a cornered mouse at a tom-cat. Amazingly, he didn't fire. For a moment I thought it was the girl; that he was holding his fire to avoid hitting her; but then the carbine fell away from him, his hands went to his chest and he leaned gently out into space and fell.

The racket of the helicopter drowned everything else and I hadn't heard the Doo. Somehow, miraculously, it was coming from behind me, slicing across the ice surface. And behind it, on the tow line, knees bent and leaning back, was Ericson. The tow line was hitched to his belt and his hands held his rifle.

The helicopter buzzed angrily away as the Doo slid to a halt beside me. When it stopped, Ericson took advantage of the momentary stillness to snap off another shot. I couldn't see whether he hit anything or not, but the helicopter pointedly moved further away.

'Good shooting!' I shouted.

Ericson's teeth showed as he grinned.

'Quick, sling her in the back!' Meldrum's face looked urgently up at me from where the cabin door had been.

I pushed the girl unceremoniously into the back of the Doo's cabin, then stood on the footboard as Meldrum roared away. A minute or two before it had seemed as though I would never make it. Now, we were there in thirty seconds.

It was a desperate situation. As I stepped off the Doo I could see the whole murderous problem spread before me. We were standing at the top of a sheer, fifteen-foot ice cliff. The loose floe on which the Otter waited lay about two miles dead ahead. Hutton was coming up fast from the left in the *Polar Star*, and behind me, to the left, the *Lenin* was clear of the pack and cracking on speed in the open, black water. And up above, now safely out of range of Ericson's rifle, the helicopter hovered, watching.

Skipper Hutton could get to us first; there was no doubt about that. But while we were clambering aboard *Polar Star*, the *Lenin* might bottle us up against the ice-pack and there were a thousand men aboard the icebreaker to swarm over us.

And quite apart from all that, Grey Smoke and Komarov would have to be carried and Chance, with that wound in his thigh still bleeding, was growing weaker. The only factor on our side was that the Russians didn't know about the Otter.

We stood anxiously, watching Hutton race the *Polar Star* towards us. Humble fishing boat she might be, but from stem to stern she looked navy. Creaming ahead on full power, making twelve knots only, but making them proudly, sitting back a little, and coming for all she was worth.

She was a mile, then half a mile away; then as the seconds ticked by she raced closer, four hundred yards, a cable's length . . . *Polar Star* dashed towards us without slackening speed, looking as though she would smash her bows into the ice wall. But then at the last moment, with one of those uncanny juxtapositions of engines and helm, she seemed to squat and pivot slowly round her stern, until she came to rest, delicately, alongside.

Hutton, duffle-coated but unmistakable, came out of the wheelhouse and crossed to the derrick, put his boot in a slung loop and waved an arm. A moment later he stood beside us on the ice. He stared round at us, then cupped his hands to his mouth and howled to the deck below: 'Stretchers.'

It was a slick operation. Two canvas stretchers soared up to us on the derrick and while I buckled Grey Smoke in, Hutton eased Komarov into position. First one stretcher and then the other sailed off the ice and down to the trawler's decks, then the derrick swung back, and one by one we were swung down, the girl conscious again now, slung over Hutton's broad shoulder, and furious.

As I left the ice, making the short, easy journey to the lifting deck of the *Polar Star* a few feet below, I gave a last glance at the two Doos, their engines still thumping faithfully. It seemed a pity to be leaving them . . .

But the sentimental moment was erased instantly from my mind as I looked round and saw the dark bulk of the *Lenin* coming up fast.

CHAPTER TWENTY-FOUR

Hutton slid the *Polar Star* smoothly away, demanding full power from the engine room and getting it quickly, taking his ship deeper into the pack.

Chance and I stood beside him in the tiny, cramped wheelhouse.

'Not the open water?' I asked.

Hutton's face turned slowly towards me, the eyes steady and clear among the creases of skin. 'She's got the legs of us. Three, maybe four knots. In fact,' and the folds of his face arranged themselves into what could have been a humourless grin, 'in fact she's got us all ways up. She's faster, she's better equipped, the ice can't damage her.'

Chance and I looked at one another. 'So?' Chance said.

'So we kid him on a bit,' Hutton murmured. 'And the darker it gets, the more we kid him.'

'Kid him?' I said. 'When he's got radar and helicopters?'

Hutton said, 'Look at our radar.'

The wheelhouse repeater screen glowed green as we looked down at it, and Hutton's spatulate forefinger traced the outline of the ice configuration.

'See, don't you?' he said. 'It's a damn funny way for the ice to crack, but you see what's happened?'

I saw. The giant floe on which the Otter was marooned was U-shaped and the hole in the pack from which it had torn itself was U-shaped too.

'Got us bottled in the U, hasn't he?' Hutton said. 'So d'you know what he'll do?'

I shook my head.

Hutton laughed. Actually laughed. 'He'll ponce up and down there like the manual of naval tactics says. And he'll have his helicopter up just in case. But he'll wait. Now then, how's the light?'

'Going,' Chance said. 'Going fast.'

'So we'll slither a bit,' Hutton said.

Polar Star began to steer a curious, random, zig-zag course through the darkening water. From the pocket of Hutton's duffle-coat an old tin emerged, and out of it came a twist of black and glistening tobacco. He began to slice it with an old and evil penknife, then rubbed the flakes in his hard fingers and filled his short stubby pipe. He lit it carefully, tamping down the brightly glowing tobacco with his forefinger, finally puffing with satisfaction. In the bitter night air, the pipe smelled remarkably good.

The light was fading quickly now; twilight to night. The visible horizon shortened rapidly. Harry Hutton reached up and moved a switch over. 'Let's have the riding lights off, an' all.'

Polar Star, darkened now, moved from side to side of the channel, picking her way among the loose ice, nosing close to the main pack, then turning, heading back towards the floe.

'On his radar, we'll look like a hysterical mouse, trying to get away from the old tom-cat,' Hutton said cheerfully. 'Look at him!'

Lenin had turned, as he had predicted, and was steaming back the way she had come.

'Right,' the skipper said. 'There's no knowing how long yonder monkey'll keep it up. He won't leave us here all night, that's for sure. But he'll probably march up and down a couple of times before he does anything. So we'll just nose over towards the floe . . .'

Polar Star's engines pushed us gently through the water, throbbing softly through the stresses of the hull. Above us, and to the south, the helicopter rode, circling slowly, her lights flashing in the blackening sky.

The hut on the floe lay almost at the curve of the U, and *Polar Star*, zig-zagging, began to move toward it. I hoped the two guys in there had everything ready, and that they hadn't cracked. They must have been through several varieties of hell since they'd been put ashore, particularly when the floe had broken away. In their shoes I'd have been a gibbering idiot, and I prayed they'd stood up to it.

The helicopter swung lazily across the night sky at us. The pilot was checking what we were doing, but he must have been pretty confident that there wasn't much we *could* do, because the pass was quick and pretty high. Hutton chuckled and swung *Polar Star* out past a chunk of ice, then back towards the floe.

'A couple of hundred yards,' I said, 'and we'll be out of sight of the *Lenin*.'

Hutton nodded. 'That's when he'll start getting jumpy.

Not at first. But in a few minutes. You know. It's when you can't see . . .'

We watched the helicopter's flashing lights, and the steady green and red of the *Lenin*'s over at the mouth of the U, as *Polar Star* eased gently in under the lee of the floe.

'Give me the derrick,' Chance said.

He stuck his foot in the loop and was hoisted clear of the deck to the surface of the ice eight feet or so above. He looked round, then called down softly.

'Hundred and fifty yards, maybe. Looks good.'

'OK.' I waved Harald Ericson forward and he was lifted quickly to the ice table where he bent and fastened on his skis.

Up above I could hear Chance's voice as he gave Ericson instructions: 'Get over there. Warn them. But no lights and no ignition until we're all up on top here. When we are, start the Otter's engine and taxi this way. We can load the injured in best from here.'

'OK.' Ericson slid off out of sight.

Chance leaned over. 'Let's get them up here.'

'Right.' I attached the hook to Komarov's stretcher first. The old boy was beginning to come round at long last, but this wasn't the time to do anything about it. In a moment he'd been swung clear of the deck and was coming down to a neat four-point landing on the ice. Grey Smoke's stretcher followed, then Meldrum stepped forward, jerking his thumb ruefully at the girl.

'Like to keep her, Skipper? She's about your bloody mark, the treacherous wee bitch.'

'She'll feel at home in Scotland, then,' Hutton said. 'Take her with you.'

We all kept her covered as she swung up to the ice, Meldrum and I from the trawler's deck, Chance from the floe.

'Now you.' I pushed Meldrum forward.

'What happens to the Tyke here?' he said.

Hutton said, 'Don't worry about me, sonny Jim. And hurry up. Your mummy'll be fretting.'

A couple more minutes and we were all on the ice, staring across the surface of the floe towards the prefabricated shed. There was no sign of any movement either in the shed or among the shadows around it. Below us, *Polar Star*'s engines picked up speed and she drew away from the side of the floe out into the open water of the channel.

A moment later there was a roar from across the floe, part of the shed fell away and I could see the flames sputtering blue and orange from the exhaust of a petrol engine. Then, slowly, the Otter emerged on to the moonlit surface of the floe. Ericson, still on skis, stood beside her, pointing towards us.

The Otter turned clumsily on its skis and began to taxi slowly across to us. The noise of its radial Pratt and Whitney with the three-bladed prop was deafening as it bumped over the icy surface, then turned into the wind and stopped a few yards from us. The door in her side opened and the steps were lowered.

'Right,' Chance shouted. 'Let's get them in!'

Meldrum and I grabbed Jim Grey Smoke's stretcher and lifted him quickly into the little cabin, then jumped down again for Komarov. Ericson had unfastened his skis and was standing five or six yards clear of the Otter, rifle at the ready. As I climbed out of the aircraft's cabin, I saw him staring into the sky, then he swung round. 'Quickly. We are seen.'

I glanced up. The helicopter was swinging fast and silently across the night sky, the noise of its engine drowned by the din of our own. As I watched, it slipped rapidly down towards the ice surface.

I nudged Chance and pointed.

'Everybody in and quick,' he shouted.

'What about the girl?' I said.

He looked at me. 'We take her. She wanted to come with us, and she's coming. Maybe the CIA can trade her in for someone else later.'

I pointed my carbine at her. 'OK,' I said. 'Get inside.'

Reluctantly she obeyed. Meldrum went in after her, then Chance, dragging that leg up the steps. Before I climbed after them, I went and stood beside Ericson, watching the helicopter. There was no doubting what its intentions were. It was hovering low, just a few feet above the floe and the door in the cabin side was open. In a couple of seconds it would be on the ice and men would be coming out: armed men; men equipped to stop us.

Ericson dropped to one knee, the rifle sliding to his shoulder. 'I must frighten the pilot,' he said softly. 'If they crash from that height, few will survive.'

He bent his eye to the sight and I watched his finger take the pressure of the trigger. There was a moment's pause as he squeezed, then a sharp, flat crack.

Peering through my night glass I saw the glass starred in the helicopter's cockpit. The click of a bolt sounded beside me, then another flat crack and another panel of glass crazed. Ericson was shooting as calmly as though he were on a range, thumb and forefinger sliding the bolt like silk, the shots snapping off. He'd fired five times when the pilot's nerve went and the helicopter lifted suddenly higher and moved out of range. He allowed himself a thin smile of satisfaction as he watched it soaring clear.

'Hurry,' I called to him.

He was slinging the rifle across his chest as he turned, and something stopped him in mid-movement. He was staring across the floe, open-mouthed. I bent until I could see beneath the Otter.

'My God!' Ericson said softly. 'Look at her!'

I saw the *Lenin*'s riding lights. They were terribly close, but for a moment I didn't understand. Then below the lights I saw the great, reinforced bows of the nuclear icebreaker.

Suddenly everything was very clear indeed. The *Lenin* was going to slice up our floe.

CHAPTER TWENTY-FIVE

I don't know what warned me: some flicker at the corner of my eye, perhaps, or an unconscious reaction to the sound of a distant engine. Whatever it was, I hurled myself flat underneath the Otter, yelling to Ericson to do the same. As my body thudded to the ice, I heard the hammering of carbine fire and the bullets stitching a line across the ice. There was a grunt and I turned to look at Ericson.

Above the helicopter was turning to make another pass. I got to my feet and whipped across to where he lay.

'Where are you hit?'

His breath hissed with the pain as he moved his body and pointed to the hole in his parka, low on his right shoulder, from which blood already oozed. There was another in his thigh.

'Go,' he said. 'Quick.'

'Like hell,' I said. I dragged him, ignoring the grunts of agony, across to the Otter, and Iain Meldrum jumped down quickly to help. Together we raised Ericson and began to half-carry him up the little staircase. The Norwegian, feeling forward with his good left leg, had found the bottom rung, and we were concentrating on lifting him up, when the three of us were knocked flying in a sudden explosion of violence that erupted and flashed past us from inside the cabin.

'What the hell?' Meldrum's voice was angry as he hauled himself to his feet again.

Chance's face appeared in the doorway. 'It was the girl.'

'Give me a carbine,' I said. In that moment. I would have killed her.

He shook his head. 'Let her go. Get Ericson inside.'

Already the surface of the ice was stained with Ericson's blood. Meldrum and I picked him up gently, and lifted him bodily up the steps and inside the tiny cabin.

Urgently I turned to Chance. 'The ship's carving up the floe, I said. 'We've got to move.'

The roar of the engine rose and I felt the Otter turning. I hurried forward to the cockpit, where the medical kit was stowed away in a locker beside the pilot, and in that moment, for the first time in my life, I forgot my patient.

Ahead, through the windscreen, I could see the helicopter, hovering low just in front of us, laying down a curtain of fire. And beyond it, the great rearing bows of the *Lenin* were racing forward at the floe.

As they hit, a shudder ran through the huge, floating sheet of ice and even in the plane, I staggered.

The *Lenin* just kept moving forward, like a wedge into a log, and in a moment I saw the crack leaping across the floe, carving a good quarter of it clean away.

'Quickly, for God's sake,' I urged the pilot.

He, too, was staring at the scene ahead, watching as the great ship began to back and turn, drawing away to give another hammer-blow to the floe. Already the chunk she had cut away was another and separate floe, with a ten-foot gap of black water separating it from us. One more blow like that, in the right place, and there wouldn't be room for the Otter to take off.

The *Lenin* was almost clear of the ice again; she seemed to be shaking herself, gathering strength for another massive blow at the floe.

Now the girl had run forward, arms waving, in front of the Otter, and the helicopter began to lower itself to pick her up. She raced round to the fuselage door and climbed in and for a moment it looked as though the helicopter would lift away. Instead, after a moment, it dropped back to the surface, a few feet in front of us.

The pilot's intention—or the girl's—was simple: by sitting there he would stop the Otter taxiing. One more pass by the *Lenin* would chop the floe up and maroon the Otter; then they could mop us up at their leisure.

I yelled back along the cabin of the Otter for a carbine and Chance clambered forward. I cocked it, switched to automatic firing, and emptied the magazine through our windscreen in the direction of the helicopter pilot. After a few shots, the helicopter ceased hovering and sat heavily on the ice, but I didn't stop firing and its motor didn't stop running.

Our pilot began to turn the Otter gently, to bring it round clear of the helicopter; for long moments I thought he wouldn't make it, that his wingtip would snag the whirling rotors of the stranded helicopter. He inched round, though, and we sneaked past about a foot clear.

Now the pilot waited for nothing. His hand reached for the throttle lever and rammed it forward. The Pratt and Whitney radial snarled as the revolutions rose. Then the pilot clipped off the brakes and the Otter moved forward.

I couldn't take my eyes off the *Lenin*. The massive ice-breaker's three propellers had turned her very fast and she was racing now for the floe, her armoured bows only feet from the edge of the ice. The Otter, with eight of us aboard and weighed down with fuel for the long flight home, would need a full three hundred yards to get off, and the only part of the floe that now allowed a run of that length was in the direction of the *Lenin*!

I stood there, tensely, helplessly, as the ice vibrated beneath the Otter's skis and the little plane drove forward towards the point where the massive icebreaker was going to shear away the ice.

The pilot's hands were steady on the stick as the Otter raced forward, its speed increasing but with an agonizing slowness. The *Lenin*'s bows moved inexorably forward: she would hit the ice at a good ten knots, head on—and she was only twenty feet away from it now . . . ten . . . five. She struck!

The ice was racing whitely beneath us as the needle crawled round the airspeed indicator and the engine boost crept up.

I saw the crack a fraction of a second before I heard it:

from the point where the bows of the *Lenin* made their appalling impact on the edge of the ice, a black line snaked suddenly forward at unbelievable speed, straight across the floe. Through the shattered windscreen of the Otter, even above the roar of the engine, the strange ker-achety-twang of the splitting ice was clearly audible.

The black crack raced towards the Otter as the *Lenin* wedged herself into the ice and her nuclear engines drove her forward. If the crack passed in front of us, the Otter was likely to trip and catapult over on to its back.

The little Otter raced forward, the pilot's face concentrating grimly on the dials. I'll never know how he kept his eyes off that black line that was coming towards us like a whiplash.

I saw his hands tighten on the column, but they didn't move. The Otter and the racing crack were moving towards a meeting at a tremendous speed, and in a second or two the crack would reach the Otter's ice.

Then the pilot's hands moved: gently, sensitively, yet strongly, the knuckles white beneath the skin, and I watched the Otter's nose come up as the lift rode beneath her wings. The crack was on us now, snaking forward across the ice. I watched horrified as it reached towards the plane: by some freakish chance it would hit us by the skis, I was sure of it . . .

A second dragged slowly by, and then there was a hell of a bump. I sank to my knees under its force, then stood, bracing myself, waiting for the crash. But there was no crash. The little Otter had dragged itself into the air.

I couldn't take my eyes off that racing crack and turned awkwardly in the Otter's cramped cockpit to stare down at the floe below. There must have been a pressure fault in the ice formation, because a strange and terrible thing happened. As the flying crack hit a point about two-thirds of the way along the floe, it ceased to be a single racing line and became star-shaped. Half a dozen or more cracks radiated from the central point, snaking over the ice, then they themselves divided into more and smaller cracks. What was happening to that sheet of ice was exactly what had happened to my windscreen that night in Central Park. I watched the network spread towards the stranded helicopter, the lines passing beneath it, over, round, until it looked as though it were enmeshed in some frightful spider's web.

For a moment everything was still; then the ice began to move, pressure on pressure, direction over direction. The vast blocks of ice began to heave and crunch, to spin and turn. I saw the helicopter begin to slide towards the black gap that appeared beside it. Then the block on which it stood must have righted itself for a moment before some huge force spun it like an ice cube in a glass and the helicopter slid into the black water and vanished amid the maelstrom of swirling ice. A great chunk rolled over where, a moment earlier, the helicopter had been, and I stared in shock and realization. In that place at that moment, people were dying: the helicopter's pilot, its crew, the soldiers. And the girl. They were choking now in the supercooled water beneath the vast, inescapable weight of the rolling, churning ice . . .

It wasn't a rapid climb, but it was as rapid as we could make it. Looking down I could see the *Lenin* still wedged in the ice and a trail of phosphorescence that marked Skipper Hutton's progress. The *Polar Star* was a darkened ship, sneaking down the edge of the pack ice towards open water. And maybe five miles ahead, a cluster of boats was heading towards her. There were dozens of them, and I grinned: the *Lenin* could hardly arrest the entire Hull trawler fleet in international waters.

I picked up the medical kit and went back into the cabin. Ericson had been lucky: both bullets had gone through and the one that struck his shoulder had missed his lung. I gave him morphine and penicillin, bound the wounds and settled to wait.

The cabin of the Otter was like a dormitory. There were men asleep everywhere. Iain Meldrum was neat in his seat; even sleeping compactly and efficiently. The wounded Ericson seemed coiled, even in repose: not far under and liable to snap warily awake. Chance, by contrast, slept hugely, noisily, grunting and snorting happily. Poor Jim Grey Smoke was chemically unconscious, the marvellous copper skin paler now, but at least he was unaware, for the time being, of the state and the pain of his legs. Tonight, at Thule, when they wheeled him into the operating theatre, I was going to make damn sure that there was one friend in that impersonal bunch of service medicos around him.

And still Komarov slept, lying on the stretcher on the cabin floor, breathing easily. My benzedrine had worn off now, and all that sleep was infectious. I began to yawn and my eyelids turned to lead and dropped. I forced them up again a few times, but finally I didn't have either the strength or the will-power.

About fifteen seconds later Chance kicked me awake, his long leg stretching across the gangway and his felt boot chopping at my shin.

'Feet,' I said.

'Your patient's awake, Doc.' He flicked his eyes at the cabin floor to save himself the effort of moving his head. I glanced down. Komarov was stirring, stretching his arms and legs and making little noises in his throat.

'Thanks for letting me know.' I looked across at Chance as I rose, but he was already asleep again. I kneeled beside the stretcher and watched Komarov's eyelids twitch, open briefly, then close again. After a moment they opened again and stayed open. They were very puzzled.

I said, 'You're on your way to America, Professor Komarov.'

'America?' He raised his head and looked around, at the sparse interior of the cabin and the weary and wounded men. 'But how . . .?'

'Your message to Professor Ward. We came to get you.' I'd tell him about Ward later.

'You came? To Novaya Zemlya?' His eyes were grey and hard and, at that moment, surprised.

I said, 'It seemed important.'

He nodded. 'It is. There is much that must be told.'

'They'll be very glad to see you in Washington.'

He stared at me, blinking. Mention of Washington had shaken him and the words, the situation, were sinking in. But for a man who'd gone to sleep under guard in one country and awakened lying on the floor of a light aircraft in the middle of nowhere, he was adjusting pretty well. After a little while, quite slowly, the skin of his forehead lost its lines of worry and eased into smooth and shiny planes and he smiled faintly.

'It will be very interesting,' he said. 'Thank you.'

There didn't seem to be anything to say.

Alistair MacLean

His first book, HMS *Ulysses*, published in 1955, was outstandingly successful. It led the way to a string of best-selling novels which have established Alistair MacLean as the most popular adventure writer of our time.

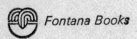 *Fontana Books*

Desmond Bagley

'Mr Bagley is nowadays incomparable.' *Sunday Times*

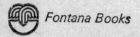
Fontana Books

James Jones

A Touch of Danger
A superb first thriller by the author of *From Here to Eternity*
set on an Aegean island where the sun and sex are corrupted by
violence and drugs. 'A believable private eye at last—not
too tough, not too lucky—and a plot built with loving care.'
John Braine, Daily Express

The Thin Red Line
His novel of the Marines on Guadalcanal—a gory, appallingly
accurate description of men at war. 'Raw, violent, powerful
and terrible, the most convincing account of battle experience
I have ever read.' *Richard Lister, Evening Standard*

From Here to Eternity
The world famous novel of the men of the U.S. Army
stationed at Pearl Harbour in the months immediately before
America's entry into World War II. 'One reads every page
persuaded that it is a remarkable, a very remarkable book
indeed.' *Listener*

Go to the Widow-Maker
A superb novel about the war between the sexes, set in the
world of rich men and those who cater to them. In Jones's
tale of dangerous living, love is for men and women are for
sex. 'Jones is the Hemingway of our time . . . There is savage
poetry in his descriptions of spear-fishing and treasure-
hunting.' *Spectator*

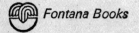 *Fontana Books*

Fontana Paperbacks

Fontana is a leading paperback publisher of fiction and non-fiction, with authors ranging from Alistair MacLean, Agatha Christie and Desmond Bagley to Solzhenitsyn and Pasternak, from Gerald Durrell and Joy Adamson to the famous Modern Masters series.

In addition to a wide-ranging collection of internationally popular writers of fiction, Fontana also has an outstanding reputation for history, natural history, military history, psychology, psychiatry, politics, economics, religion and the social sciences.

All Fontana books are available at your bookshop or newsagent; or can be ordered direct. Just fill in the form and list the titles you want.

FONTANA BOOKS, Cash Sales Department, G.P.O. Box 29, Douglas, Isle of Man, British Isles. Please send purchase price, plus 8p per book. Customers outside the U.K. send purchase price, plus 10p per book. Cheque, postal or money order. No currency.

NAME (Block letters)

ADDRESS
